MY FELLOW AMERICANS

MY FELLOW AMERICANS

Keir Graff

This first world edition published in Great Britain 2007 by
SEVERN HOUSE PUBLISHERS LTD of
9–15 High Street, Sutton, Surrey SM1 1DF.
This first world edition published in the USA 2007 by
SEVERN HOUSE PUBLISHERS INC of
595 Madison Avenue, New York, N.Y. 10022.

British Library Cataloguing in Publication Data

Graff, Keir
    My fellow Americans
    1. Terrorism - United States - Fiction 2. Undercover
    operations - Fiction 3. United States - Politics and
    government - 2001- - Fiction 4. Suspense fiction
    I. Title
    813.6[F]

ISBN-13: 978-0-7278-6522-9   (cased)
ISBN-13: 978-1-84751-024-2   (trade paper)

Typeset by Palimpsest Book Production Ltd.,
Grangemouth, Stirlingshire, Scotland.
Printed and bound in Great Britain by
MPG Books Ltd., Bodmin, Cornwall.

One

The building was gone. It was like a hole in the city. In the pit where the foundations had been, its earthen walls shored back by towering iron plates, men crawled like red-jacketed ants over the caterpillar-tracked ground, over piles of girders and heaps of scarred stones and broken concrete. Though it was morning, the metal-halide lamps ringing the site shone like noontime sun, flooding in bright white light the blue-black diesel smoke of the bulldozers that snorted and growled as they pushed fill from one place to the next. Men guided the machines, beckoning the bulldozers and front-end loaders with circling arms, peering into deep holes and then summoning towering cranes with a single pointed finger. The cranes trembled stick-like like praying mantises, holding twenty-ton columns like twigs. A column descended into the ground; while workers shoveled dirt into the gap, a cement truck began backing up, ready to set the new skyscraper's foundation.

Across the Chicago River, on the sidewalk of Upper Wacker Drive, Jason Walker tugged the legs of his camera tripod to their full length and splayed them on the sidewalk. He unzipped his camera case, selected a camera and lens, and screwed them together. Though he found the construction scene diverting, he was much more interested in completed buildings. When billionaire developer Ronald Flush had announced his plans to tear down the *Chicago Star-Tabloid* building and erect in its place a goliath tower that combined a hotel, office suites, and condominiums, Jason Walker had neither grieved for the newspaper building, which was an eyesore, nor been thrilled by the anticipation of another mirrored-glass skyscraper. But he had been excited by the news nonetheless.

Immediately to the west of the site was one of the last works by the Dutch architect Willem de Vries, the boxy, steel-and-glass headquarters of technology giant HAL. The HAL building wasn't on any top-ten lists of Chicago architecture, and even architecture buffs weren't particularly fond of it. But Jason Walker loved the rectilinear Internationalist style, and de Vries was considered its master. This wasn't his best, but it was good. And this brief period of construction next door meant that, for a few months, the massive east wall would be completely unobstructed. Perfect for a picture.

The sun warm on his arms, an almost-cold lake breeze tousled Jason Walker's hair as he threaded the camera on to the tripod. He was running late. He had meant to arrive before sunrise in order to catch the orange dawn in the building's windows. But, early as it was, the color had already left the sunrise. Still, he thought he would get some good pictures. He squinted into the viewfinder and adjusted the focus. The looming monolith took shape, brilliant on one side, black on the others. He took a picture, adjusted his settings, and took another. He was always surprised to find that most people thought this building and others like it were ugly. The average person preferred red-brick Victorian piles, Gothic castles, and Greek and Roman temples—the older the better. Accordingly, the average architect designed buildings that, but for skewed proportions, inferior materials, and shoddy workmanship, looked like them.

Jason Walker despised those buildings. He didn't mind the originals, and studied them for their contributions to the evolution of design, but to mimic them now was pure sentimentalism, a longing for a safer and simpler time that would never return. It was like bringing Disneyland into the real world. Buildings, he believed, reflected the times in which they were built. No wonder Americans didn't know who they were, he thought, living in an architectural theme park.

Postmodernism that paid tribute to the classical styles and their periodic resurgences obscured the true beauty of the building: its engineering. The modern skyscraper had been born in Chicago, and it was here that architects first boldly showed the public the steel girders that held these slender buildings in the sky. Then, slowly, they began to let go of all that was unnecessary. De Vries had been more minimalist than most, but he still produced beautiful patterns through repetition and subtle variation of the lines of his building materials. Where others saw a bleak black box, Jason Walker saw a chest of jewels.

He zoomed in until he couldn't see anything but a grid of bronze-tinted glass and dark aluminum facing. The frame of the camera and the angling-away building made a trapezoid; the shadows of the raised window mullions made the pattern hypnotic. Between them, the windows flashed like fire in the rising sun. He took more pictures, adjusting his focus, angle, aperture, or shutter speed slightly after each one.

He felt suddenly uneasy. Though the scene in his viewfinder was beautiful, something about it troubled him. Then he realized what it was. Years earlier, giant color photographs in the newspaper had shown similar details of a somewhat similar building. Only those photos had been hazy with smoke. And people, tiny as ants, had been falling to their deaths.

He stepped back from the camera and rubbed his eyes. He took a deep breath and stretched his arms. It was a beautiful spring day. This early, traffic was light and the sidewalks were clear. The gray wall of buildings behind him seemed empty. In the shadow of the Michigan Avenue Bridge, the neon sign for boat tours burned red, having been left on overnight.

With an explosive flutter of its wings, a seagull landed on the balustrade overlooking the river. Cocking its head, it squawked petulantly. He laughed. The bird was filthy, its mottled gray-and-white feathers stained with soot. One of its eyes was milk-white and its beak didn't appear to close properly. But the bird had picked the wrong mark. He didn't have any breakfast for it.

Slinging his camera case over his shoulder, Jason Walker carried his tripod a hundred yards west and set up for a straight-on shot of the building. The photo would be uninteresting, but while he was here, he thought, he might as well shoot every angle.

The bird followed him, walking as if its feet were sore, hectoring him with a voice that sounded as if the bird had spent the night in a smoky blues bar. He wished there were other people around for the bird to bother.

He took a half-dozen shots, then crossed the Wabash Street Bridge and cut across the plaza. Standing close to the HAL's west side, he shot nearly straight up, catching the heavy dark wall overflowed by the brilliant sky. He liked the image, and thought it was ironic that he could have taken this picture any time at all.

The bird kept following, sometimes flapping aloft and circling, sometimes hobbling along on the ground.

Jason Walker circled the HAL, on the east side tramping across an elaborate pedestrian bridge of scaffolding and plywood that permitted a close view of the construction site. Detaching his camera from the tripod, he shot a dozen pictures of things that interested him—trucks pouring concrete into forms; the retaining wall that held back the river; an area where an underground street would service Flush's new building—before continuing several blocks north to shoot the HAL from that direction. He thought he had lost the bird. He was actually scanning the sky when a tubercular croak behind him told him that he hadn't gotten rid of it yet.

Two hours had passed by the time he finished shooting. He'd taken two or three dozen photos of the building itself. But he'd also taken plenty of the area around it. The *Star-Tabloid* had not been a particularly tall building, but it had blocked some arresting views. There was a rust-brown steel parking garage immediately behind the site that was strangely beautiful. The blue sky in the newly made gap was like a breath of fresh air. It almost made Walker wish Flush wasn't building a new monument in the *Star-Tabloid* building's place.

He stowed his camera gear and recrossed the river to a bakery. He bought coffee and a bagel for himself and a poppy-seed muffin for his avian assistant. But when he came out of the bakery the bird was gone.

He decided to walk to the photo lab, which was maybe a mile or two away. It was a beautiful morning. The exercise would be good for him. It also meant he could delay starting work.

Crossing the river a third time, heading north once again, he noticed that the flags on the Michigan Avenue Bridge were flying at half mast. He didn't know why. When he was a boy, he remembered flags flying low on several occasions: the death of President Johnson; the capture of the American embassy in Tehran; the bombing of the Marine barracks in Beirut. After the September 11, 2001 terrorist attacks, the flags had gone down again and the nation had mourned for months. Now there were so many tragedies, it seemed that the flags went up and down as if on mechanical pulleys. Bombings of U.S. troops and contractors in Afghanistan, Iraq, Iran, North Korea, Venezuela, Cuba; a reservoir poisoned in Ohio; a school bus burned in Washington, D.C.; a small plane crashed into Reunion Tower in Dallas, killing a table of four and their waitress.

Gina Saraceno, the woman Jason Walker was seeing, had a wicked sense of humor. 'Soon,' she said, 'they'll lower the flags when the White House cook burns the president's toast.'

He liked that about her. He admired the fearlessness of her opinions even if he didn't share her political passions. She cared deeply about strangers in other lands who were hungry and oppressed, and talked about little else.

'War is the natural state of man, and the world isn't fair,' he told her once, pretentiously. 'Once you can accept that, it's like a weight off your shoulders. You can't change things. Wishing you could will only make you miserable.'

She had called him a miserable misanthrope and told him she hoped she wouldn't have to rely on him if she ever went to jail, and then they had made love.

Gina Saraceno was beautiful, a short, dark-skinned Italian with frizzy black hair and a tremendously curvy body. She was uninhibited, and genuinely seemed to like him despite their differences. But as much as he liked her, there were times he wouldn't answer her calls because he didn't feel up to her. Her arguing, sometimes even her affection, made him tired. He hated to admit it, but he was also made the tiniest bit nervous by her vocal criticism of the president. True, the president's declaration of martial law had not meant that the streets of Chicago were suddenly filled with jack-booted soldiers. And true, his third term had not resulted in the gutting of every other article of the constitution, as civil libertarians had predicted, but you never knew who might be listening.

Jason Walker made his way up the broad sidewalk of Michigan Avenue, splitting a quickening stream of office workers, chic shop assistants, and early tourists. The boulevards were beautifully planted with exotic flowers, all in full bloom. Parks in the neighborhoods were undergoing something akin to war rationing, but Boul Mich and the Loop remained as festive as ever.

At Superior, where he planned to turn west, a battered sedan had been encircled by a half-dozen police vehicles and two Homeland Security vans. The occupants, who looked African-American or perhaps African, stood with their hands against the vans, feet spread wide. Two policemen stood guard with short machine guns while a third searched the suspects. The rest of the police stood in a loose circle, talking casually. He walked past Superior to Chicago and turned there. Before he passed the corner he saw a man in black slacks and a black windbreaker standing halfway up the block and talking into a radio as if describing the scene.

Jason Walker was sweating when he finally reached the photo lab in the shadow of the El tracks. The shop catered to professional photographers and was too expensive for someone of his means. But he couldn't stand to stop using them. Even if he was the only audience for his own work, he loved the excellent quality of the prints in his portfolio. Typically, he had the lab make only contact sheets at first. From the contact sheets he chose a number of small prints. From the prints he chose one or two enlargements.

He had been told endlessly that he could save time and money by using a digital camera, but he had invested quite a bit in his camera gear several years before the digital revolution, and he couldn't bear to consign the tools to the scrap pile just yet. He had an almost sensual love of the precision-machined, German-made camera, from the click of its shutter and the tiny tremor that shook the camera body, to the fluid rotation of the lenses. He knew how to use a darkroom, too—although he rarely did anymore—and even enjoyed that.

Watching an image emerge from a white sheet of paper as he gently agitated it in the developer pan was one of the few times technology masqueraded as magic. And what was the point, he wondered, in making a hobby more efficient?

The girl at the counter was twenty, tattooed, wearing a top that seemed to be made of red cellophane.

'Film camera, huh?' she said when he dropped his rolls on the counter. He still found that construction irritating.

'Just don't call me a Luddite,' he said.

'Don't sweat it. It's cool. But I don't know how much longer they're going to make this stuff.'

She swept the little yellow canisters into a vinyl envelope, sealed it shut, and called up his personal information on a computer. She printed out an order ticket, peeled off the back, and stuck the ticket on the envelope.

'End of the day OK?' she asked.

'Tomorrow is fine, if that's easier.'

'Don't sweat it. End of the day. We close at six.'

As he stepped on to the sidewalk, Jason Walker pulled out the neck of his shirt and blew on his chest, trying to dry the sweat. Had the counter girl been teasing him? He really wasn't that sweaty. Still, the day was going to be a hot one, and he thought he might shower before he returned in the afternoon.

He took the train to Argyle Station, walked to Marine Drive, and turned right. He turned right again and walked up the semicircular drive to the entrance of his building. He showed his photo ID to the bored guard behind bulletproof glass, then swiped its magnetic stripe and the interior door opened. He rode the elevator to the fourteenth floor. It was actually the thirteenth floor, but Jason Walker lived in the last building in the world where superstition still reigned. He didn't know if the condominium's board of directors was also afraid of black cats, walking under ladders, and warty old women, but they had nonetheless neglected to update the unit numbers and the buttons on the elevator panel.

He walked stealthily down the hall, but as he turned his key in the lock, he heard a scrabble of toenails in the apartment next door. Schatzi, his neighbor's 100-pound Rottweiler, gained traction and raced down the hall. As he closed his own door behind him, the dog slammed full body into his neighbor's door, threatening to splinter the shuddering wood. Frustrated, it commenced a deafening barking.

'Just call her by name,' the dog's owner, Richard Zim, had told Jason Walker when he moved in. 'She'll quiet down once she knows you.'

Calling the dog by name had actually extended the barking jags, sometimes by as long as an hour. The two apartments shared both a floor plan and a twenty-five-foot wall that was only four inches thick. With a glass to the wall, he could hear every word of Richard Zim's phone conversations (he talked almost exclusively about his twenty-two-foot sailboat, *Schatzi II*). Even without a glass, he could hear Richard Zim clearing his throat. He found that if he took his shoes off and walked in stockinged feet, Schatzi would stop barking within five to fifteen minutes. But until she did, it was difficult to think. He remembered Richard Zim saying that he didn't bother to lock his door. And with an alarm system like that, he wouldn't need to.

Jason Walker showered, changed his shirt, and sat down at the dining-room table. This was his desk, covered with computer gear, phone and fax, and piles of folders and loose papers. Tapping the keyboard to wake up the computer, he checked the to-do list in his day planner. There was only one item: *Edit green ball*. He wouldn't have forgotten it, but had duly entered it out of a habit established several years ago when his schedule was full. Now he wished he hadn't bothered. It was pathetic to make a list with one item. More than that, it reminded him how precarious his financial situation had become.

Five years ago, at age thirty-three, Jason Walker had moved from Seattle to Chicago to edit a small magazine called *Billiards Journal*. It wasn't exactly *Playboy*, but he had jumped at the chance to leave *Claims Weekly*, a trade newsletter for insurance claims adjusters, where he'd been the assistant editor. He didn't even know how to hold a cue stick, but the publisher had assured him that his handicap wouldn't be a problem. He applied himself to learning the rules, the nicknames of the professional players, and the issues of interest to the magazine's readers. Soon he felt comfortable at least writing about the game, even if he never became good enough to sink more than three balls in a row. And this was despite several professional tutorials.

Three years later, *Billiards Journal* was facing bankruptcy, about to become another victim of the deteriorating publishing economy. The publisher, who also owned *Bowling Digest*, *Darts Quarterly*, and *Tavern Sport News*, slashed staffing and consolidated the production of all four publications into a single office, naming himself the new editor-in-chief. Jason Walker was laid off, then offered a part-time job as website editor at drastically reduced pay. He refused in what was for him dramatic fashion, walking out of a lunch meeting before the food arrived at the table.

The next day, he ordered new business cards and began looking for freelance editing and writing jobs. The first year had been tenable, but this year was terrible. Days and sometimes weeks went by without assignments. Most of his clients were publications too small to have either an in-house copyeditor or an accounts payable person. What money he did earn was usually late. His best client was *Chicago Socialite*, which paid poorly and late but demanded short turnaround and scrupulous attention to detail.

The piece in front of him was, like most stories in *Chicago Socialite*, not professionally written. Many of the contributors were actual socialites, who described their exotic vacations or praised their pet causes in return for the large glamour shots that ran in the contributors section. In this one, a Mrs. Gennifre 'Bubbles' Greensward profiled the Green Gourmets' annual fund-raising ball, an 'ecologically conscious,' $1,000-per-plate, 1,000-head fête. The hand-printed invitations were made of recycled, handmade paper, for instance. It shouldn't have bothered him as much as it did that the writer confused *its* for *it's* in every instance.

With a deep sigh, he began work and, with only 271 minor amendments, was able to offer an article near enough to grammatical correctness for the readers of *Chicago Socialite*.

Technically, he was only supposed to correct errors of fact, spelling, and locution, but in actuality he performed line-by-line rewrites.

It was lunchtime. He walked to a red-vinyl diner, ordered a sandwich, and read the paper while he ate. The first six pages contained news of seven car bombs, two terrorist trials, an Israeli–Palestinian clash, and a missing truckload of radioactive material. Sometimes, out of a vague desire to feel informed, Jason Walker actually tried to read these articles. Usually he flipped past them, feeling the only difference would be the details. On page nine, a three-inch story reported that a man named George Libby had declared himself an independent candidate for the next presidential election. 'That is, if we're having one,' he said sarcastically at his own press conference. Republican and Democratic leaders alike had declined to comment on George Libby's candidacy. Ever since the constitutional amendment allowing the president's third term, and his subsequent declaration of martial law, both political parties had agreed that it was important to support the president in time of crisis.

Jason Walker imagined Gina Saraceno's take on the story. 'Well, George Libby must be tired of walking around free as a bird,' she might say.

I should call her, he thought. Maybe tonight.

Finally, he reached the entertainment section. He enjoyed the movie news and reviews. Most of the movies were about soldiers, policemen, and spies, which struck him as ironic, given the headlines. Didn't most people want a break from all that?

The hostess was glaring at him. The restaurant was full and she wanted the table. He folded his newspaper, paid, and went home. He checked his work on the *Chicago Socialite* piece and then emailed it back to the editor, asking whether she had any more work for him. She responded right away.

Something later today, she promised.

Missing the last check, he reminded her.

She didn't reply to that one. He spent an hour emailing other editors, asking about copyediting work and suggesting stories he might write. When he ran out of ideas, he turned off the computer. He thought about opening a beer and looked at the clock. It was only quarter to four. If he started drinking now, where would he be at eight o'clock? He decided to pick up his contact sheets. He would have been just as happy to wait until tomorrow, but given the circumstances, he welcomed the errand.

Schatzi sent him off with a fanfare of barks. He could still hear her even after the elevator doors had closed, even as the car started its descent.

Outside it had grown even hotter and the air was heavy with moisture. He walked slowly so he wouldn't arrive at the lab looking like he'd been caught in a spring shower. When the train stopped at Wrigley Field, the doors opened to let in a throaty roar. People said the Cubs had a real chance this year. They said that every year. After an excellent start in April and May, losing streaks in June and July had relegated them to fifth place in a six-team division.

He was only slightly damp when he arrived at the lab. He found the same clerk still at the counter.

'It's the film-camera man,' she said.

'That's me,' he said.

'Your order isn't ready. We're having a problem in the lab. They think they got a bad shipment of chemicals.'

Jason Walker wasn't upset. He wasn't in a hurry.

'No sweat,' he joked.

She didn't bat an eyelid. But she didn't seem as friendly as before, either.

'Sorry about that,' she said. 'Noon tomorrow, I'm sure, but call first.'

He said he would and then left. He stood on the sidewalk outside for a few minutes, feeling the hot pavement softening his shoes, listening to the clatter of trains overhead. What now? The movies, definitely. He checked his watch, thinking he remembered the start time for the new Benny Sandler comedy. He started for the theater.

The comedy had been sold out, so he had bought a ticket for a jokey spy spectacular. The hero was like James Bond if James Bond had been a muscleman instead of a ladies' man.

He delivered quips even as he leapt out of a burning airplane to wrestle the villain for the last parachute. Jason Walker couldn't say he didn't enjoy it. The hero's women, for one, were gorgeous and often naked. But it was also a nice feeling to be lost in a crowd that was laughing, groaning, and gripping the arms of their seats as one.

The lights came up and the crowd began filing out. Sitting reading the credits, he felt alone and deserted. In addition to Gina Saraceno, he should call David Darling. David Darling would want to go to a Cubs game, but that was all right. Jason Walker didn't have many friends to show for his five years in the city. Of course, he had never had very many friends.

He let the crowd carry him down the escalators and out to Oak Street. The theater was cheek-to-jowl with shops that sold $10,000 watches to women who wore $30,000 fur coats. Fortunately, the movie tickets were only $12, the same as everywhere else. Above him, a thousand tiny white light bulbs burned on the underside of the old-fashioned marquee. If anything, the air outside the theater felt even hotter than before. The tiny bulbs might have been making it worse. It was near dark, yet it seemed as if everyone on the street was reluctant to call it a day. Chicago winters were so long, and springtime was so stormy, that Chicagoans were determined to wring as much as they could out of summertime.

Jason Walker watched the traffic inch along for a while, then decided he might as well go home and eat dinner. A beer, maybe two, then bed. He'd hustle for work in the morning. Maybe something had already come in. He stepped toward the curb, thinking he'd jaywalk.

A white van with tinted windows glided to a stop in front of him. The cargo door was thrown open from inside. His arms were gripped, two hands to each arm, and he was half-pushed, half-dragged into the van. Twisting his head, he glimpsed open-mouthed pedestrians pointing at him in shock, while others strolled by unaware, smiling and laughing.

And then the door slammed shut and someone pulled a black cloth bag over his head.

Two

He was pushed so hard into the seat that he felt the metal springs under the foam rubber. Fingertips burned his muscles. The van's tires chirped once and then it accelerated smoothly into traffic. His hot breath filled the bag. The sudden blindness was terrifying. He would have given anything to tear off the bag but he couldn't move an inch. No one said anything.

He had no idea what to do. An hour ago, watching the movie, he would have thought that he would fight back or at least demand to know what was happening. But he was paralyzed. Except for his lungs. He was breathing faster and faster. His breaths were shallow. He couldn't get enough air.

'Relax,' said someone in the front seat. 'Breathe into the bag.'

Someone holding him chuckled. It sounded more like a cough.

The van turned left, then right. The driver seemed to be observing the speed limit and stopping at the lights.

Jason Walker didn't pass out. His convulsing chest calmed, his breathing slowed, and he found that he was getting oxygen again. He could almost think. He was being kidnapped. But by whom? And why? He wasn't worth money and he hadn't offended anyone that he knew of. He formed a single sentence in his head: *Where are you taking me?* He thought that if he said it aloud things would stop spiraling out of control.

'Where—'

The words died in his throat. Maybe they were going to kill him. Despite the heat, his skin prickled with cold. His stomach dropped. His thoughts were like birds, banking and diving just out of reach.

Then he thought: white van, tinted windows. Homeland Security. Something was wrong, but they weren't going to shoot him. Until he found out why they wanted him, it was best to keep quiet. That was one thing he could do.

He had no idea how long they drove—half an hour, an hour, fifteen minutes? In darkness, immobilized, his brain had no point of reference. He tried to concentrate on his senses.

The fabric over his eyes was thick and tightly woven. Sometimes he saw the oncoming glow of headlights, but that was all.

He was still pinned. The men had slackened their holds a little, but not enough for him to move. He felt slick sweat where their hands gripped his arms. His sweat and theirs.

His mouth was dry. His saliva was sticky. It felt as if he was chewing on tissue paper.

For a few minutes a warm aroma of burnt cocoa filled the van. It had to be from the sweets factory just northwest of the Loop. And then the scent was gone.

The van turned left, then right, then left three times. He had no idea what direction they were headed in. For a while the traffic sounds had been compressed and echoey, making him wonder if they were on Lower Wacker Drive. Then they were clearly above ground again. They inched forward, starting only to stop. He heard only car engines, diesel gasps, and the occasional squeak of untuned brakes. He thought that he and his abductors must be on an expressway, stuck in traffic.

His adrenaline was still pumping, but the moment of panic went on and on. He wished he didn't have time to think. The people who stumbled down the smoking stair-wells of the World Trade Center had been terrified, but they had had one clear objective. The people held hostage in the Tehran embassy had faced the slow terror of imagining a thousand possible outcomes.

He felt embarrassed that he had gone without a fight, hadn't even raised his voice. He tried to form another sentence.

And then the van turned sharply, slowed to ease over a speed bump, and stopped. The two front doors opened. The cargo door slid open. He was pushed out, struggling to keep his feet. The doors slammed. From the reverberations it sounded as if they were inside a parking garage. They marched forward, holding his arms to his sides. He kept flinching, sure they would guide him into a low overhang, breaking his nose without giving him a chance to put up his hands.

There was a soft plastic sound and then doors slid open. They walked forward, stopped, and the doors closed behind them. They waited. After a moment, another set of doors opened. They walked through.

'Who you got?' said a voice.

'Jason Walker,' said one of his captors.

'Seven.'

They started moving again.

They knew his name. This wasn't a case of mistaken identity. They knew who he was, so they had found him, followed him, and grabbed him.

Why?

He was half-led, half-pushed down a long hall. A door opened. They pushed him through and let go. He fell to the floor. The door closed behind him

He tore off the mask and immediately had to close his eyes against searing bright light. Squinting, he saw that he was alone. Alone in a cell. The room was roughly eight feet by ten, with its smooth concrete walls, ceiling, and floor all painted white. The metal door was painted white, too. A steel bunk was bolted to one wall and there was a strange-looking fixture that provided both a toilet and a sink. There was no cover or seat for the toilet. There was no bedding, no towel, no toilet paper. It was all very clean, as if it had just been built and he was the first occupant.

Jason Walker sat on the bunk. The metal was so cold that his hands recoiled. The whole room was cold. Looking up, he saw on the ceiling two vents covered with heavy steel grates, four fluorescent tubes under a locked Plexiglas enclosure, and a half-dome of smoked glass. He knew there was a camera under the bubble; it looked exactly like the camera enclosures on every downtown street corner. And he knew why it was there. But he didn't understand why chilled air would be rattling out of both vents. His arms were reptilian with goosebumps. Exhaling, he saw a wisp of his own breath.

Standing up, he windmilled his arms to get his circulation going. He felt warm blood rushing to his skin. He did twenty jumping jacks. That helped, too, even if he felt self-conscious in front of the camera. He started pacing the cell, hoping to keep the slight flush of warmth alive.

Maybe someone he knew was in trouble. He had heard people talk about this, that sometimes perfectly innocent citizens were taken into custody and treated like criminals in order to get them to talk about their friends. The practice was deplorable, of course, and yet he could almost understand why Homeland Security would choose to do it. Loyalty was part of friendship, and friendship might cause someone to excuse a friend's suspicious behavior as harmless, or lead them to dismiss genuinely inflammatory statements as jokes. To be treated roughly was frightening, but it would tell any potential witnesses right away that the proceedings were serious. They might then be able to see their friend's behavior with fresh eyes.

He was ashamed to realize that he was thinking of Gina Saraceno. That was ridiculous. She was a dissenter, certainly, but no criminal. Maybe she'd angered the wrong person, who in turn had accused her. In that case, he would be pleased and able to set the record straight.

Or would he? Did a few dozen dates, half of them ending in bed, tell you whether someone was capable of treason or terrorism?

He wouldn't have been thinking like this if he wasn't shut in a cell. It was best to wait and find out what they wanted.

Several hours later, he was shivering uncontrollably. The concrete floor felt so cold on his feet that he'd spent half the time standing on the steel bunk. If heat really did rise, he hoped to avail himself of whatever few degrees might be hovering near the ceiling. He wasn't sure he could tell the difference.

He thought that at any minute he might go into convulsions. He knew that shivering was the body's attempt to warm itself, but if anything, the shivering was making him feel colder. He tried holding his quaking arms against his chest and breathing deeply, but he always started trembling again.

Surely they don't know how cold it is, he thought. They wouldn't treat an innocent person like this.

He was hungry, too, and tired. It had to be after midnight. But if he had felt sleepy, he would have been sure that he was dying. In Jack London's story 'To Build a Fire,' the man, freezing to death, falls asleep.

The cell door swung open and a man stepped on to the threshold. He wore black slacks and a white shirt with no insignia or name tag. Forty-ish and soft in the middle, with steel-rimmed glasses and a brushy mustache, he looked like a high-school teacher, except for the heavy belt hung with a pistol, a stun gun, a canister of tear gas, handcuffs, and a nightstick.

'Turn around, face the wall,' the man said.

Jason Walker complied.

'Kneel on the ground. Hands behind your back.'

The man's voice was also like a high-school teacher's, bored with his students.

Again, Jason Walker did as he was asked. He heard a jingle and then cold metal handcuffs clicked on to his wrists. With a fleshy hand in his armpit, the high-school teacher lifted him to his feet and guided him out the door.

Two soldiers were waiting outside. They looked like regular army, but he had no idea how to read their various insignia. These men didn't wear name tags, either. They began walking, one soldier ahead, one behind, the high-school teacher next to him. It was much warmer in the hallway and he felt grateful just to be out of the cell.

The hallway was white with cell doors set in at regular intervals. To the right of each door, about five feet off the ground, four-inch video screens showed fish-eye views of a series of cells just like the one he had come from. The first few were empty, and then he saw a man sitting on his bunk, convulsing as if from racking sobs. Jason Walker listened but heard nothing.

'Eyes forward,' said the high-school teacher.

He obeyed.

'Where are you taking me?' he asked.

None of the men gave any indication that they had even heard him. They kept walking.

They entered an elevator. He learned from the bank of buttons that the building was three stories tall with two lower levels. They rode from LL1 to LL2, then walked down another hall and went into a room. This room was just as white as the first but had, instead of a bunk and a toilet, a table and three chairs. Two men were already seated. Still handcuffed, he was pushed into the remaining chair. The high-school teacher and the soldiers left.

He sat on the edge of his chair. If he leaned back, it hurt his wrists. At least this room was warm.

'Jason Andrew Walker?'

He nodded. The man who had asked was gaunt and gray, his skin like crinkled tissue paper. Someone who was willing to pay ten dollars for a pack of cigarettes.

'Say yes or no. We're recording this.'

'Yes, that's my name.'

The man read a Social Security number.

Jason Walker said that that was his, too.

The man dug around in a large envelope. He coughed several times—dry, sharp reports—then cleared his throat several times. He was wearing gray slacks, a blue blazer, a white shirt, and a red tie. The other man was wearing blue slacks and a gray blazer, with the same shirt and tie. The other man was short and round and red-faced with a fixed scowl. He glared angrily.

Jason Walker tried to smile but failed.

'Can I ask why I'm here?' he said.

Neither man reacted. He was beginning to feel as if he didn't exist. But if he didn't exist, why had all this fuss been made over him?

Smoker pulled a fat stack of glossy 4x6 photos out of the envelope and began laying them out in a neat row on the table. They were prints of the photos Jason Walker had taken that morning. Shot after shot of the HAL building. His stomach dropped. This was not about Gina Saraceno, or one of her friends, or one of his friends. This was about him.

After several rows, Smoker looked at the stack in his hand and seemed to decide that it would take too much effort to finish the job. He set the rest of the stack down.

'Did you take these photos?' he asked.

His voice didn't match his face. It was youthful, almost musical.

'Yes. I was—'

Smoker silenced him with an upraised palm.

'This morning. You took the pictures. Alone?'

He thought of the seagull.

'Yes, I was alone.'

'Several dozen pictures of the HAL building. You're not a tourist. Did you have a professional reason for taking the pictures?'

'No, I—'

The hand again. He fell silent. Scowl looked as if he was hoping for an excuse to leap over the table and start beating him. No, not hopeful; resentful that he had to wait.

'You are a . . .?'

Jason Walker didn't know how to finish the sentence.

'Your profession?'

'I'm an editor. Freelance.'

'Not a photographer.'

'It's my hobby.'

'Pictures of buildings? Dozens of pictures of the same building?'

'I'm interested in architecture.'

Smoker showed the top photo on the stack to Scowl, even though the table was covered with photos just like it.

'Not a very pretty building, is it?'

Scowl scowled harder. He shook his head.

'I think that's subjective,' said Jason Walker, wishing he hadn't.

'Really? You like it?'

Smoker almost sounded interested.

'It's also a significant building. It was the last building de Vries built in America.'

Smoker leaned forward.

'Why did you really take these pictures?'

'I told you. I'm interested in architecture, and it's a significant building.'

'So you say. Well, then, if you like buildings, why'—he riffled through the stack of photos and removed a smaller stack, then began laying them out on top of the others—'these? This isn't a building.'

They were the photos of the Flush Tower's foundations.

'I don't know why I took those. I just thought they seemed interesting.'

'Picturesque,' agreed Smoker.

Scowl frowned.

'Who did you take these pictures for?' demanded Smoker.

'Myself. For my own interest,' said Jason Walker.

'For your aesthetic pleasure.'

'I have binders full of shots like these at home. I've been taking them for years.'

'Really?'

For some reason, he knew that Smoker had already seen the photos, that his portfolios might even be in an adjacent room.

'I notice,' said Smoker, 'that you often take pictures from all points of the compass. Why?'

Jason Walker knew this was an odd habit for a photographer. Real architectural photographers, professionals, would shoot only the most attractive angles. But Jason Walker had a compulsion to document buildings, not just make pretty pictures. And so, in addition to artistic shots, he always recorded all the prominent views of each building he photographed.

'There's no good reason,' he said. 'I'm not a very good photographer. I'm recording them. For my own interest.'

Smoker and Scowl didn't reply. They stared at the pictures, looking tired or bored.

When he had arrived in this room, Jason Walker had started to relax. Though it had been terrifying to be thrown into a van and then a cell, he had clung to the hope that, once he was allowed to talk, everything would be made right. And he had been prepared to assume that the two men at the table were reasonable.

But now he was getting frightened again. They didn't believe him, or they weren't listening, or they didn't care. He wished he could lean back. He was so tired. His back was starting to hurt. Everything seemed to be crashing down on him. If he wasn't able to convince these two bored functionaries that he was innocent, then he would keep falling, through interrogation rooms, secret courts, into cell after cell. Now it was too hot. He couldn't think. He could barely breathe. A bead of sweat rolled from his armpit down his side and lodged in his waistband.

'You think I'm a terrorist?'

Smoker and Scowl seemed to perk up slightly.

'Did someone at the lab report me? Because there's nobody waving at the camera?'

'We're not at liberty to say,' said Smoker. There was a trace of encouragement in his voice, however, hinting that that was exactly what had happened.

'If you've been to my apartment, what did you see? Photos of buildings, yes. But didn't you notice anything else?'

He was unable to read their expressions.

'They're all modernist buildings. From the International school. Would a terrorist target a particular school of architecture?'

'We noticed that the buildings are government buildings,' said Smoker. 'And corporate headquarters. And homes of millionaires. But what we want to know is why you're interested in the HAL building right now.'

'I have books about architecture! Magazines!'

He was feeling desperate.

'Well, maybe you have colleagues who can vouch for your activities. Who can tell us how you spend your days.'

'I work alone. I work with people over the phone and by email.'

'Leaving you plenty of time for photo-taking excursions.'

Scowl stood up. His arms and legs were so small in proportion to his barrel-shaped torso that in other circumstances he might have looked comical.

'We're tired of fucking around,' he said, his voice high and reedy. 'It's time for you to stop squirming and start talking.'

'I'm telling you the truth.'

Scowl shoved his chair back and walked around the table. He grabbed Jason Walker's cuffed hands from behind and jerked them upward. Jason Walker fell forward until his cheek slapped the table. His shoulder joints burned. Scowl kept up the pressure.

He repeated everything he had already said. Scowl pulled his arms even higher and he repeated it all again, faster, stumbling over the details. Scowl tugged again and he felt as if his arms were about to come out of their sockets. He was blind with tears. Smoker started questioning him again, throwing in some new ones. He answered as fast as he could, hoping the pain would stop. He was just a freelance editor. He was practically unemployed. He enjoyed taking pictures. He didn't give them to anyone. Yes, he showed them to his friends. Who were his friends? Just people. None of them had asked him to take the pictures. None of them opposed the government's war on terror. That he knew of. No, he didn't suspect any of them. Was he sure? He thought he was sure. No, he did not oppose the war on terror. No, he was not a terrorist. No, he did not plan to bomb any buildings.

Scowl let go. Jason Walker lay on the table for a moment. Then, trembling, he sat up. His shoulders and elbows throbbed and his fingers felt almost numb. He was panting. His clothes were drenched with sweat.

Smoker looked tired. Scowl had sat down again. He was more red-faced than before, but his expression had softened. The workout had been good for him.

'Think he's telling the truth?' Smoker asked Scowl.

Scowl shrugged. 'Could be. Could be pretty good at this doofus act, too.'

'It's hard to say.'

He realized that everyone lied to these men. Probably most of the people they questioned were guilty, and of course guilty people would lie. Even innocent people would tell some lies. After all, they were afraid. He hadn't said anything about Gina Saraceno. He didn't really suspect her of anything, but it was true that she didn't support the war on terror. Had he said that, Smoker and Scowl might have paid her a visit. So that was a lie of omission.

Smoker and Scowl's job was to read fear, to read pain. How strange that words, his strength, were useless here. He was telling them the truth about everything that was significant, and they heard his words but ignored them while they looked into his eyes and listened to the quaver of his voice and smelled the rank sweat slickening his skin. This was real horror, to have strangers judging the quality of your character, the content of your soul.

'We're going to leave you here for a moment,' Smoker said abruptly.

As they stood up, he asked them if he could have a drink of water. Once again it was as if he didn't exist.

When they had left, he thought about trying the door, but there was a camera on the ceiling just as there had been in his cell, so he sat patiently until they returned.

They came back twenty minutes later, Smoker smelling of cigarettes, Scowl smelling of coffee and pastry. He wished he'd had a chance to use the toilet one more time before being dragged into this room. He hoped he'd be allowed to shower soon. He was beginning to wrinkle his nose at his own acrid smell.

'Tell us about the pictures again,' said Smoker.

He told them, and told them, and told them. Smoker seemed reasonable, almost friendly this time, although he was relentless in his insistence on the details, grilling Jason Walker over and over about the smallest inconsistencies in his telling. Still, after what might have been another hour or perhaps three, he thought he was making progress. Scowl hadn't hurt him again, and Smoker had taken to nodding frequently, as if it was all making sense to him now.

Finally, at what might have been dawn or noon, they pushed back their chairs again.

'I think we're done here,' said Smoker.

'So I can go home?'

'I think we're done here.'

Smoker and Scowl left. A guard and two soldiers, different ones this time, walked him back to his cell. His sweat turned clammy in the refrigerator-like cold, but he was grateful to have a rest from the questioning. Besides, there was a green wool blanket folded at the foot of the bunk.

He was urinating into the toilet with shivering relief when the door opened again. Over his shoulder he saw someone drop a plastic tray of food on the floor. When he was done, he inspected it. Meatloaf, macaroni, gray spinach, and a bottle of water. He ate ravenously, snapping the tines of the plastic fork in his hurry. On any other day he might have been disgusted by the food, but right now it tasted better than Charlie Trotter's best.

There was a strange bitterness to the water, but he was so thirsty that he drank it all in practically one swallow.

He was trying to roll himself in the thin blanket when sleepiness seized him like paralysis and he fell heavily into unconsciousness.

Three

Jason Walker woke up on the floor. Sitting up, he saw that the bed was gone. So was the toilet. He was damp with sweat. The room was hot. His head throbbed painfully and there was a coppery taste in his mouth. He felt as if he was peering through the wrong end of a telescope. Slowly, he realized that he was in a different cell.

The walls of this cell were sand-colored and smooth. The floor was dirty gray concrete and sloped to a grated drain in the center. A plastic bucket with a mismatched lid sat next to the drain. On the ceiling, four fluorescent tubes glowed under a locked Plexiglas enclosure, next to a half-dome of smoked glass. There were no windows, but two armored hatches had been set into the gray steel door, a small square one at eye level, and a thin wide one at the floor.

He tried to stand up. The pain in his head grew worse the higher he rose, so he sat back down with his back against the wall. The cell was sour with the reek of urine and vomit. He stank, too. Certainly no one had bothered to bathe him in the time he'd been asleep. Looking at his knees, he noticed that he wasn't wearing his own clothes anymore. He had been dressed in an orange boiler suit.

The pain in his head dulled slightly and he became aware of an urgent need to urinate. He stood up cautiously, supporting himself on the wall, then took halting steps to the bucket. He lifted the lid and peered in. It had been emptied since the cell was last occupied but not washed. The smell reminded him of overflowing outhouses he'd encountered on hot summer hikes with his parents in the Cascade Mountains. He fumbled some buttons open and started to pull down his underwear. His underwear felt funny. He was wearing a diaper. Angrily, clumsily, he pulled off the diaper and threw it in the bucket. The diaper was filthy. He urinated in the bucket and replaced the lid. He hobbled back to the far side of the room and slid down to the floor again.

He had been drugged. The diaper was proof of that. They hadn't wanted a mess.

The previous cell had seemed soundproof, but here he became aware of many distant sounds: shouting voices, slamming doors, the high-pitched whine of machinery. Why had they moved him? Did they want him out of the city for some reason? He was grateful, at least, that the awful cold had stopped.

He waited. Hours passed. He grew thirsty. His tongue seemed swollen. The heat was like an oven. He grew so thirsty that he wondered how long he would wait before he drank his own urine from the bucket. Then the air grew cooler and the temperature became almost bearable. The lights didn't dim, but he guessed evening was coming. His new cell was definitely not climate-controlled.

The air turned chilly. He wondered if he had been forgotten. He went to the door and banged on it with his fist, his thumps dull and puny. He shouted, but hearing his own ineffectual voice made him ineffably depressed. He sat back down on the floor, then became tired and lay down. After a while, he fell asleep.

It was a cliché, but Jason Walker had met Gina Saraceno at the supermarket. Depressed over his dwindling finances, he had vowed to stop eating his meals in restaurants. He would use some of his newfound free time to cook huge pots of hearty food, then freeze the portions and reheat them as needed. Without any experience in the kitchen, however, he had little idea of the ingredients he needed and even less idea of the quantities.

He inched through the produce section, loading his cart with sacks of potatoes and onions and carrots, heads of cabbage, and a mound of turnips, beets, and squashes. They seemed ridiculously cheap when purchased this way.

'Hearty,' he murmured, as if in a trance. 'Hearty.'

In dry goods he bought twenty-pound sacks of rice and beans. In canned goods he bought peas, corn, and tomatoes, and peaches, pears, and pineapple. In the meat department he bought family-value packs of hamburger, sausages, and the cheaper parts of chickens. He splurged on five pounds of bacon. He bought several bags of flour, sugar, and salt. He bought two gallons of cooking oil. He bought eggs, butter, and milk.

By the time he was done, pushing his shopping cart, which had one balky wheel to begin with, was like pushing a stove. Panting with the effort, he made his way to the checkout lanes, occasionally stooping to pick up fallen cans or beets.

Ahead of him in line, a short, curvy woman was winding a lock of dark hair around her finger and reading *Hello Goodbye*. The cover story promised exclusive photos of a public spat between the movie-star couple known as AngieStan.

The dark-haired woman glanced up reflexively, then folded her magazine and put it back on the rack. Jason Walker and his shopping cart apparently offered more titillation than the spilled drinks of famous people.

'Let me guess,' she said, 'it's your turn to shop for the cult.'

'Excuse me?' he said.

'You're locked in the basement reading scripture all week long, but every weekend, someone has to buy food so the group doesn't starve. You draw lots, or flip coins, or split newborn children to see who's left holding the bigger half. And the lucky winner gets to visit the real world to buy food.'

He had never been particularly quick when people teased him. In fact, he often composed word-perfect retorts on paper after the fact, committed them to memory, and then hoped for the same situation to arise again. But no one had ever accused him of being in a cult before. And this woman was very, very pretty. He didn't want to come across as stupid as he felt. So he played along.

'You're wrong,' he said. 'We don't draw lots. This is my job every week. Other people wash the idol, or scoop dead bugs out of the holy water, but I always do the shopping. I do the cooking, too.'

The woman smiled.

'How many people are there in your cult?'

He had an inspiration.

'One more after you're done talking to me.'

'I don't think so. I kind of like the idea of a cult where the men do the cooking, but you'd have to come up with something better than hamburger and cabbage. It looks like you're going to reenact the first edition of Betty Crocker.'

The line moved forward, but it was long and slow. He was grateful.

'Jason Walker,' he said impulsively, offering her his hand.

She took his hand, a crooked smile on her lips.

'Gina Saraceno. Seriously, are you fleeing to the hills? What's with the stew fixings?'

He told her. She laughed and, when she was done laughing, coaxed him out of line. She guided him around the store, making him put almost everything back. Her own cart contained only a tub of yogurt, a cantaloupe, two eggplants, and a bunch of basil.

'You don't need three hundred pounds of food,' she said. 'You need cooking lessons.'

They bought Italian sausage, fresh tomatoes, eggplants, garlic, capers, basil, olive oil, balsamic vinegar, ricotta and mozzarella cheese, anchovies, and several kinds of pasta—also bread, salad greens, and wine.

'Start with Italian food,' said Gina Saraceno. 'It's easy to make—it's easy to make a *lot*—and it tastes good when you reheat it. Italian families are big, so Italian moms know what they're doing.'

'How many brothers and sisters do you have?' he asked.

'One sister,' she said. 'Thirty-two cousins.'

She abandoned her cart and helped him carry his groceries home. She was determined to see this through, she said. He had thought he was about to watch a cooking demonstration, perhaps being invited to slice cheese or wash tomatoes, but he was wrong. As soon as they reached his kitchen, she pulled up a chair, uncorked the bottle of wine, and began giving commands. An hour and a half later, he felt as if he'd been through boot camp. He was sweating and his nerves were frayed, but there on the table was a delicious-looking meal of pasta puttanesca, salad, and garlic bread, and there was a ready-to-bake lasagna in the refrigerator.

'This looks good,' she said. 'I wish I could stay and eat it with you.'

Crestfallen, he couldn't think what to say.

She punched him in the arm. 'I'm only kidding, Mister Literal. Unless you only own one fork.'

Jason Walker ate and Gina Saraceno talked. She told him that her father, who was now dead, had been a history professor at the University of Illinois. Her mother, who was still living, was a community activist, although old age and health concerns had slowed her somewhat. Gina Saraceno was a late-life child. She had arrived ten years after her sister, apparently a surprise to her parents.

Gio Saraceno, her father, had been a 'throwback,' an unrepentant, card-carrying communist who addressed his friends as 'comrade' and never shied away from speaking his mind. His specialty was labor history. His daughter grew up with bedtime stories not about knights, princesses, and dragons, but labor organizers, protesters, strikebreakers, and bosses. As a girl, she observed with a child's sensitivity that many people considered her father to be a harmless kook. But even though she had not grown up to espouse his particular vision of world harmony, she had inherited his self-confidence in the face of contradictory opinion and also his desire to help people. As a social worker making home visits to at-risk children, she worked odd hours, a mix of days, nights, and weekends.

Gina Saraceno made Jason Walker feel poorly read and ill-informed. Worse, when he did have an opinion, his shyness made him an ineffectual debater.

'Everyone talks about supporting the president in time of crisis,' she said. 'What if the president helped create the crisis?'

'By inviting the terrorists to attack us?'

'Of course not. But he doesn't make them not want to attack us, either.'

An invisible question mark formed over his head.

'I'm not the first person to say it, but it seems obvious that every time some Iranian mom loses a son, we've got five more potential terrorists who hate us even more than they did already.'

'Innocent people have died in every war. We can't let that stop us from protecting ourselves.'

'Why not protect ourselves at home? Look, I understand that reasonable people may disagree on things. I just miss the disagreement. I just don't understand how the country sits idly by while the judicial and legislative branches all rush over to the same side of the scale. What happened to checks and balances? Look, in his second term, the president had what, a twenty-eight percent approval rating?'

He nodded.

'And then there was a wave of attacks and it was eighty percent.'

'The same thing happened around September 11.'

'Right, and then, well, you know what he did with that mandate. Only this time he can't get reelected, so he arm-wrestles Congress and the states into changing the constitution. And while they're doing that, they sneak in the "homeland language" and "sanctity of marriage" amendments, too. Is he planning on being president for life?'

'I hope not. But I understand why people don't want to change things when things are bad. What's happening might be bad, but they know there's always the possibility that it could be even worse. They like to stick with what they know.'

'Don't tell me you're one of those people,' said Gina Saraceno, draining her wine glass.

'I'm just saying how some people think,' said Jason Walker, draining his own.

They were on more even footing while they listened to his music collection. But when they went to bed, Gina Saraceno once again decided to teach him a few things. Not that he minded a bit.

He was dreaming that he was lying in bed, holding Gina Saraceno, when he was awakened by a loud clang. The door to his cell had been thrown open. Rolling over, he opened his eyes in time to see a black bag come toward his head and then the bag was in place and he couldn't see anything. The bag smelled like sweat and halitosis. Hands lifted him under the arms and dragged him forward. He found his feet and stumbled along, guided by pushes from behind.

Dizzy, he staggered into a wall. He heard laughter. He had hit his forehead. He tried to put his hand under the bag to check if he was bleeding but his hand was swatted away. He was pushed forward again, then kicked in the rump. He lurched ahead with his hands held out in front of him to prevent further collisions.

After what might have been fifty yards he was grabbed by the shoulders and turned to the right. He scraped against a doorjamb, struck his thighs, and fell face-first on to a table. He was lifted off the table and thrown into a chair. Someone struck his head. He cried out. Footsteps retreated and the door clanged shut. It was silent. He thought he must be alone again.

He lifted the bag off, squinting in bright light. Across the table were two men wearing black T-shirts. They both had close-cropped hair. One had a crooked nose with a scar on it. He looked like a man sent from central casting to play an Italian mobster in a B-movie. The other one had a round, soft face and looked like a college fullback.

Jason Walker turned his head and saw two men in khaki uniforms standing against the wall behind him. Their faces were brown and they both wore full, black mustaches. The sleeves and pockets of their uniforms were blank.

'So,' said the mobster. 'It's the architectural photographer.'

He pretended not to hear the irony in the man's voice. He said, simply, 'Yes.'

'Can you tell me why one of the buildings you photographed so—artistically—was bombed six months later?'

His stomach felt cold and hollow. They were still trying to make him into a terrorist.

'You have heard of the BOL Building?' said the mobster.

'I must have photographed at least two hundred buildings.'

'The bomb was in a truck, in the parking garage, next to a critical support column. It was lucky that the charge wasn't packed correctly, or it could have brought down a dozen floors.'

'I never photographed the parking garage.'

The mobster smiled, his thin lips crooked like his scar. 'You didn't?'

His mind raced. Had he? He didn't remember. He might have. Maybe there was something about the way the columns lined up that looked good through the viewfinder. But even if he had taken a picture, he certainly hadn't made any prints. Or had he? That was two years ago, at least. How could he be sure?

'Who did you take the pictures for, Jason?'

'For myself.'

'Did you also plant the bomb?'

'No.'

'Then who did?'

'I don't know. It's just a coincidence.'

'It's extremely rare that we meet someone like you by coincidence. You'll have to convince me.'

'I don't know if I can.'

'Oh,' said the mobster, 'I think you can.'

The mobster nodded at one of the men behind him and Jason Walker's head lurched to the left. He saw tiny lights, like cinders floating up from a campfire. The pain made his eyes fill with tears.

'Who did you take the pictures for?'

'For myself. For my hobby.'

'It's your hobby to take pictures of buildings from all four sides? To document engineering details? To take pictures of building foundations and structural details?'

He tried to lift his hands to his throbbing head. They were slapped to the table with a wooden baton.

'Keep your hands down.'

'You can't do this to me.'

'We are doing this to you.'

'I'm an American citizen. You have to let me call a lawyer.'

'We don't have to let you do anything.'

'This is America. You can't do this in America.'

'What makes you think we're still in America?'

Jason Walker froze. It was like waking from a nightmare to find his bed intact and the house blown down around it. Surely the man was lying. But what if he wasn't? Before the third term, there had been stories in the newspaper about secret jails in other countries. Stories about suspected terrorists being flown out of the country for questioning.

He turned to look behind him.

'Eyes to the front!' said the mobster.

One of the guards was stepping toward him, baton raised, but he couldn't help it, he had to look. The men had light brown skin, dark brown eyes, and black hair. It meant nothing. But their uniforms.

The guard speared him in the side with his baton, then banged his head on the table and held him there. When his head hit the table, it was like the shutter of a giant camera blinking once, slowly.

Panting, he didn't resist. Where were they? What could he say to make it stop?

Suddenly, the football player's face was in front of his. He looked kindly, corn-fed and Midwestern. Something in his expression told Jason Walker that he was genuinely sorry to see him suffer.

'This doesn't have to happen,' said the football player. 'You don't have to keep hurting. You can make it stop.'

'Please,' he said.

'We don't want you. We know you're not a bomber. Who gets the pictures after you take them? It's possible that it's someone that you don't even know is a terrorist. Maybe it's someone, a friend, a family member, who pretends to like your pictures and then uses them. If you didn't know about it, we couldn't hold you responsible. You wouldn't have meant any harm. So all you have to do is give us a name.'

He tried to think of anyone who had shown an undue interest in his photographs. It was preposterous. No one was interested in them. The two gallery owners he'd shown them to, years ago, had closed the portfolio after the first half-dozen images. His own friends were politely interested, but no one had asked for copies. He hadn't yet told Gina Saraceno about his hobby. As far as she knew, the crisp, black-and-white enlargements that lined his walls had been bought in a store.

'I'd tell you,' he said, 'but there's no one. Maybe it's someone at the photo lab?'

The football player's face fell. He looked personally disappointed. He moved back around the table and sat down.

The mobster didn't look ready to give up quite yet.

'Think hard. Maybe someone set you up. Someone who has access to your photos.'

Jason Walker pictured Gina Saraceno looking at his photos. He wondered if she sometimes leafed through his portfolios when he was in the shower. He stopped, angry with himself. He had only known her for a few months. Even if somebody he knew had used his photos of an underground parking garage to plan a bomb attack, it would have been long before she entered his life.

Moreover, why wouldn't that person take their own photos? Why would they go to great lengths to use his? It was a public garage. All that was necessary to see it was to pay to park a car.

'I can see your mind working, Jason. You're thinking of someone, aren't you? Just give us a name.'

He couldn't keep himself from flushing.

'Someone who is critical of the president, of the country. Someone who seems angry that we are at war.'

And wouldn't a terrorist pretend to be a supporter of the war on terror?

Perhaps he took too long to reply. Or perhaps he looked recalcitrant. The mobster nodded over Jason Walker's shoulder and thick, callused fingers grabbed his left hand. He felt a quick tug and heard a sound like a snapping pencil.

He shouted in disbelief. He pulled his hand away and they let him take it. He saw his left little finger sticking out at a wrong angle. He couldn't move it. Pain lanced up his arm.

'I wish we could give you the time you need to weigh the pros and cons and come to the right decision on your own,' sighed the mobster. 'But innocent lives are at stake and we don't have the luxury of time.'

'You can't torture an American citizen!'

The mobster spread his hands guilelessly.

'We aren't torturing you. We're just asking you some questions.'

The football player looked sorrowful.

'Give us a name,' said the mobster.

Names raced through his head. Friends, enemies, the payroll accountant at *Chicago Socialite*. If he just said a name they would stop. And then they would bring him back again, asking for the correct name. Unless whoever he named named someone else. Perhaps the whole chain of misery would spiral away from him and disappear forever.

He just wanted everything to stop. He wanted to go home.

'I can't,' he said.

'Let's do it,' the mobster said to the men behind him.

He heard thumps and scrapes, the sound of furniture being moved. He turned to look and was rapped on the head with a baton. The camera shutter blinked again.

'No, let him look,' said the mobster.

Jason Walker turned, holding his throbbing left hand. The black-haired men had pulled two sawhorses out from the wall and set them five feet apart. One sawhorse was six inches higher than the other. They laid a long piece of plywood across the sawhorses. The plywood was stamped Idaho Lumber and had bloodstains on it. They came for him and lifted him, struggling, on to the board. One of the men pinned him in place, leaning on his chest and pressing a baton hard against his throat, while the other man wound duct tape around his chest and arms and his legs. Then the second man wound tape around his head. He couldn't move. Staring straight up into a fixture with four fluorescent tubes, the kind he saw regularly in offices throughout Chicago, he wondered when he would beg them to kill him.

'You can stop this at any time,' said the football player.

'Stop it now,' he said. 'Stop it now, please.'

They wound plastic wrap around his face, the kind he kept in a drawer at home to cover leftovers. They wound it around and around until the room looked blurry. It was like he had

Vaseline in his eyes. They left a little bit of slack around his mouth and chin. He could breathe but not deeply.

'Tell me when you're ready to tell me what we want to know,' he heard the mobster say.

He felt his pulse quickening. He badly needed to defecate. He had the strangest feeling, as if he were burning up with fever and falling backward through the air.

He heard a handle turn with a squeak. He recognized it instantly as a tap for a garden hose. Why was there a garden hose in this room?

A few drops of water flecked the plastic, like the first spits of a rainstorm on the windshield. And then water covered him like a torrent. His chest convulsed, his jaws pumped, but he couldn't breathe. He struggled against the tape but couldn't move. He was drowning. He closed his mouth against the water. Otherwise he would swallow it all and his lungs would fill with water. But with his mouth closed he couldn't breathe. He was going to die.

Jason Walker screamed at them to stop. He told them he would tell them what they wanted to know. He would tell them everything.

The handle squeaked again, an innocent sound, like his father turning the water off after giving the lawn a good soak. The water slowed to a trickle and then stopped.

He was desperate for the plastic to come off but it seemed like an eternity before it did. No one said anything. The silence stretched out and he wanted to fill it. He became so frustrated at waiting that he was ready to blurt out his full confession unprompted. Except that he still didn't know what to say. But he would say anything to avoid drowning again.

'Well?' said the mobster.

His chest convulsing, he choked out the words. Yes, he took photographs of buildings. Yes, they were for someone else.

Who were they for?

A man.

What was the man's name?

He didn't know. The man never said.

Why did he help this man?

For money. It was a lot of money. He needed it.

What did he do with this money?

He deposited it in the bank.

How long had this been going on?

For several years. Maybe longer.

Did he hate America?

Yes. No. Sometimes. He just wanted the money. He didn't know what the man was going to do with the photographs.

The black-haired men cut the tape. They didn't bother to pull it off his clothing or his head. He sat up, his limbs trembling, and tried to pull the tape off his forehead. It pulled hair and he quit trying. He fell off the board. He climbed into the chair. His interrogators exchanged a look. He didn't know what the look meant.

The mobster inclined his head toward the door and the black-haired men filed out without saying anything.

'Do you feel better now?' said the football player.

He nodded. He felt only an animal instinct to cling to life.

'I think we're done here,' said the mobster to the football player. To Jason Walker he said, 'Wait here.'

They left. He sat, trying to gather himself. His entire body was sore, even in places where he hadn't been beaten. Once, when he was in his twenties, he had been in a car wreck. A pickup truck had run a light and hit the car he was riding in, spinning them around in the middle of an intersection. He had been wearing a seatbelt and hadn't received a scratch, and yet he had limped for a week. The moment of fear, when every muscle in his body had contracted, had bruised him invisibly and worse than the wreck itself. He felt worse than that now. He examined his hand. The finger and the meat of the hand near to it were turning purple. It hurt but the pain was no longer excruciating.

He was alone for a long time. He was exhausted but he couldn't sleep. He was starving. His mind was racing but he couldn't hold on to a single thought.

A man walked in and sat down, placing a pack of cigarettes on the table. He smiled. The man was Jason Walker's age but taller and more muscular. He had blue eyes, a slightly upturned nose, and a thick thatch of blond hair that seemed playfully tousled. His skin was tan and dotted with light freckles. He was wearing chinos and a red polo shirt that was snug on his muscular biceps.

'My name's Chad Armstrong,' he said.

He slid the cigarettes across the table.

'Go ahead and smoke if you want to, Jason.'

Jason Walker didn't smoke. He never had. Surely they knew that. Except Chad Armstrong didn't seem to know that. He needed something and the cigarettes were all that was on offer. He ripped open the pack, wincing at the pain in his left hand. He pulled a cigarette out with his fingernails and held it to his lips. Chad Armstrong pulled an expensive butane lighter out of his pants pocket and thumbed it open, producing a hissing blue flame. Jason Walker leaned the cigarette into the flame and inhaled. He coughed long and painfully. The nicotine shot through his fragile nervous system, nauseating him. He coughed again, dropping the cigarette on the floor.

'Not up to it yet? Don't worry about it. Keep the pack for later.'

Chad Armstrong was still smiling. Chad Armstrong looked earnest. Jason Walker clung to the name Chad Armstrong like a lifeline. It was the first piece of information he'd been given. The fact that he was being given a name seemed like a miracle. And yet Chad Armstrong looked like someone he might meet at a bar on Rush Street, a cocky young guy with a business degree, someone he had gone to school with and envied for his confidence. How had the two of them arrived at this table?

'First,' said Chad Armstrong, 'I believe you. Your first story, that is. I appreciate that you tried to help us out, but you're a terrible liar. You're pretty upset right now, and I can understand that. We made a mistake. But protecting freedom has its price, and I guess I'd rather make a mistake with one guy than a whole planeful of people. I'm sure you agree with that, don't you?'

He didn't know. He guessed so.

'Can I go home?' he asked.

'Of course. We're going to get you expedited and get you home just as soon as humanly possible. But I need to ask for your help. Not here, but when you get back. You see, we don't just pick people up at random. We believe a terrorist cell in Chicago is planning something big. And when we got a tip about you, we thought we might just have gotten lucky. Now, of course, we know that that was wrong and you're innocent. But you can still help us.'

Jason Walker pictured a plane slicing into the Sears Tower. He saw ash-white people fleeing a rolling cloud of black smoke on LaSalle Street. He shivered. He couldn't imagine how he could possibly help.

'How big?' he asked.

'We think they're planning to bring down a building,' said Chad Armstrong. 'We don't know which one, or when. The chatter we've been monitoring indicates that it's going to be sooner rather than later. We plan to stop them.'

Chad Armstrong was matter-of-fact and serious, but nothing in the way he spoke seemed equal to the gravity of the situation. Jason Walker thought that it was as if Chad Armstrong was discussing a rival company's plan to take his customers. And yet here they were. Water pooled around their feet.

'The activity we've monitored all centers around a community center. It's supposed to be a place for Lebanese folks to get together and swap recipes and sing songs or something. We think it's a front for militant jihadis. We're not sure if they meet there, pick up messages there, or recruit suicide bombers there. Possibly all three. But they're very disciplined. So far they haven't screwed up and let us know anything useful. What we need is a man inside. What we need is a Lebanese guy.'

Jason Walker's mouth went dry.

Chad Armstrong leaned forward.

'You,' he said.

Four

'I'm not Lebanese,' said Jason Walker.

'Your mother was Lebanese,' said Chad Armstrong.

'Yes, she was Lebanese, but I'm an American.'

'You have a Lebanese passport.'

'I travel under my American passport, not my Lebanese passport. Because I'm not Lebanese.'

Chad Armstrong eyed the pack of cigarettes as if he was thinking about taking them back. He spun the lighter idly on the tabletop.

'OK, you're not Lebanese. You just happen to have been born in Lebanon to a Lebanese woman and you still have a Lebanese passport. Really, you're Irish.'

Jason Walker remembered sitting at the kitchen table in Seattle as his mother served an elaborate meal of baked kibbeh, tabouleh, falafel, hummus, stuffed grape leaves, fresh fruit, green salad, and flatbread. He remembered calling the kibbeh 'weird' and asking if he could have a hamburger instead. He remembered his mother's silent acquiescence.

'I don't really remember Lebanon,' he said. 'My parents didn't talk about it much. I wouldn't fit in at a Lebanese cultural center.'

'It doesn't matter if you don't know anything. In fact, that makes it even better. You're half Lebanese, but you don't know anything about the culture. Great. It's the perfect excuse to walk into a place like that. You tell them you want to connect with your heritage. Tell them you don't know who you really are.'

'I'm not a spy.'

'Don't flatter yourself,' said Chad Armstrong. 'We know you're not a spy. We have plenty of spies. I'm a spy. We're not going to ask you to rappel through the skylight with a lock-pick and a minicam. You'd simply be an informant. All you have to do is start visiting the place. Keep your eyes open, tell us what you see and who you meet. That's it. No James Bond stuff.'

He took one of the cigarettes. He lit it, inhaled deeply, and inspected the burning tip with satisfaction.

'What if I don't do it?'

'Look. Me personally, I don't think you're guilty of anything but having a dorky hobby and bad taste in architecture. But you looked suspicious enough to someone that they were willing to fly you here, at considerable expense to the taxpayer, to find out for sure. Somewhere there's an ambitious lawyer who's willing to make the case that you're public enemy number one. But if there's not enough evidence, they could also send you to Camp X-Ray, where you can cool your heels for a few years while they find or create the necessary evidence. And while you think about that, bear in mind that most of the guys in X-Ray aren't mild-mannered, marginally employed, half-American Christians like yourself. They're the real deal. Hunger-striking, Koran-quoting beardies who want to chop your balls off just because you like reading the *Sports Illustrated* swimsuit issue.'

'I need time to think.'

'Sure, take all the time you want. We've got a room in this hotel that you'll love. The ceiling is four feet high and there's six inches of water on the floor. It's like having your own pool. The water is—well, I wouldn't want to drink it but there's probably nothing wrong with crouching in it. There are better rooms, but we're pretty booked right now. In fact, we just let two Saudi brothers have the room you were in. They were planning to firebomb a Toys'R'Us.'

His hand hurt. His head felt hot. He couldn't think well enough to argue. Of course he had to say yes. He just didn't want to. He wanted to go home.

Chad Armstrong sighed.

'Or, you could go back to Lebanon.'

'I'm an American citizen.'

'But you're also a Lebanese citizen. That makes things easier. If you were only an American citizen nobody would want to take you. You'd be a man without a country. But if we strip you of your citizenship, repatriate you, they have to take you. Maybe that wouldn't be so bad. You could start a new life.'

His father had had three photographs of Lebanon on the wall of his study. One showed a man in a suit leading a donkey down a dusty road. Another showed the sun setting on a beach with palm trees. The third showed the hotel his father had co-owned, its facade demolished by shelling.

He himself had only a few memories of Beirut. One of them was of his father waking him in the middle of the night and carrying him through hotel corridors to the basement. He supposed that they had lived in the hotel. Another was from when he was twelve years old, living in Seattle. On the news there was a report that the marine barracks had been bombed.

'These people prefer to live like animals,' his father had told him with disgust. 'That is why we will never go back.'

One of his friends who knew that his mother was Lebanese had said, 'So, do you think it was your mom's friends who did the bomb?'

Jason Walker regarded Chad Armstrong dubiously.

'All you want me to do is look around and meet people?'

'That's all. Maybe take a class if they offer any. Who knows? It might be a real learning experience for you.'

'All right,' he said.

He told himself that he would do what he was asked and no more. Less, if he could.

'Glad to have you on board,' said Chad Armstrong. 'Remember, if you tell anyone about this we'll probably have to kill you. Now let's see if we can find you some Band-Aids and ibuprofen for your hand.'

A bored-looking man—possibly the one who'd broken Jason Walker's little finger, he wasn't sure—bandaged his left hand, taping the finger to a tongue depressor and then to his ring finger so he couldn't move it.

Then he was taken back to his cell. There was no sign of the two brothers who wanted to firebomb a toystore. Perhaps Chad Armstrong had been joking. Or perhaps the brothers were in the interrogation room, taped to boards laid across sawhorses.

He was given two blankets, two bottles of water, and a tray with lentils, lamb stew, and two pieces of flatbread. He was intensely hungry and wolfed it down, wiping the plastic tray with pieces of the bread to soak up every last bit of gravy. He felt much better. The worst was certainly over. He lay on one blanket and covered himself with the other and tried to sleep. The moment he closed his eyes he began shaking uncontrollably. He put his face into the scratchy blanket and wept. He screamed into the blanket, beating the concrete floor with his fists until they were bruised and sore.

Chad Armstrong probably knew more about Jason Walker's family history than Jason did himself. Chad Armstrong had the resources of the American government at his disposal. All Jason Walker had had were his mother and father.

Jean Walker was an elegant, taciturn man who wore a suit every day of his working life. After his retirement, he allowed himself the luxury of not wearing a tie on Saturdays and Sundays, though he wore a blazer unless the temperature was above ninety degrees, and he always wore leather shoes. Jason Walker never saw his father in shorts.

Like his son, Jean Walker was of mixed heritage, having had an American father and a French mother. His father, a career diplomat, was relocated often, and he reached adulthood speaking five languages fluently but having no close friends. He entered the world of business and became a hotelier, eventually buying a half-share in a Beirut hotel during the 1960s. He was already in his forties when he fell in love with Rima, the daughter of his Lebanese business partner. Fifteen years younger, she was bright and vivacious but not educated, having been encouraged to pursue only domestic achievements. They had one child.

When the Lebanese Civil War started in 1975, Jason

Walker was four years old. The glamorous city of Beirut huddled under the hail of bullets. State buildings were shelled. Mansions were occupied and then burned once no longer useful. His father sold his share of the hotel for a pittance and moved the family to Seattle, where a business acquaintance had offered him a job as assistant manager of a hotel in a large and well-known chain. Jean Walker was a man apart, quiet, thoughtful, witty only when the situation required it. He never spoke of the past or complained about his lot, reduced to working for another man when he'd once commanded a staff of nearly 200. But he didn't have much guidance to offer his son as Jason Walker navigated the strange new world of grade school.

As a high-schooler, Jason Walker had been pained by his father's difference from the other fathers. While they wore Bermuda shorts and T-shirts and sandals, at every gathering Jean Walker looked like a board chairman suffering through an attempt at good fellowship with his employees. Older than the other fathers, he was too well dressed to join in backyard football games. And in any event, he preferred to sit drinking tea and reading his precious international newspapers, which arrived days and sometimes weeks later than the Seattle paper.

Rima Walker also could not shrug off the gloss of culture she'd acquired in her life, but unlike her husband, she made every attempt to assimilate. She bought every *Better Homes and Gardens* cookbook, cooked every buffet delicacy, no matter how foreign—she thought that serving miniature hot dogs in cocktail sauce was the depth of barbarism—and volunteered to help with every potluck, bake sale, and church social. She joined the other housewives for soap operas and coffee klatches, and reserved her nostalgic meals of Lebanese food for family affairs.

Her attempts to assimilate didn't always succeed, but Rima Walker put a brave face on every subtle social snub and encouraged her son to try even harder to fit in. With English that became less accented every day—she had stopped speaking to him in Arabic—she knew he had a better chance. He was a shy boy but, with her approval, gorged himself on American culture. He ate Big Macs, watched *The Dukes of Hazzard*, and listened to *American Top 40* on the radio every Sunday. He rode a skateboard. When video games debuted, he spent his after-school hours in the arcade, wearing his baseball cap backward, dropping quarter after quarter into the machines. His mother countenanced all this with greater forbearance than her fellow parents, relieved that her son had the same addictions as their boys. But clearly some part of her hadn't wanted him to cut his last tie to his heritage. Why else would she have insisted—even going so far as to send the money to pay for it—that he keep his Lebanese passport renewed?

Best of all, Jason Walker was fair-skinned and his name was normal. Unless his friends met his mother, they never realized he was from the Middle East. And even when they did meet his mother, many of them thought that this short, slender, raven-haired woman with Mediterranean skin was Italian. Like any growing boy, he was acutely attuned to the ways in which his family wasn't normal. But often he was the only one who noticed.

Jean and Rima Walker had traveled extensively in the Middle East, Europe, Asia, and even Africa. But Seattle was the last stop on the itinerary. Though the East was only a direct flight away, Jean Walker stopped traveling and never said why. He never betrayed anger at what life had handed him. But he had never shown any kind of passion. When Jason Walker became old enough to understand that his father had once been an important man, and that they had once enjoyed a way of life that included servants and a penthouse overlooking the Mediterranean, he took his father's seemingly placid acceptance for a character flaw. And when a life-long love of Gauloise cigarettes caught up with Jean Walker, killing him with fast-spreading lung cancer, it didn't seem to even his own son that a bright light had been extinguished. The candle had simply burned itself out. Years later the son would wonder whether he'd judged his father without ever really knowing him.

He had expected his mother, so much younger and so full of life, to start over, but she never stopped being a widow. When he settled in Chicago, he encouraged her to move there and rent a unit in his building, but she kept offering vague demurrals. After she died, he learned the reason why she hadn't wanted to start over: a nonsmoker herself, she had nonetheless been battling lung cancer, too. Without telling her son, she'd had first one lung removed, then endured endless months of chemotherapy and radiation on the tumor in her remaining lung. When she had finally told him what was happening, she had had less than a month to live.

Jason Walker was a perfectly assimilated American and all alone. He'd never met his French or Lebanese relatives. He had met his American relatives, who lived in Virginia, only once. Though he'd tried hard to be like his mother, who always won people over eventually, he was more like his father, often alone, not very good at making friends. Naturally, he had gravitated toward a job that he could do alone. No one—not Gina Saraceno, not David Darling—could say with certainty that Jason Walker was who he said he was.

Lying in a cell somewhere outside of America, Jason Walker wasn't sure that he could, either.

For most of the night—if it was night—he slept without stirring. When finally his mind began to rise out of the black well of unconsciousness, he thought he was outside, wandering through the streets of a ruined city. Children kicked a soccer ball in a dusty lot. Old women squatted on curbstones, cooking foul-smelling meat. A man walked toward him, leading a donkey. The man was wearing a suit. He saw that the man was his father. Jason Walker rushed forward to embrace him. But when Jean Walker opened his mouth, he spoke in a language his son couldn't understand.

Where do we go?

Iskat habim, said his father. *Leono hurga.*

Frightened, Jason Walker shook his father's arm.

I can't understand. Take me with you. Show me.

Jean Walker smiled and gently removed his son's hand. He shook his head and walked off, still leading the donkey.

Jason Walker stumbled into a building and climbed seven floors up a crumbling staircase. On the top floor, he found a ladder leaning against the wall. He climbed the ladder and threw open a trap door. He climbed on to the roof.

The city stretched as far as he could see, an unbroken horizon of ruined buildings. Columns of oily smoke climbed into the sky. Nearby, behind him, gunfire chattered. He whirled, half expecting to see bullets flying at him. He ran to the trapdoor but it was gone. There was no way off the roof. He was stuck there forever.

Five

He woke frightened, his head snapping back. Gritty metal struck his cheek. They were torturing him again. He couldn't see. He felt another blow and gasped. His hands were cuffed behind him. He struggled to breathe. His head had again been covered with a black bag. His feet were cuffed together. He saw tiny pinpricks of light through the black fabric. Eventually he realized that he was lying on the floor of a van, bouncing with each bump in the road and landing hard.

The driver braked and Jason Walker slid forward into the struts holding up the van's back seat. The driver cursed his luck hitting a red light.

The windows were down and he could smell the streets. Rotting garbage and grilled lamb. An intense burst of cumin— a spice he'd never known the name of before he met Gina Saraceno. The air was hot and dry. Horns honked incessantly and drivers cursed each other with rehearsed indignation. A muezzin's call echoed from an unseen minaret.

Talking baseball, the men in the front of the van made no mention of their human cargo. They drove for what seemed like more than an hour. Gradually the noise of the city abated.

They turned off the road and rolled to a stop. They waited. A gate rolled back on squeaking wheels. The van drove through. After a few minutes and several turns they drove inside a building, perhaps a garage. The van's engine sounded closed in. Its tire chirps reverberated. The men got out and slammed their doors, leaving him alone.

He thought he should try to escape. But escape to where? How would he get home with no money? And when he got home, they knew where he lived. He had no means of going anywhere else. Jason Walker lay quietly on the floor of the van, feeling sweat dampen his hair.

After a while they came back.

'Hurry up, mime is money,' said one.

The other one laughed.

They dragged him out the back of the van and marched him stumbling through the garage. They took him through a door and sat him down on a bench.

Nothing happened for a moment, as if they were thinking.

'Should we feed him?' said one.

'Oh, fuck,' said the other.

'Long trip.'

'No, I know. It's just—I dunno who has the key to the fridge.'

They moved away, talking in low voices. Eventually one of them came back and uncuffed his hands, then recuffed them in front of his body. The man thrust something crinkly into his hand. Candy bars.

'Sorry, this is all I got. There's some water on the floor by your foot. In a bottle. You gotta keep the mask on.'

The man walked away.

It was like a party game. Unable to separate his hands, he opened the first candy bar, worked it under the foul-smelling black bag, and put it in his mouth. He bit down into the soft, perspiring chocolate. It was a Three Musketeers, a candy bar he'd loved as a child. Now it seemed cloyingly sweet and pitifully small. But he was hungry, and had a long trip ahead of him, so he ate the whole thing. He ate the other two. He felt sick. Drinking the bottle of water helped a little bit. He thought it might be drugged, but time passed and he didn't feel sleepy.

He felt stupid, sitting alone, afraid to risk a look. Raising his hands, he lifted the edge of the mask until he could just see. A man who looked barely old enough to buy beer was sitting ten feet away, his feet up on a desk. He was reading a comic book about superheroes. He sensed the movement and saw Jason Walker looking.

'Fucking told you not to look,' said the man irritably.

He started to rise.

Jason Walker dropped the mask and was that much less prepared when the man struck him in the face. He raised his hands protectively but another blow didn't come. He sat quietly and waited.

His finger hurt. Every time he moved it throbbed dully, reminding him that it was broken. Every time he smashed into something or flinched at a blow, pain shot up his arm.

In his brief look he'd seen that he was in a small office. There was a window but the window was dark. It might have looked out into the garage.

Other men came and went. He tried to follow their conversations but he couldn't. They spoke in jargon, numbers and code, terms that may have been everyday vocabulary for them but which were impenetrable to him.

He jumped at the sound of a large engine firing. Then another, then another and another. The sound was deafening. A hand under his arm lifted him to his feet. He walked back out the door into what he now realized was obviously an airplane hangar. Propeller wash staggered him as the blades churned faster. He baby-stepped up a ramp into the plane and tripped twice en route to his seat. It was a bench seat, and he sat with his back against the bulkhead of the plane. A chain was run through his cuffed arms and legs. He heard a lock snap shut.

'Enjoy the flight,' someone shouted, and then he was alone. Or maybe he was one of a hundred hooded men, all thinking they were alone.

The plane taxied forward, turned, sat waiting, and then rumbled forward again. It took off so slowly that it had probably been airborne for several minutes before he realized they were off the ground.

He couldn't stand it. He had to look, even if it meant getting punched again. He lifted the hood. He really was alone. He was in a cavernous, utilitarian plane. Shafts of light punched through several small windows. The only other cargo was three pallets of boxes, covered in camouflage netting and tied down with yellow nylon webbing.

Rising from his seat and leaning forward, stretching his

chain to the limit, he could just see out the corner of a window. Dun buildings rolled away under them toward a low, smoggy skyline. The plane banked and settled, and he saw below him, looking as tiny and insignificant as a child's school-fair diorama, three sand-colored pyramids.

Egypt.

And then the plane banked again and he saw only blue sky darkening with the approaching night.

The flight was long. When he tried to sleep, he was awake. When he decided to stay awake, sleep pulled at his eyelids with insistent fingers. The metal bench seat was narrow, and his tether wasn't long enough to allow him to lie on the floor. When the plane gained altitude, it became cold.

It was not a direct flight to America: the plane set down three times. The first time, the pilot descended toward the dark desert so quickly that Jason Walker thought they were crash-landing. At the last moment, however, he saw tiny flickering lights, like bonfires, and a half-dozen red-capped flashlights urging the pilot toward the bonfires. The landing was so rough that it may as well have been a crash landing. Holding on as tightly as he could, he still managed to bang his head and bruise his back. His finger signaled its hurt with the same persistent stab as a toothache.

Once they had landed, a man wearing a blank uniform and a holstered pistol came back from the cockpit. Seeing Jason Walker looking at him, the man cursed and put the black bag on him again, knotting it behind his neck.

The cargo door opened with a long hydraulic groan. A half-dozen men boarded the plane. They spoke a language he hadn't heard before. The plane's crew didn't seem to speak the language very well. There was some confusion, ending in an adamant:

'This one. No, this one. *This one!*'

There was grunting and heavy breathing as the men struggled to shift the pallets. Someone stepped on his toe. The pallets scraped their way down the ramp. Everyone sounded much happier once the cargo was out of the plane. The voices became more distant. The plane sat on the ground for an hour or two, its cargo door open to the cold desert air. It was perfectly quiet except for the ticks and hums of the cooling plane and the sounds of Jason Walker's own body.

Eventually, feet tramped back up the ramp, the door groaned shut, and the plane's engines fired. Nobody spoke to him. He was getting hungry. The plane taxied like a bus bumping over railroad ties, then somehow climbed into the air again.

He waited fifteen minutes, then untied the knot holding the black bag on his head. The cargo hold was lit only by three small red lights strung along the ceiling. Two of the pallets were gone. On the remaining pallet, letters and numbers stamped on the cardboard boxes were obscured by the camouflage netting. He wondered what it was necessary to drop off on a sand landing strip in the middle of the desert in the middle of the night. Weapons, probably. For whom? Was America arming the Libyan rebels? Or was someone else shipping cargo on an American plane? Was this even an American plane?

Slowly, his eyes became accustomed to the dim red light. On the other side of the hold it looked as if someone had slung a bag of clothes between two girders. The bag shifted and he realized that it was a body. A man, sleeping in a hammock, his face turned toward the bulkhead. Another prisoner? He didn't appear to be handcuffed. A passenger? Someone who needed to travel without a passport, anyway.

The plane climbed higher than before and the cargo hold grew colder. Jason Walker watched the man through his own fitful slumbers but never saw him stir.

He woke with a jolt, bounced off his seat, and grabbed frantically for a handhold. The plane was landing. Gray light came in the small windows like winter sun through wax paper. The rest of the landing was smooth.

Across the hold, he saw the man in the hammock lift his head sleepily, then run his fingers through his sleep-tousled hair. The man looked at him with reptilian disinterest. Then he climbed out of his hammock and made his way to the front of the plane, disappearing behind the cockpit door. Jason Walker had been staring right at the man but couldn't have described him if his life depended on it. Darkish hair, unshaven, T-shirt and jeans. Brown skin, or maybe just a deep tan. A look of deep weariness. That was all.

He stretched his chain to the limit and peered out the window again. Gray clouds and spitting rain. Criss-crossing runways. In the distance, behind a tall fence topped with barbed wire, a glimpse of steepled roofs and stone architecture.

Then they put the bag on him again and opened the cargo door once more.

They stopped one last time, on a rocky, windswept spit of land near the ocean. It might have been an island. The passenger had gotten off at the last stop and the hold had been filled again with pallets. These pallets held white boxes with long numbers stamped on their sides in black boxy typeface. They had been wrapped so many times in shiny clear plastic that they must have been both waterproof and airtight. The plane waited for hours and hours. Finally they remembered or deigned to feed him. Someone he hadn't seen before and would never see again boarded the plane with a tightly covered aluminum pot of stew and a bottle of water. The man gave him a flimsy plastic spoon and allowed him to take off the hood while he ate.

When night fell the plane took off again and climbed over the white-capped ocean into the clouds. In the middle of the night the clouds became patchy and he saw that they were over land again. He saw the fragile lights of towns and cities below like tiny microorganisms, like dew on spiders' webs. He thought at times that he might know where they were but always he was proven to be completely lost. Only in the forty-watt light of dawn did he discern the shore of Lake Michigan and the slender towers of the Chicago skyline below them.

The plane landed at O'Hare and taxied to a halt among freight planes. He was hooded, led from the plane into a van, and then unhooded again. His hands were uncuffed, but the back of the van, where he sat, was a cage. The van drove for several minutes along the airport's service roads and took him to a gate where a staircase was being wheeled up to a small plane.

The man in the passenger seat came around to the back of the van. He opened the rear doors and then unlocked the cage. He handed Jason Walker a shopping bag with the name of a discount menswear store on the side.

'Put these on,' said the man.

He closed the door again.

Jason Walker reached into the bag. He found a white button-down shirt, tan chinos, a blue blazer, a braided brown leather belt, and a pair of penny loafers. With no room to stand, he knelt and began changing into the clothes.

Outside, business commuters were climbing off the plane on to the tarmac. They looked crisp and well-rested. Perhaps it was an early morning flight from New York. The people were in Chicago to sit in meeting rooms, to have lunch, to have drinks and dinner. They would fly home tomorrow and never give thought to the man watching them from a white van near the gate.

He finished changing and put his coverall into the shopping bag. He rapped on the van window to let the guard know he was done. The guard was wearing a blue coverall with patches and laminated identification tags that marked him as a member of airport maintenance. The guard waited until the last commuter had entered the gate and then let him out of the van. The guard handed him a cheap aluminum briefcase.

'Enter through the gate,' he said. 'There's cab fare in the briefcase.'

The man climbed back into the van. The van didn't start. They would watch until he went into the airport.

He left the van and crossed the tarmac to the gate. The morning shadows were still long, but it was already so hot that he felt sweat prickle his forehead. This familiar airport, where he'd come and gone so often and so carelessly, was just another dreamscape.

He opened the glass door of the gate and went inside.

He climbed concrete stairs, turned right down a short hall, and found himself in a departure area. It was full of businesspeople, and a few tourists, drinking coffee and talking on phones. They were waiting for the small planes that would scatter them throughout the Midwest. Even this simple scene was almost too much. He kept his head down and hurried through into the terminal. He was certain that everyone could see through his cheap disguise. He was obviously not a hungover salesman who'd managed to injure his finger on the minibar.

At the cabstand he was asked twice if he wanted to share a cab going downtown. He simply shook his head and waited his turn. In the taxi he finally remembered to look in the briefcase. Inside were a blank day planner, a two-day-old newspaper, and a ballpoint pen. Inside the planner were three twenty-dollar bills and a boarding pass for the flight he'd supposedly arrived on, flight 7511 from Philadelphia. Cab fare and no more. No attempt to buy him off or compensate him. If there had been a mistake made, it was his, for liking to take pictures. For having been born in Beirut.

Chicago alongside the expressway looked too normal, too sunny, to be the real thing. And when the taxi pulled up outside his building, he had the strangest sensation that the building only looked like his.

Fortunately, the guard in his building had never seemed to like him, so he got inside without having to make any small talk about where he had been. As he came down the hall, Schatzi's barking—which he had somehow forgotten to anticipate—almost scared him back into the elevator. Fortunately, Richard Zim was home and quieted his dog.

At first glance, the apartment looked the same as before. Closer inspection revealed that it had been thoroughly searched. Everything, from socks to silverware, had been shifted. His portfolios were gone, as were a number of his files: credit card receipts, bank statements, tax returns. Proof that he had little enough money, however he had gained it.

But there was nothing more upsetting than that. No drawers torn from the desk with their contents scattered on the floor. No books ripped apart for spite.

There had been five newspapers stacked in front of his door. He had forgotten to collect his mail, but he had seven messages: three from Gina Saraceno, who wondered why he was ignoring her; one from *Chicago Socialite*, asking why he hadn't edited the emailed files; one from David Darling, just saying hi; one from his dentist, reminding him that he was overdue for his semi-annual teeth cleaning; and one containing only several seconds of silence and a brief burst of static.

He was to tell no one or be killed. Was that the way someone like Chad Armstrong made a joke? Or was that the way—smiling, congenial—someone like Chad Armstrong told the truth?

He made a sandwich and ate it. He showered and shaved, then painstakingly groomed himself. His bathroom looked familiar enough, but something had changed. He felt like an actor on a set. If the surroundings hadn't changed, then he had. He had read about people with brain injuries who suddenly believed that the people closest to them had been replaced with actors or robots. Some of them also believed that their surroundings had been replaced with exact replicas. The brain viewed things differently so they were different. The unquestioned narrative of daily life had been replaced with some strange fiction whose purpose could only be guessed at.

Now what? he wondered. He was supposed to tell no one, to carry on as if nothing had happened. But he couldn't imagine doing anything he had done before. If the familiar world had been revealed to be a movie set, how did he ignore the cameras? How did he walk to the store to buy bread?

What day was it? Wednesday. The empty day ahead made him nervous. He didn't want to stay in the apartment. He didn't want to leave the apartment, either. Would they be following him?

He sat down at his computer to work, hoping to occupy his mind, but he found himself wanting to replace the entire text of Mrs. Amanda Levine-Mandelbaum's travelogue about taking her small children and household staff on a

Grand Tour of Europe, with a capital-letter, boldface screed against the Levine-Mandelbaums and their progeny. He read a few of his emails and then powered down the computer.

The phone perched on his dining-room table like a gun. Would they kill him for telling? Not for telling the newspapers, but his friend? His lover?

He had to tell someone. David Darling or Gina Saraceno. He picked up the phone and dialed a number. The phone on the other end rang once, twice, three times.

What if it were tapped? Of course it would be tapped. They wouldn't trust him not to tell. They wouldn't take his word as to whether or not he had disobeyed them.

He thumbed off the receiver so hard his knuckle cracked. He could tell no one. Anyone he did tell would be in danger. They might find themselves booked on the same airline he had just flown with.

The phone rang in his hand. He stared at it dumbly, then answered.

'Why did you hang up?'

Gina Saraceno. Like everyone in the world but him, she had caller ID.

'I—sorry. Someone called on the intercom and I had to answer it.'

'Oh. Do you need to answer the door?'

'No. They'll come back. I mean, it was a wrong—they pressed the wrong number.'

There was a moment of silence as Gina Saraceno tried to make sense of his stumbling excuses. Evidently, she decided to ignore them.

'Well,' she said, 'I'm not used to playing the role of the spurned woman, so you'll have to forgive me if this comes out funny, but why the hell haven't you been returning my calls?'

'I'm sorry,' he said.

'We're not married, we haven't exchanged promise rings or poorly thought-out tattoos, but still, I kind of thought we were past the point of me having to worry, "Will he call? Will he call?"'

'No, of course . . .'

'So I was going to call one last time and then wait for your call explaining that you'd met another woman, trying in your halting fashion to let me down easy. That was her on the other line, wasn't it?'

'I don't have call waiting.'

'At the door, then.'

'Gina, wait,' he said. 'You're wrong. I *am* sorry. I got a job—'

'You got a *job*?'

'An assignment, sorry. In Philadelphia. Completely last-minute. I just had to pack and go. I didn't have time to call you before I left—'

'And once you were there?'

'I was too busy. I just got back. I literally just walked in the door.'

Another moment of silence while Gina Saraceno weighed his words.

'Who was the assignment for?'

'*Philadelphia Magazine*. Kind of a glossy lightweight, you know.'

'What was it about?'

'The National Park Service wants to renovate Independence Hall. It's too small for the number of visitors they get every year, so they want to build an addition. The preservationists are furious, of course. They want to just limit the number of people who can get in, and they say that if it's changed, the visitors won't really be seeing Independence Hall, anyway. But the Park Service says you can't keep people out, so you have to find a way for them to get in.'

He had no idea where this was coming from. He didn't know anything about Independence Hall. Hopefully it was administered by the Park Service.

'So it's a big deal for you, right?'

'A big paycheck, anyway. The story is kind of a typical point–counterpoint kind of thing. I just stated the facts, summarized the arguments, and prettied it up. But it beats copyediting.'

'Why did they ask you? Why didn't they get someone local?'

'A college friend of mine owed me a favor. He's an editor there and he knew I needed work. He told his boss that it would be best to get an out-of-towner, someone who wouldn't be biased. A lot of people are upset about it.'

'I can imagine.'

'There's a chance that the article might get picked up by a national publication, too.'

He had no idea why he added the last part. It was hard to stop.

Gina Saraceno seemed to relax. Her voice warmed. He hadn't been cheating after all. In fact, he had a verifiable excuse for his absence.

'I'm sorry I was so pushy, honey,' she said.

'Did you just call me "honey"?'

She laughed.

'I know, that's weird, isn't it? I'm just sorry and I wanted to sound like a sweet girl instead of the pushy broad I am.'

'I don't think you're pushy.'

'That's because you're a push*over*. So can I come over? I want to have make-up sex. It wasn't much of an argument, but I want the sex anyway.'

'Me, too, definitely, but—'

'I heard a "but" coming.'

'I'm just so bushed. I was writing until three last night and I had to get up at six thirty. Can we make it tomorrow? *Honey?*'

'As long as you call me "honey," OK. But the sex had better be great.'

'It will be, I promise. Whips, chains, and cannoli, just like you like it.'

She laughed again.

'It's a date. See you tomorrow, *honey.*'

'Bye, *honey.*'

They hung up.

Jason Walker wasn't used to lying. While he was lying, he kept adding details to the lie to make it sound more believable. Now that he was off the phone, each one of those details clanged in his ear like an alarm he couldn't shut off. He knew that there was a *Philadelphia Magazine* or something like it. He hadn't been sure of the exact name. And he thought he had read something somewhere about proposed changes to Independence Hall. But for all he knew, construction was already under way. For all he knew, *Philadelphia Magazine* had already written an article about it. It would be easy enough for Gina Saraceno to find out.

He rubbed his eyes until he saw purple stars. He exhaled, exhausted. There was no reason for her to look at old issues of an out-of-state magazine.

The real issue was that she'd be expecting a new article to appear. She would want to help him celebrate.

Jason Walker wasn't much of a drinker. He enjoyed beer with dinner, wine at a party, and Champagne on New Year's Eve. But he found himself standing outside the liquor store on Argyle Street as they opened the doors at 10 a.m. The owner showed him to the whiskeys, then helped him pick out a bottle. When the owner found out that he wasn't really a whiskey drinker, he suggested a bottle of rye, which he called 'training whiskey.'

Walker carried the bottle home in the hot sun, absently twisting the paper bag around the bottle's neck. In his apartment, he poured a three-finger measure into a glass and took a sip. He stifled a cough and opened the freezer, looking for ice. His ice cube tray hadn't been touched in a month. The ice cubes had evaporated into rectangular slivers. He shook them out into his hand and dumped them in the glass, where, popping, they began to dissolve. Running the tap until the water cooled to lukewarm, he added half an inch of water.

He drank, then drank again. He sat down in front of the television and turned it on. On a cable news channel, a video clip showed Homeland Security agents marching six Middle Eastern-looking men out of a ranch-style house in St. Louis. He turned up the volume.

'Neighbors say the six men kept to themselves,' said the voiceover. 'In fact, only one of the neighbors our reporters spoke with remembered seeing any of the men coming and going. All six worked as drivers for the same taxicab company, and Homeland Security officials inform us that they are examining this company closely for further terrorist connections.'

The camera cut back to a blonde anchorwoman. Her wispy hair and red lipstick did little to soften the hardness of her face.

'Once again,' she said, stacking a prop pile of papers, 'our top story: six men arrested in suburban St. Louis and charged with conspiracy to commit a terrorist act. Homeland Security informs us that the men wanted to blow up the landmark St. Louis arch on the anniversary of September 11, when it would have been full of tourists: men, women, and children. Officers seized photographs, maps, diaries, and what they are calling a "terrorist cookbook with recipes for destruction." We'll have more on this story at the top of the hour and as it develops.'

The woman, whose name was Amanda Nicole, promised a story when she returned about a high-speed car chase gone humorously wrong.

Jason Walker finished his glass of rye and poured another. He didn't add water this time. By noon he was asleep.

Six

He saw Gina Saraceno the next night. She was curious to know how, while writing a story about a planned renovation of Independence Hall, he had broken his finger. Consumed with the larger lie, he had forgotten to mention it.

'The doorman at my hotel closed the cab door on it,' he said.

'Oh my god,' she said. 'Did you go to the hospital?'

'Of course. They said there's not much you can do, though. Just keep it wrapped and wait.'

Jason Walker had not visited the hospital. He had let his medical insurance lapse once the monthly premiums grew larger than his rent. But a Web search had satisfied him that in fact there wasn't much more to be done for a broken finger than to keep it wrapped and wait.

'They must be freaked out, the people at the hotel. You could sue them for something like that.'

'The manager gave me a letter saying the hotel would cover my medical expenses, and he comped my bill.'

'Wasn't the magazine going to cover your hotel bill?'

'Well, yes, but what was he going to do? Give me a stack of twenties?'

'He could have fired the doorman.'

'Gina, it was an honest mistake. The guy felt terrible. You should have seen the look on his face. I actually ended up trying to make *him* feel better.'

'Does it hurt?'

'Some.'

Bourbon had numbed the pain the previous day, and today he hadn't noticed it much unless he tried to use his left hand. But talking about it made the wound pulse anew.

Gina Saraceno cocked her head. She looked at him strangely.

'If I were the suspicious kind,' she said, 'I'd think that you ran away for some crazy drunken weekend, screwed a married woman, and broke your finger in a fight with her husband. And I guess maybe I am the suspicious kind. But you're not the lying, cheating type. You're just really unlucky.'

Jason Walker agreed that he was really unlucky. Gina Saraceno told him his bandages looked disgusting and gently unwound them. His skin was white and puffy where the adhesive had stuck. Around the break it was the color of an overripe plum. He gritted his teeth against nausea while she gently cleaned his hand with a washcloth. She held it lightly while it air-dried, finishing the job with gentle puffs of breath from her pursed lips. Then she wound new tape around the splint. Slowly, the throbbing in his hand subsided.

They made love with unusual care and sweetness. He lay on his back, his left hand elevated on a pillow, while she sat astride him, moving as if trying to ravish him without his knowing. Usually loud and abandoned, she contained her energy, keeping her eyes on his, seeming almost on fire from within at the effort required to be so gentle. In the end, she wasn't able to have an orgasm but she smiled warmly when he did.

Jason Walker thought that, in spite of everything, he was very, very lucky. He promised himself that he would never lie to Gina Saraceno again, a promise that he took back instantly when he remembered that telling the truth would mean putting her life in danger. Lying merely jeopardized their relationship.

Chad Armstrong had told him to tell no one, to resume his normal life and wait for instructions. Resuming his normal life proved impossible. He didn't care whether or not Chicago socialites were revealed to write as poorly as they spoke. Even the checks he so desperately needed seemed worthless. Why hustle after a few hundred dollars when, for all he knew, he might not live to spend them? Before, his days had been ordered around the search for work and, when he could afford it, small pleasures like taking pictures and watching movies. Now he waited only for the phone to ring. Some anonymous voice would tell him to go to a street corner late at night to receive instructions. Or maybe he would just be bundled into a van as he had been before.

He did make a half-dozen half-hearted attempts to find work, but he didn't follow up on them. He wrote a letter of apology to his editor at *Chicago Socialite* and received a reply accepting his apology, but no work. There was no promise of further work, either.

He thought about writing down what had happened to him. But to write would be to create evidence. And that surely somehow violated the command to tell no one.

His neighbor, Richard Zim, went on vacation. He knew this because Schatzi was barking more than usual. She barked at sirens, at people in the hall, at him when he forgot to walk softly. The woman who looked after the dog while Richard Zim was gone seemed annoyed by the favor she had agreed to perform. Morning and night she arrived with a slam of the door, left to walk Schatzi with another slam, returned five minutes later with a slam, and left again immediately after that with one more slam for luck. The dog's long nails clicked back and forth, back and forth, and sometimes she curled against the connecting wall, keening for her owner. The thin wall only amplified the sound.

Jason Walker found it difficult to sleep. He watched cable news late into the night, the grainy green video of precision-guided bombs as they fell through the night, rushing groundward, suddenly arriving on the roofs of terrorists' homes. He watched khaki-clad reporters standing in the aftermath of suicide bombs, in markets strewn with bricks, fruit, and body parts. He watched experts explain the threats to power plants, water supplies, and tall buildings.

Only a few years ago, politicians had done battle over Iraq, whether it was time to stay or go. Then the terrorists had begun to strike again on American soil, and now American soldiers were in Iran. Operation Desert Wind, a full-scale attack of that country, had gone almost as swiftly as the takeover of Iraq. But now the difficulties of occupation had doubled.

American soldiers weren't yet on the ground in North Korea, Venezuela, or Cuba. But air strikes, missiles, and artillery shells launched from South Korea, Panama, and Florida had neutralized those countries' militaries. Soldiers were in short supply, so the new battles would be fought from afar. The word *front* had become elastic. Robot planes took photos and logged coordinates for precision-guided missiles. Without troops on the ground, it was not known exactly how well the targets had been chosen. But the countries had already been angry at America anyway. The goal, said the president, was to 'neutralize both the schools of terror and to contain the countries who wish us harm.' Things were not going well at the U.N. Several European countries had withdrawn their ambassadors, but the U.S. had not.

Senators who had once argued engagement and retreat now debated whether enough resources had been allocated to the fight. Many of them had seen their own states attacked. Some favored sending more troops, others favored building more planes. Only George Libby seemed willing to disagree with the very idea of fighting. His campaign slogan was 'Bring them all home.' He did not receive very much attention from the media. When the news networks did discuss his campaign, the anchors had smiles in their voices. The man campaigning to be elected on a date that had not been declared was treated as a harmless eccentric, a human-interest story.

Jason Walker grew more accustomed to the taste and effects of bourbon and drank it more often.

Two weeks after his return to Chicago, he received a check from *Philadelphia Magazine* for $3,500. It was postmarked two days earlier and came sealed in a convincing-looking envelope with the magazine's logo above the return address. There was no correspondence inside, just the check and, attached to the check by a perforated fold, a standard-looking accounting pay stub. The charge line read *Cover Story—Independence Hall.*

Obviously they were listening to his phone conversations. And yet his first reactions were relief and pleasure—relief that Chad Armstrong or some other government operative was helping him sustain his lie, and pleasure at having $3,500. At what would probably have worked out to a dollar per word, it was an amount appropriate to the story he would have written, had he written it. All he had to do was to leave the check in some casual but prominent place where Gina Saraceno would notice it. If she did have any lingering suspicions, this simple forgery would allay them.

And he needed the money. It would cover all his living expenses for two months. After what the government had done to him, backing up his lie with money was the least they could do.

But then it occurred to him that it really was a paycheck. Both the payer and the services rendered had been disguised. In fact, the services had not yet been rendered. It was an advance for services due. It was what they would pay him for spying. Or 'informing,' as Chad Armstrong had called it.

He had agreed to become an informant because he had no choice. Would taking money make him a collaborator?

He folded the pay stub behind the check and set it on top of the envelope on the small table where he kept a dish for his wallet, keys, and loose change. Let Gina Saraceno see it, anyway. He wouldn't have to cash it.

He had hardly left his apartment in two weeks. Suddenly it seemed stifling. He called David Darling at work. They went out together about once a month, and it was his turn to call anyway. He reached voicemail and left a message. David Darling called back while he was in the shower. Finally they were on the phone together. He told his friend that he had a sudden urge to see a baseball game.

'Cubs? Tonight? Why, do you have tickets?'

He said that he did not.

'You do realize that they're playing St. Louis? Besides all the down-staters, there'll be lots of locals who just want to see how good baseball is played. We'd have to scalp.'

Jason Walker looked at the check. He couldn't really

afford scalpers' prices, but he didn't care. He wanted to go out. And he knew that David Darling, a die-hard Cubs fan, would relent.

'You always say I never do anything on impulse,' he said.

'I didn't mean that you have to suddenly do something that'll cost a hundred bucks.'

'If you'd rather go to a movie, we could do that.'

David Darling paused. Jason Walker could hear him drumming a pen on his desk.

'No, no. I feel like I should give you positive reinforcement here. But we better get there early. Meet you at the Gingerman at five thirty?'

'Deal,' he said.

'First round's on you,' said David Darling.

They met at the bar, the far northern outpost of Wrigleyville and an oasis of relative calm. Jason Walker ordered two pints of summer ale from the skinny, tattooed bartender and tried not to look at her breasts. Given the tight tank top she wore, not looking at her breasts meant staring soulfully into her eyes throughout the transaction, which seemed to annoy her.

'You're better off just looking at her breasts,' said David Darling when she walked away.

'How did you—?'

'How did I what? Oh come on, sometimes you're painful. I swear you were raised in Afghanistan, all the women wore burkas.'

The beer was cold and good and he was glad to be out of his apartment. The normality of the bar on game day made him feel almost as if the last week and a half had never happened. Cubs fans in blue and Cardinals fans in red insulted each other with feigned good nature, and the jukebox played the same dozen songs it always had.

David Darling wasn't a writer or an editor. He was a leasing agent for apartments. They had met when Jason Walker first moved to Chicago and walked into AAA Apartment Finders—the business was listed first in the phone book—looking for help. He had filled out a questionnaire and returned the clipboard to the receptionist, then watched as a short, rather disheveled man picked up the clipboard, scanned it, and then called his name.

'David Darling,' the man had said, sticking his hand out. 'Any jokes about the name and you find your own damn apartment.'

On the first day, David Darling showed Jason Walker six apartments. On the second day, he showed him seven. Jason Walker was indecisive and politely choosy. At first, David Darling seemed irritated, but by the second day he seemed amused. On the third day he began pointing out obvious flaws in the apartments he was showing and insisting that they look at 'at least one more.' Jason Walker responded by becoming more aggressive in his demands. It became very funny to both of them. They spent the afternoon of the fourth day at a Cubs game, and that night in a half-dozen bars.

Eventually they found an apartment they could both agree on, and Jason Walker moved in. They remained friends despite the difference in their temperaments. Jason Walker envied David Darling's nonchalant attitude toward life. David Darling enjoyed his job, his friends, and his allegiance to a terrible baseball team, and didn't seem to feel a need to change anything. Jason Walker had once been ambitious, and his thwarted ambition sometimes made him feel embarrassed to be alive.

They left the bar and strolled down Clark Street toward Wrigley Field, sometimes stepping off the curb to pass stalled clusters of baseball fans. David Darling talked money with several scalpers before finding a price he deemed 'extortionate but fair,' and money changed hands.

The weather was weird. Patches of sunny blue sky were suddenly obscured by fast-moving clouds that disappeared minutes later. Some of the clouds looked heavy with rain while others were fluffy and shining white. The air didn't smell like rain, but with a steady fifteen-mile-per-hour breeze, a summer downpour could arrive by the third inning. He hoped they hadn't spent their money to wait out a rain delay. But it was better than waiting at home.

They stood in line at the turnstiles and then entered the

cool, dim stadium concourse. They bought hot dogs, peanuts, and beer and found their seats, which were on the right-field line, about thirty rows up from first base. Between mouthfuls of food and beer, they talked about movies and the weather. They stood for the national anthem, putting their hands on their hearts and fixing their eyes on the American flag snapping over the scoreboard in center field.

Jason Walker had never considered himself to be particularly patriotic. But he had always felt a surge in his breast in the moment before a baseball game started. Among the quieted crowd, listening first to the singer's voice echoing off the stadium walls, then the rising cheers as the song reached its crescendo, he felt a sense of surrender, of community, that he wished he could capture and revisit. And what was wrong with loving something—a country, the idea of a country, a game—with forty thousand people all at once?

Today he found himself mouthing the words of the song and studying the faces of the people around him. Some of them looked as reverent as he once had. Some of them merely looked bored. Some of them talked on their cell phones. David Darling held his sweat-stained Cubs cap over his heart and sang lustily, smiling all the while.

The applause became a roar. The song ended. The spectators sat down and the players ran on to the field.

'Did you see the story about the guys who wanted to blow up the St. Louis arch?' said Jason Walker.

'Yeah,' said David Darling. 'Why couldn't they target Busch Stadium instead?'

'It seems weird. It's not like they caught them with a truck full of fertilizer.'

'Yeah, well, the idea is to catch them before they build the bomb. If they get the bomb built, it's too late. These guys have no qualms about setting it off, even if they're sitting on top of it.'

'It just doesn't seem like a lot of evidence. If they could arrest you for a book you have, well, I have a book about Nine-Eleven, but I'm not going to fly a plane into a building.'

'You can't prove you're not going to do something. They have to look for signs that say you're a likely risk to do it.'

'You're right. But if they show the men, it seems like they should have to show the evidence.'

'The government can't let the defense lawyers know what it does and doesn't know,' said David Darling.

He glanced almost imperceptibly over his shoulder.

'Look, don't think I don't love debating the pros and cons of Homeland Security, but let's not do it at a baseball game.'

Jason Walker shrugged agreeably.

David Darling suddenly seemed to notice the white-taped fingers of his friend's left hand.

'What happened there? Close your laptop too fast?'

Jason Walker didn't feel like telling the whole Philadelphia story.

'I cut it when I was cooking,' he said.

He instantly regretted it. That was two lies to keep straight.

'Gina still trying to teach you, huh?'

He nodded, forced a chuckle, and agreed that it was a hopeless task.

On the field, the St. Louis leadoff man, who had been walked on five pitches, stole second. The second batter hit the first pitch down the right-field line, scoring the runner.

David Darling booed gleefully.

'You guys are killing me!' he shouted.

Despite the fact that Chicago's other baseball team, the White Sox, had won the World Series twice in recent memory, and despite the fact that the Cubs continued not to win the World Series, or even to have winning seasons, Wrigley Field was full of fans. Cellular One Ballpark, where the White Sox played, was fuller than it used to be, but rarely sold out. Cubs fans insisted that they wanted their team to win, too, but they saw no point in punishing bad teams by ignoring them. Especially when the sun was shining and the beer was cold.

The St. Louis team did not appear to be distracted by revelations of a terrorist plot in their hometown. They scored five runs in the first three innings. In the fourth inning, with the bases loaded and only one out, the Cubs' manager finally walked to the mound and took the baseball from his starting pitcher, who looked relieved to be given the rest of the afternoon off.

Jason Walker excused himself past a half-dozen resigned-looking fans and made his way to the toilets. Thousands of other people had had the same idea, so progress was slow. He shuffled down the stairs, then down a ramp, and stood in a slow-moving line.

When he emerged, he headed for a food counter to buy a pretzel and two more beers. There was only one person in line ahead of him. Traffic in the concourse was thinning. Play had resumed, as evidenced by the indignant shouts that echoed down the ramps.

'And they call this baseball,' said the man behind him.

He turned. The voice belonged to Chad Armstrong.

It was his turn at the counter. Stammering, he ordered. His fingers fumbled with the sweat-damp bills in his wallet.

Chad Armstrong gestured Jason Walker's money away.

'This one's on me,' he said.

He ordered a beer of his own and gave the cashier a twenty.

They walked slowly away, Chad Armstrong sipping his beer and smiling. Jason Walker held a small carton with two beers, the pretzel, and a packet of mustard.

'How was the trip back?' asked Chad Armstrong.

'It wasn't very comfortable,' said Jason Walker.

'Finger feeling better?'

'I guess so.'

'You were probably wondering when you were going to hear from me again.'

He nodded.

'Well, here I am. I had to buy standing-room-only seats. Your plan was last-minute, and even Homeland Security can't get seats for Cubs–Cards on game day.'

'Couldn't you just show them your badge?'

Chad Armstrong grinned. 'Of course. But then people here would have known there was an undercover agent in the park. And people talk. This way'—he sipped his beer—'I'm just one more lonely guy with poor planning skills and an afternoon to kill.'

They had stopped near a wall. Whether Chad Armstrong

had guided them there, or whether Jason Walker's desire
to hide had caused him to stop, they were in an almost
private spot.

'You get the check?'

He nodded.

'Good, good. So, about your assignment. Your assignment
which you have chosen to accept. It's time to get started.
Time and terrorism wait for no man. You're still with us?'

Jason Walker said that he was.

'OK, did you bring a pen? No? Just kidding, you don't
need a pen. Go to the Lebanese Cultural Center tomorrow.
Look around. Be friendly. Tell them you want to learn more
about your Lebanese heritage. Take a brochure. Leave. Don't
be too eager.'

He gave an address on North Kedzie Avenue.

'Don't you want, I don't know, pictures?'

'Leave your camera at home. You don't think we can
take pictures? We can take pictures. We're just short on
half-Lebanese guys right now. The idea is to make contact.
Don't worry about memorizing everything. You'll remember
the important details. We'll debrief you and find out what
we need to know. But if you show up acting like you're
ready to move in and be their new mascot, Mr. Falafel or
whatever, they won't trust you. So be shy, awkward—be
yourself. Whatever you do, don't try to act like someone
else. And if I catch you introducing yourself as "Walker,
Jason Walker," I'll crush your nuts with a hammer.'

He laughed.

Jason Walker tried to laugh.

'When will you debrief me?'

Chad Armstrong drained his beer, crumpled the cup, and
dropped it on the ground.

'Don't worry, we'll be around,' he said.

He winked and walked away.

Jason Walker walked up the ramp and began climbing
the stairs toward the field boxes. Tripping on a step, he
caught himself but spilled the beers. His shoes were soaked.
Cursing, he made his way back to the food counter and
bought two more beers.

When he returned to his seat, David Darling saw his sour look and the wet spots on his pant legs.

'Need to work on your aim, Jason,' he said.

Helping himself to one of the beers, he gave an animated, accelerated play-by-play account of what had happened in the last inning-and-a-half. When the Cubs' reliever started pitching, the Cardinals' third baseman had taken three balls, then hit the fourth pitch out of the park on to Waveland Avenue, a grand slam. When a fan threw the ball back into the park, it hit the Cubs' left-fielder in the back of the head. The player was removed from the game for evaluation. Then the Cardinals singled, grounded out, singled, and made an out on a deep fly ball to center field. In their half of the inning, the Cubs had struck out, ground out, and lined out. The Cardinals were at bat again, with one out and a runner in scoring position.

Jason Walker listened with poorly feigned interest. He was thinking about his new line of work. The job itself didn't seem so bad, he thought. It was his new boss who was going to make matters difficult.

Seven

The indecisive weather had made up its mind. It would rain. Rumbling, steel-gray thunderheads bullied their way over the city, throwing down billowing sheets of rain. Storm drains clogged with newspapers and shopping bags and overflowed the curbs. Taxis, making no concession to the driving conditions, sluiced by bus stops, throwing up long fantails of dirty water.

Jason Walker sat by his window and watched the flooded scene below. Though his air conditioner sounded as if it was choking on a piece of broken plastic, it was cool and arid in his apartment. He had meant to go to the Lebanese Cultural Center before noon, but at mid-afternoon found himself still waiting by the window. He was nervous and glad to have the rain as an excuse to delay. If it rained all night then he would risk angering Chad Armstrong by putting the trip off until tomorrow.

But in the late afternoon the rain stopped falling. The cloud ceiling rose and on the far horizon the falling sun squinted toward the lake. Street lamps, which had blinked on early in the day and stayed on, shined their purple light through limp and sodden leaves to the rain-slick sidewalks below.

He pulled on a light windbreaker, tucked an umbrella under his arm, and headed out. Schatzi bid him farewell with a volley of barks. Despite their long through-the-door acquaintance, she still sounded as if she wanted to eat him.

He walked down Marine Drive, the wind shaking raindrops from the trees, to Lawrence, where he waited for a westbound bus. The rush-hour traffic crawled. Even after he was settled in a window seat, he watched the same pedestrian overtake the bus three times before the bus finally pulled ahead for good.

The bus passed through the newly nice center of Uptown, then through Lincoln Square, the gentrified remnants of a working-class German neighborhood. After that, the signs on the stores were written in the blocky Korean alphabet. He got off the bus in front of a pool hall, then crossed Lawrence and walked south on Kedzie.

All of Chicago was salted with Mexican restaurants and groceries, but here he also saw various Middle Eastern businesses, even the gold dome of a mosque. A few blocks south, across the street, he saw the cultural center. A faded red-and-white awning with green cedar trees, a modified Lebanese flag, gave the center's name in both English and Arabic. A few old men sat sipping tea on dirty white plastic patio sets under the awning. They appeared to have long ago exhausted their topics of mutual interest.

His skin prickled with fear. He opened the nearest door and walked in. He was standing in a Lebanese restaurant. Impulsively, he ordered kidney bean stew and pita bread. He ate slowly and without appetite.

At last he could wait no longer. He paid for the meal and walked to the cultural center. The old men out front watched with blank faces as he approached.

A bell jangled as he opened the door. He stopped just inside. The bell jangled again as the door closed. Had he thought to imagine it, he might have expected a smoky room where evil-looking men sat cross-legged on silk pillows, smoking hookahs. But the room was bright and cheerful.

A half-dozen tables with mismatched chairs were scattered up front near the windows. Along one wall stood a small food counter with an antique-looking cash register. Plates of plastic-wrapped pastries filled a glass-fronted cooler, and silver urns with hot water and hot coffee were positioned for self-service use. The walls of the room were covered with outdated travel posters featuring scenes of a cosmopolitan, prewar Beirut, and a floor-to-ceiling corkboard panel was covered with a patchwork of posters, flyers, and notices. Paint peeled from the pressed-tin ceiling and the floor was covered in worn linoleum tile. In the back of the room, where the lights had not been turned on, there was a small stage, to one side of which dozens of folding chairs were stacked.

A half-dozen men were playing chess. Two others read newspapers. Even though he lingered in the doorway, looking lost and feeling like an idiot, no one greeted Jason Walker or even acknowledged him. With the food counter unmanned, it didn't seem as if anyone was running the place.

Now what? he thought.

Then he noticed what appeared to be the library. Against one wall were a bookshelf, a magazine rack stuffed with well-thumbed magazines and newspapers, and several stacks of travel brochures.

He walked to the bookshelf and chose a book at random. He recognized the writing on the cover as Arabic. A glance at the spines of the other books showed more Arabic titles and several in French. Unable to think of any other excuse to stay, he pulled out a chair at an empty table and sat down with the book. There were several pages of color plates in the center, depicting various old buildings that he assumed were in Lebanon. He studied the pictures and their incomprehensible captions with the intensity of a religious scholar searching for a sign in a sacred text.

When he had committed the features of the dun-colored buildings to memory, he picked out another book. Unfortunately, this one didn't have any photographs. He pretended to read. It was looking as if he wouldn't have anything to report to Chad Armstrong unless a bomb went off.

Then he realized that one of the men was no longer reading his newspaper. The man was looking at him. Jason Walker smiled, nodded, and resumed pretending to read. But the man kept looking at him. A few minutes later, the man pushed his chair back and walked over.

'Is the book good?' asked the man in uninflected English.

'It's interesting,' said Jason Walker.

'Have you read on this subject before?'

'No, this is my first time.'

'You know,' said the man, 'it will probably be even more interesting if you read it right-side up.'

He looked at the book in his hands, embarrassed. 'I don't read Arabic,' he said.

The man laughed a friendly laugh.

'Well, you will not learn if you do not try,' he said. 'My name is Leo Haddad. What is yours?'

'Jason Walker.'

They shook hands. Jason Walker put the book down and Leo Haddad picked it up. He read the title page.

'Even if you could read this, I think you would find it very boring. It is a history of commerce in the area now known as Lebanon. Are you Lebanese?'

'I guess so. I was born in Beirut, but my parents came here—'

'—because of the war. Yes. I came here, too, because of the war.'

Leo Haddad appeared to be in his mid-thirties. His skin was light brown and his hair was jet black. He was clean-shaven and neatly dressed, but his hair looked as if it had been cut at a deep discount.

'How long have you been here?' asked Jason Walker.

'I have lived in Chicago for several years. Before that, my family lived in Montreal, Canada, where my father felt comfortable because he spoke French. Before that, Lebanon.'

'Are you Muslim?'

'Are you Christian?'

'I guess I am as much as I am Lebanese. I don't know very much about either.'

'You have come here to learn more about Lebanon, and also yourself?'

'That makes it sound pretty noble. I thought I'd come here so I wouldn't feel so stupid.'

'To know yourself is the most noble thing there is.'

Leo Haddad insisted on buying him a piece of baklava and a cup of strong, sweet black coffee. He obtained the latter by sticking his head through a curtained doorway in the back and calling for someone. A moment later a big man with a milky eye and a burn-scarred hand came up to the counter. Leo Haddad asked for coffee and the man began preparing it without a word. Jason Walker couldn't take his eyes off the man's hands as he poured sugar and water into a small copper pan and brought it to boil on a hot plate. Removing the pan from the heat, he poured in finely ground coffee and heated it until it frothed, stirring rapidly all the time. He removed it from the heat and then repeated the procedure two more times before pouring the coffee into two demitasse cups. He accepted Leo Haddad's money with a grunt, put the pastries on small plates, and then walked away and disappeared behind the curtain.

'There is coffee in the urn,' said Leo Haddad, 'but it is not coffee. If you want to be Lebanese, this is the coffee you should drink.'

The coffee was strong, black as engine oil.

'Who is that man?' asked Jason Walker.

'That is Ghassan. I believe he was injured by a bomb.'

He didn't know what to say.

'Maybe you imagine that he was a terrorist?'

Jason Walker shook his head. 'No, I don't think that.'

'When many people think of Lebanon, they think of Hezbollah. The Lebanese are peaceful, most of them. The country has an unfortunate history. It is like a ball that children fight over. Spoiled, stupid, and very large children. I think that, without outside intervention, we might have been a model for the Middle East. We are diverse and the people had learned, most of them, to live with one another. But now we have become poor, and like in poor countries, those who live there are angry. And that is why more Lebanese live outside of Lebanon than within.'

Leo Haddad changed the subject, saying that it was impolite to speak of politics with someone he had just met. He asked about Jason Walker's background and was amazed to learn that Jean Walker was a Frenchman. He was incredulous that Jason Walker spoke neither French nor Arabic nor any language but English.

Jason Walker tried to explain about his mother's desire to assimilate.

'That is strange,' said his new acquaintance. 'The Lebanese, as a rule, do not assimilate. They form communities and make a new, little Lebanon wherever they go. They adapt handsomely, but they do not forget they are Lebanese.'

'My mother didn't forget that she was Lebanese, but I think she thought that I should only be American.'

Leo Haddad shook his head.

'We should have many things in common, you and I, and yet we are strangers to each other. If you spoke Arabic, if you spoke French, if you had been raised with familiar customs, it would be like meeting a long-lost friend. Do you want to learn more about your native country?'

Jason Walker said that he did.

'Then you must begin the same way a schoolchild would, with a book.'

Leo Haddad returned the book about Lebanese commerce to the shelf and selected one that Jason Walker had overlooked. Written in English, it was called *Lebanon for Beginners*.

'I am sure this book will not be intelligent enough for you,' he said, 'but we have very few English books here. And I do think it will whet your appetite.'

Jason Walker, embarrassed by the man's friendly generosity, thanked him. Leo Haddad dismissed him with a smile.

'I am glad that you were brave enough to visit here, knowing no one. In these times, I am sad to say that even some Lebanese choose not to visit us here. They love Lebanon, they love their country, but they feel worried to be seen walking out of a building with Arabic lettering on the sign.' He shrugged. 'And who knows? Maybe they are right. Maybe we are being watched. But I cannot wash Lebanon off so easily.'

Leo Haddad said that he hoped they would meet again, and the two men said goodbye. Jason Walker walked north to Lawrence Avenue and waited for a bus under the glare of a street light.

He felt bad for spying on someone like Leo Haddad and

thought he might pretend to forget the name. But even if he had to talk, the worst he could say was that he'd met a man who loved his country and had loaned him a book. Surely, even now, that was not a punishable offense.

The following night Jason Walker met Gina Saraceno for dinner at a small Italian restaurant near the El tracks in the gallery district. Seemingly unchanged since the 1940s, Club Lago had a small, crowded bar up front, and a small, crowded dining area in back. Before the indoor smoking ban it had been loud and smoky. Now it was just loud.

He was amazed at his girlfriend's seemingly inexhaustible appetite for Italian food. While he could occasionally convince her to try some other cuisine—usually Greek or something equally heavy—she ate most non-Italian foods with indifference. Mexican food was pretty good, she allowed, and Thai food wasn't bad, but she became animated only on the subject of a truly great linguini vongole or veal saltimbocca. She had eaten at seemingly every Italian restaurant in the greater Chicago area. And in many of them, as in Club Lago, she was on first-name terms with the owners.

He had arrived first. Following her standing instructions, he ordered a bottle of her favorite Chianti. Shortly after the wine arrived, she did too, sweeping in with even more enthusiasm than usual. Her grin, always generous, spread from earlobe to earlobe.

'Why so happy?' he asked.

She sat down, took a gulp of wine, and rummaged in her bag, all without saying a word.

'I'll bite,' he said. 'Why so silent?'

She found what she was looking for.

'Close your eyes,' she said.

He closed his eyes. Feeling a tug on his shirt, he opened them involuntarily. She was sitting in her chair, grinning, arms at her sides. He looked down. A red, white, and blue badge, about three inches across, was pinned to his shirt. *VOTE LIBBY*, it proclaimed.

'I decided to volunteer,' she said.

Jason Walker took the badge off and set it on the table.

'Very funny.'

"'If they let you vote, Vote Libby.'"

'Is that the official slogan?'

"'Join the Libby Lobby!'"

'You're making these up.'

"'If they count the votes, then your vote counts: George Libby.'"

He felt embarrassed. Gina Saraceno's sense of humor could be inscrutable at times. He wasn't always sure if he was supposed to laugh with her or just let her laugh at him.

'Stop it, Gina,' he said.

'OK, sorry. I got a little carried away.'

'So, really, where did you get the button?'

'At campaign headquarters.'

'Which is a novelty shop?'

'Actually, it's the house of a hippie in Hyde Park. He has a card table in his den, covered with buttons, flyers, and bumper stickers.'

'Which would explain why the city is not exactly plastered with his slogans.'

"'George Libby just wants a few good men.'"

'Gina.'

She drank more wine.

'All right, sorry. I shouldn't wind you up. But I am volunteering.'

'There's no election.'

'Exactly.'

'So you're telling people to vote for George Libby if and when there's an election?'

'Exactly. And you're my first sale. Vote Libby, Jason.'

'You know, a lot of people think his campaign is unpatriotic, that it's unfair to distract the president when Americans are dying right here in America.'

'I know. Vote Libby.'

'I'm not saying, you know . . . I'm not saying I . . . it's just . . . what's gotten into you?'

'Are you going to Vote Libby or not, Jason?'

'Well, I'll read the brochure. And if they call an election, I'll give him careful consideration.'

Gina Saraceno sighed and picked up a menu.

'Fair enough. But the point is that people should be upset that they don't at least have the opportunity to vote for George Libby, even if they don't *want* to vote for him.'

'I can hardly imagine people beating down the doors of the polling places on behalf of a candidate they don't want to vote for. Are you going to stand on the sidewalk and pin these things on people's shirts?'

'Probably. Or go door to door.'

'Aren't you worried?'

'What, that they'll send me to Guantanamo? Just because they're not holding an election, it doesn't mean they've outlawed campaigning. I want to exercise a few of the rights I have left, while I still have them.'

'I would have thought you were too cynical to campaign for anybody.'

'Well, if it were an election year, you'd probably be right. George Libby isn't exactly my idea of a policy dreamboat. He's kind of a one-issue kind of guy. But he is brave, and I'd probably campaign for anybody who I thought could make the world safer.'

'How will he make the world safer?'

'Well, he can't make it any un-safer, can he? He has a novel idea: he wants to let other countries figure things out for themselves. The more we try to fight terrorism over-seas, the more terrorists we create. We back off, tell everyone we want to do things diplomatically from here on out, and watch the bombings stop.'

'He doesn't know that will work.'

'Of course he doesn't. But it's at least worth a try.'

'As soon as we pull out, all these countries will just rearm themselves. And they'll be even angrier than they were before. And we won't be able to do anything until they attack us here.'

'They're already attacking us here. At least we'd have more troops at home to protect us.'

Jason Walker took a sip of wine. He didn't know what to think. If anything, recent events had made it even harder for him to keep an argument clear in his head. And even under the best of circumstances, it was hard to win an argument with Gina Saraceno.

'You're probably right,' he said, 'but pulling the troops out is a big decision. It's not like you can just decide to put them back.'

'They should never have been sent in the first place.'

It was time to either argue or order. They both began scrutinizing their menus.

'What are you having?' she asked.

'Probably the usual.'

'Me too.'

They folded their menus. Embarrassed, they looked at each other and laughed.

'So, are you going to Vote Libby?' she asked, teasing.

'Stop it.'

'If you want to volunteer, I have extra badges and brochures.'

'What's in it for me?'

She smirked. 'For every day you volunteer, you get one full-body massage with a happy ending.'

'George Libby gets you for free, but I have to use the barter system?'

They realized the waiter had been standing behind them. He was waiting for a break in the conversation. His face was red.

Gina Saraceno covered her face with her hands. 'Oh, my god!'

'I can come back later,' suggested the waiter.

'I think we'd better order,' said Jason Walker.

That night, after a wonderful massage he'd been given as an 'advance,' Jason Walker lay next to Gina Saraceno in her bed. She was sleeping, her thick black hair almost entirely covering her face. She lived near Taylor Street, the Italian neighborhood that had been almost entirely swallowed by the University of Illinois, in the garden apartment of her family's ancestral three-flat. Maria Saraceno, her mother, still lived on the main floor, and Tina Saraceno, her older sister, lived on the top floor with her husband and two daughters.

He liked the apartment. It was small—the rear half of the basement was taken up by the building's furnace and laundry room—but cozy. She had painted the walls a warm yellow and collected an eccentric array of lamps to light the rooms. The small windows looked out on to crocuses and daffodils. On summer mornings he saw birds beaking in the mulch for bugs, and spiders' webs thrumming with capture and kill.

Gina Saraceno's plan to campaign for George Libby made him nervous. He didn't like the idea of his girlfriend drawing attention to herself by making a public and unpopular stand. And he especially didn't want her doing it when her boyfriend was working for Homeland Security. He felt as if he were contaminated, as if he would infect her idealism merely by coming into contact with her. He wondered if he should break up with her. But he couldn't do it. He couldn't be that alone, especially not now.

Fortunately, she had brought her plan up away from his home, and then they had come to her home. He didn't know how closely he was being watched, but he doubted that Chad Armstrong would approve the expense necessary to follow a low-level informant twenty-four hours a day. Even if he wanted to, it was doubtful his superiors would. The bureaucracy of Homeland Security might have been Jason Walker's best ally.

It bought him time. Not much, but enough time to figure out what to do. He wondered how long he could keep Chad Armstrong from knowing about Gina Saraceno's volunteer work.

Eight

J ason Walker visited the Lebanese Cultural Center five more
times over the next two weeks. He stopped by in the
morning, in the afternoon, and in the evening. He tried to meet
more people but the others showed less interest than Leo
Haddad. They were content to let him read books upside down
and even backward if he chose. When he did build up the
courage to introduce himself, he was received politely but with
no warmth. He gave up trying and started going only in the
evenings, when he knew Leo Haddad was likely to be there.

Though the two men were almost the same age, their
relationship was like that of uncle and nephew. Leo Haddad
quizzed Jason Walker on what he'd read, then chose more
books for him. Their conversations were wide-ranging and
friendly, but Leo Haddad made sure they were educational,
too. He had taken at face value Jason Walker's claim that
he wanted to learn.

At home, the informant made careful notes of the things
he'd seen, the names he'd heard, the things he had discussed
with his target. But he became less and less certain that he
would be willing to share those notes with his government
handler. Leo Haddad was obviously not a terrorist. Beyond
even that, Jason Walker liked him. He was kind and generous
and a good listener.

But there was a terrible paradox. If Jason Walker didn't
want to be deported to Beirut, he had to keep spending time
at the cultural center. The only man making that time possible
was Leo Haddad. And the more time they spent together, the
harder it would be to keep their friendship secret. Once again
he felt like a plague carrier. Every time Leo Haddad smiled
at him, he felt black and poisonous inside.

Leo Haddad introduced him to the center's director, a smiling, bearded man named Ahmad Saad, who invited him to become a member of the cultural center. The annual dues were $100, which helped with rent and other expenses and paid for the complimentary tea and coffee. A portion of the money was donated to a charity that did 'good works' in Lebanon. Membership, explained Ahmad Saad, also provided a discount on special activities. For example, in several weeks, a group from the center would be attending a lecture and slide show on ancient Mediterranean art at the Museum of the Art Institute.

The invitation seemed promising. The activities were obviously innocent, but Chad Armstrong had wanted him to get involved, so he would join. Of course, he had also been told not to appear too eager. He thanked Ahmad Saad for the opportunity and told him he would think it over.

When they shook hands as they said goodbye that evening, Leo Haddad clasped his hand a moment longer than was necessary.

'I can see that you are no dilettante,' he said. 'I admire you very much. Many Americans would rather remain in ignorance about the rest of the world. And as you learn about this unfamiliar place, you will learn about yourself.'

Jason Walker waved him off, laughing. 'I'm afraid your high opinion of me is somewhat misplaced.'

'I am certain it is not.'

He received his credit card bill. On the itemized list of debits was a charge for round-trip airfare to Philadelphia, with dates corresponding to his own trip to Cairo. There was also a charge for a five-night hotel stay, complete with realistic minibar and pay-per-view movie charges, and a single credit for the amount of his entire hotel bill. It looked as if the manager had indeed comped the bill. But the airfare was apparently his to pay. And in a cruel joke, the charge was for a first-class seat.

He eyed the check for $3,500.

In forging evidence, Chad Armstrong's people had backed up his story. But they had also given themselves deniability.

*   *   *

That night Jason Walker rode the train south to Gina Saraceno's to eat dinner with her family. The train car was hot and crowded and the driver seemed determined not to go too fast in case the wheels fell off. There was a music festival downtown and passengers carried coolers, lawn chairs, and beach umbrellas. War on terror or no war on terror, Chicago held festivals all summer long. Jason Walker couldn't remember what this one was celebrating. Blues? Country? Gospel? Or maybe it wasn't a music festival at all. Maybe the city was showing a movie in the park again.

He tried to concentrate on the book he was reading, about the Lebanese civil war. It was the first time he'd seriously tried to sort out the events that had brought him to America. Even though he'd picked small pieces up from his parents, it was hard to make sense of it all. There were so many factions, for one: Christians, Muslims, and Jews in a half-dozen varieties, from Syria, Israel, Palestine, and even Lebanon. It was hard to see how a country so diverse, so young, so artificial, could spawn so many people who claimed to love it. Even after leaving it.

The train pulled into a station and the doors opened. The dozen or so people who wanted off had to fight their way through the standing-room-only aisles. The man next to Jason Walker got up and shouldered his way out, and someone instantly took his place.

Chad Armstrong.

'That book any good?' he asked.

'Yes.'

'Glad to hear it. I can never keep all of those nut-jobs straight. So, long time no see. How've you been?'

'I've been fine, thank you,' said Jason Walker.

'In a hurry to get somewhere? I hope not.'

'Well . . .'

'Have a drink with me. I know a place. I won't keep you long. Two stops.'

They got off the train two stops later, Chad Armstrong talking until then as if they were old acquaintances who'd happened to run into each other.

They walked to an Irish pub that had been ordered out of

a catalog. Only a few years old, it looked as if it had stood there since before Chicago was a city. The floor was canted, the woodwork worn smooth as if by countless hands, even the mirrors were darkened as if by age and smoke. It was amazing what could be faked.

The crowd of drinkers, however, shattered the illusion. They wore slacks and dress shirts and tiny cell-phone headsets or they wore shorts, flip-flops, and loud T-shirts that advertised the places they spent their money.

'It's not exactly the casbah,' said Chad Armstrong, 'but no one will notice our nefarious dealings. They're all drunk on Guinness shooters. So, tell me about your vacation.'

'My vacation?'

'It's code. We're in the espionage business, see? Tell me about your trip to the you-know-where.'

Chad Armstrong didn't seem to take his work very seriously, thought Jason Walker. But still he told him, more or less, about his various trips to the Lebanese Cultural Center, reporting what it looked like, what the people there looked like, and what he had done there. The one part he left out was his growing friendship with Leo Haddad. It wasn't that hard, actually. He invented several people who had, he said, bought him coffee or loaned him books.

Chad Armstrong did not appear to be a very good listener. He ordered Guinness shooters for them both and drank his own very quickly. He stared at attractive women. He kept one eye on the crawl of sports scores on a nearby TV. He ordered a second round even though Jason Walker had hardly touched his own drink. But there were moments when Jason Walker thought he saw something else in Chad Armstrong's eyes, like a calculator doing sums.

It took ten minutes to tell everything. Chad Armstrong didn't seem to notice that he'd stopped talking. Instead he inclined his head at a nearby blonde.

'Why aren't hot chicks like that ever involved in the war on terror?' he said. 'I've got cameras in the houses of maybe twenty guys and most of 'em are gnarly beardos. And the ones with wives make their wives wear that head-to-toe shit practically until bedtime.'

'Burkas?'

'Burkas, hijabs, kaftans, muumuus—whatever. Anyway, now that you've told me about your vacation, I want to show you pictures of my vacation. Sound good?'

'All right.'

'Don't you want to ask where I went?'

'Where did you go?'

'That's classified.'

Smirking, Chad Armstrong pulled a small photo album out of his back pocket.

'Look at each one of these. Take your time.'

Jason Walker took the album. It was flimsy plastic, four inches by six, the kind some photo shops give away for free with an order of prints. The first photo was of a man looking over his shoulder. It was grainy, as if it had been shot with a zoom lens under low light and then dramatically enlarged. The photo had been cropped just below the shoulders. The man wore a mustache, a checked head scarf, and a wary look. Jason Walker had never seen the man. He shook his head.

'Keep looking,' said Chad Armstrong.

He turned the page. The next photo looked like a mug shot. A man glared at the camera in black-and-white, his skin washed out by the flash. His chin rested on the bottom of the photo as if the photographer had refused to lower his tripod. He was clean-shaven with short dark hair, very unattractive. Also a stranger.

Jason Walker shook his head and looked at the next photo.

They were all different. Some posed, some candid. Some crisp, some out of focus. Some men unaware that they were under observation, some defiant despite having been captured. But the captured ones must have been released. Or escaped.

He found himself imagining stories for each of them. The photos were clinical and yet hinted at entirely alien circumstances. This one was a petty thief who'd thrown his lot in with the Taliban in hopes of making something of himself. This one was a career mercenary. This one was a devout Muslim who'd reluctantly taken up arms.

Chad Armstrong just watched his face as he lingered over each photo. He'd never seen any of them before.

Until he saw the picture of Leo Haddad. He tried not to react, but he felt his pupils contract to pinpoints, felt his heart stutter and race. His first instinct was to turn the page, but he forced himself to linger as he had with the others.

After thirty seconds, he shook his head and turned the page.

Chad Armstrong said nothing until he had closed the photo album.

'So you didn't see any of these guys?'

'No.'

'You're positive?'

'Well, I mean, I think so.'

Chad Armstrong riffled through the book and showed him one of the pictures again. Though it was impossible to tell, he thought the man in the photo might have been riding a camel.

'Positive you didn't see this guy?'

'Yes, positive.'

Another second look, this time a prison mugshot.

'Positive you didn't see this guy?'

'Yes.'

Another look at the photograph of Leo Haddad.

'This guy?'

'Positive.'

'Because it looked like you recognized him.'

'Well, he could have been there. I'm sure I don't remember everybody I saw. Maybe I looked at it for an extra second because I thought I had seen him. But I really don't think so.'

Chad Armstrong pursed his lips.

'OK. You haven't seen him. You haven't seen any of these guys. It's weird, because we do know that a few of them like to hang out at the cultural center. Maybe it's just bad luck or whatever. I know you wouldn't hold anything back.'

'Of course not.'

'Because you don't want to go back to Beirut.'

I don't want to go *to* Beirut, you asshole, he thought.

'OK, new tactic. I know I told you just to show up and look around and not to do anything specific, but now I want you to do something specific. Keep your eyes open for this guy'—he tapped the photo of Leo Haddad—'and try to make friends with him.'

'That wasn't the deal.'

'New deal.'

'But I'm not a spy. Like you said.'

'I promise no grappling hooks and no safecracking. You won't have to strangle him with piano wire. Just introduce yourself and be friendly.'

'And then you'll change the deal again.'

Chad Armstrong shrugged. 'Look, I don't have the same thing for breakfast every day, either. Change is part of life. Adapt or die. I mean, I'll try not to get you killed. But while we're on that subject, watch out for this guy. You'll be safe if you hang out with him in the cultural center, when there are a bunch of people around. But don't walk down any dark alleys with him. He's what we in the business call a "bad guy"—industry term.'

He finished his drink and stood up.

Jason Walker was suddenly afraid that he shouldn't have held back information.

'They asked me to become a member,' he said.

'They what?'

'They asked me to become a dues-paying member.'

'Who?'

'Ahmad Saad. The director.'

'How much? The dues?'

'A hundred dollars.'

Chad Armstrong opened his wallet and took out a hundred-dollar bill. 'There you go. Don't buy drugs with that or anything. We log the serial numbers on those puppies.'

He also gave Jason Walker a phone number with a local area code.

'If you need to reach me, leave a message after the tone. I'll get it right away. You're helping us, but you may need our help, too.'

He walked to the train. He had to transfer to another train and then the bus before he arrived at Gina Saraceno's house. He was late. Dinnertime had begun. He kissed his girlfriend, apologized, and sat down at the table in her mother's dining room.

The apartment, with lace curtains framing the windows and framed photographs lining the wall, felt very old-world to him. And the big, noisy family—besides Gina Saraceno, her mother, and her sister's family, there were an aunt and uncle and an elderly neighbor—felt very old-world as well. It was a stark contrast to the way he'd grown up. Maria Saraceno had cooked all day long, and every inch of the table was covered with food. They ate and drank heartily—even the kids were allowed to have tiny glasses of watered-down wine—and laughed and told stories.

He had long ignored the idea of starting a family. And it would have been terribly premature to raise the subject with Gina Saraceno. But suddenly he wondered if she wasn't his last, best chance to not be alone. And he knew he was realizing this too late.

Tonio Longhetti, the uncle, attempted to talk to him about work. It was an uncomfortable subject and he tried to laugh it off. The uncle was a building contractor with four crews and had often offered employment 'if that computer thing doesn't work out.' Jason Walker had explained several times what he did but apparently hadn't been sufficiently clear. Since Gio Saraceno's death, his wife's brother seemed to feel a fatherly sense of obligation toward Gio's daughters.

After dinner he thought that maybe he and Gina Saraceno would go for a walk. They could stop for a drink, perhaps, then spend an early and enjoyable evening in bed.

But Gina Saraceno had other plans.

'Let's take my car,' she said.

She drove east to Lake Shore Drive, then south toward Hyde Park.

'Are we going where I think we're going?' he asked.

'Yup,' she said.

'Vote Libby,' he sighed.

She laughed.

'Oh, *honey.*'

It had been a day of nearly unlimited sunshine, and as the sun descended the wind grew stronger. A few bikers, joggers, or skaters traveled the path in the park. Beyond them, tiny whitecaps splashed gold in the dying sun. Gina Saraceno turned off Lake Shore Drive and drove past the Museum of Science and Industry. Because it was considered to be a family museum, the current show was controversial to some: 'Military Machines.' Simple, interactive exhibits explained how armor plate stopped roadside bombs and how robot planes located the enemy in the wasteland. Jason Walker hadn't seen the exhibit for himself, but it was a far cry from exhibits on Leonardo da Vinci and space travel.

Gina Saraceno made several turns, got stymied by a one-way, and looped around a block to compensate. She wasn't lost, she explained, but she couldn't remember exactly where it was. They were right on the border between genteel Hyde Park and slightly shabby Kenwood. After fifteen minutes, she brightened and pulled the car over.

'Here it is,' she said.

The red-brick three-flat had seen better days, but not recently. The mortar was falling out in chunks. Some years ago a decorative cornice had been replaced with sparkly Permastone, and repairs to the walls had been made with mismatched bricks. The wooden porch listed dangerously to one side. A bicycle rack in front of the building was jumbled with two-wheelers in various states of disrepair.

They walked up the front steps and into the vestibule. Boxes of produce were piled to shoulder-height. Jason Walker had to shift a few of them before Gina Saraceno could operate the intercom.

'It's a drop-off for an organic farm,' she explained. 'People buy shares in the farm and then once a week the farm delivers the vegetables to the city.'

He folded back the corner of a box and saw a bunch of carrots damp with earth. There were also beets, lettuce, and something white that looked like part of an alien creature. He raised an eyebrow.

'Kohlrabi,' said Gina Saraceno.

Hand-printed signs read *BREAK DOWN BOXES AND STACK THEM OUTSIDE* and *PLEASE TAKE ONLY ONE NEWSLETTER PER BOX*.

To Jason Walker, it seemed an even less likely headquarters for revolution than the Lebanese Cultural Center.

The door buzzed open and they went up to a second-floor apartment. The man holding the door for them stood about six-and-a-half feet tall and weighed about a hundred and fifty pounds. He wore his hair in a long ponytail and was missing his upper right lateral incisor. He was either fifty years old or a hard-won forty.

'Gina,' he said warmly, 'glad you could make it.'

'I'm a woman of my word,' she said. 'This is my boyfriend, Jason Walker.'

'Greetings, Jason. I'm Scott Fink.'

Fighting an urge to say 'Vote Libby!' he shook the man's hand.

Scott Fink led them through a foyer into a small living room crowded with house plants and people. The walls were lined with posters. Some encouraged citizens to protest against war or workers to organize labor unions. A few others encouraged music lovers to attend Grateful Dead concerts.

'Everyone, this is Gina and Jason. Gina and Jason, this is everyone.'

Everyone denoted about eight people. Jason Walker wondered if Scott Fink had dropped their surnames deliberately. Would a George Libby campaign meeting take security precautions? He hoped so.

The meeting was informal. Scott Fink served cans of beer and bowls of chips and homemade salsa, noting with pride that the tomatoes in the salsa were organic. He asked each person to give their name, an interesting personal fact, and the reason they were interested in campaigning for George Libby. They all gave first names only.

Eric, a writer, was incensed that his civil liberties had been abrogated by the president. George Libby wasn't remotely liberal enough for him, but he would campaign for anyone who opposed the president. Amber, a student, was there with her boyfriend, Jarrod, a political-science major, worried that political campaigns were becoming obsolete. Mike, a tough-looking lesbian, said she hoped to put her 'foot up the president's ass.' Demeter, a beautiful hippie, said she lived downstairs and looked to Scott Fink for guidance; 'where he leads, I follow.' Javier, a bike messenger, said that the reason he was there should be obvious to any thinking person. Cornelius and Dorothy, retired professors of African American studies, said they would fight the president not because they believed they could win, but because 'the juggernaut must be slowed, even if it means throwing our own bodies under the wheels.'

There was a moment of silence. Scott Fink nodded his head thoughtfully. Jason Walker was next. He had no idea how to follow such conviction. He gave his name and occupation and said that he hoped George Libby would be given a fair chance to make his case once an election was called.

He didn't exactly bring the house down. Even Gina Saraceno looked mildly embarrassed.

'I'm Gina,' she said, 'and I believe we need to get that election on the calendar.'

The group gave scattered applause and a few whoops. Scott Fink smiled and nodded approvingly.

'All right,' he said. 'Let's begin.'

Scott Fink introduced himself as a 'veteran activist and an activist veteran.' He had served in the peacetime army and was proud of his 'perfect record,' having never fired a gun in conflict. He had contacted George Libby after reading a newspaper article and volunteered to organize the Chicago campaign. It was an unpaid position, and, he said, everyone in the room could count on their efforts being pro bono as well.

Jason Walker thought of the check for $3,500 sitting on his sideboard. It was a bit worse for wear since it had blown off on to the floor and he had stepped on it. But with or without the shoe print, it was still legal tender.

With apologies to those in the group who had heard his spiel before, Scott Fink offered a short biographical sketch of George Libby and outlined the planks of his candidacy. The candidate had served one tour of duty in Vietnam with the Marines and two tours of duty in Liberia with the Peace Corps. He had earned a bachelor's degree in history on the GI bill and then a master's in business. He managed a furniture store in the Southwest, then started his own, then bought out two competitors and founded a national chain. Wishing to grow even more, he built factories and began to build his own wares. He used direct mail and TV info-mercials to market, sell, and ship directly to customers in areas where he did not have stores. Would-be investors urged him to take his company public.

Then, in the 1990s, he became the target of demonstrators who claimed that the FurnishMart factories were poisoning the groundwater with improperly-disposed-of chemicals.

'George Libby could have ignored the demonstrators,' said Scott Fink. 'He could have asked a judge to issue a restraining order, saying they were interfering with his business. He could have tried to crush this rag-tag band with all the money and power at his disposal. But he didn't do that. He investigated their claims. He found that they were right. He invited them inside the gates. He listened. It was a teaching moment.'

The future presidential candidate wasn't about to shut down his operation, of course. But he took immediate, good-faith steps to reduce the harmful impact of his factories. He hired community liaisons and gave his employees half-pay for any volunteer work they performed. He hired consult-ants to create a 'zero-impact' plan that would have FurnishMart in environmental balance within twenty years. Construction materials would be sustainable and biodegrad-able. Waste would be recycled. Showrooms would offer affordable repair services. Unavoidable waste would be balanced with gains in other areas. For example, if tests proved that airborne emissions were still harmful, extra trees would be planted on the surrounding hills.

George Libby had been profiled in *Mother Jones*. Scott Fink passed a hand-worn copy around the room. The cover image showed a sixty-ish, avuncular white man with male-pattern baldness, his arms folded over an ill-fitting shirt. Emblazoned across his legs were the words 'The Future.' Environmentalist groups saw him as a savior, someone who had access to the unsaved and who spoke their language. And George Libby did enjoy giving speeches to his peers, urging them to enjoy the benefits of a clean conscience as he did.

But he showed no political ambition whatsoever. He was still a capitalist. He enjoyed making money and believed that, once they realized the long-term benefits of doing good, others would join him. He preferred to lead by example, not by legislation. It took war and a constitutional amendment to change his mind.

First, a close friend lost two sons in the Iran offensive. Then his own son was shot down on an air raid over Colombia. George Libby wanted to protest by voting against the president, but there was no candidate. There wasn't even an election scheduled. He wanted to get an election scheduled. Calls to his congressman and senators, whom he knew well, left him unsatisfied. He thought about it for one week and then declared his candidacy.

'How do you know all this stuff?' asked Javier, the bike messenger.

'Half of it is on his website and in his campaign brochures,' said Scott Fink. 'He told me the other half himself, over the phone. We need to get the whole story into the Chicago media.'

George Libby had been painted as a single-issue candidate. His slogan was 'Bring them all home.' And he freely admitted that his son's death had been the inspiration for his campaign. He believed America's many small wars were exacerbating, not ameliorating, the problem of terrorism. But in order to be taken more seriously as a candidate, he had added stances as necessary. He was pro-environment, of course. He was also pro-choice, pro-gun control, pro-assisted suicide, pro-healthcare, pro-union, pro-stem cell research— all unfashionable stances since the start of the president's third term. George Libby had also been called an isolationist. He believed that America could help countries faced with famine, disease, and genocide, but felt that any such help should be modest. He believed in limiting tax relief to multi-national corporations, but his refusal to condemn them outright bothered some of the radicals who would otherwise have been his base.

It seemed to bother Javier, too. He had protested at several meetings of the World Trade Organization and the G8.

'Half the reason we're in half these wars is because they're making money off the arms deals, man,' said Javier. 'If Libby doesn't see that, then he doesn't realize that they're never going to bring the troops home while there's still a buck to be made.'

'I'm not saying he's the perfect candidate,' said Scott Fink. 'But tell me one who's better.'

Javier mumbled that he wasn't trying to be difficult, but he wasn't sure if he could volunteer his time for someone who wasn't opposed to multinational corporations.

Scott Fink said he understood. Despite his ponytail and his less-than-inspiring appearance, he had a calm, commanding presence. He said that although he needed help, he didn't want anyone who wasn't committed to the cause. He also understood, he said, that simply wearing a George Libby badge or sticker didn't mean what it would have meant in an ordinary year. To ask to vote might be considered a subversive act. It seemed as good a time as any, he said, to ask who was in and who was out.

Jason Walker assumed that everyone in the small group would be in. It wouldn't be nearly enough people, but anyone interested enough to come to a meeting was probably likely to do more. He thought the candidate sounded appealing. He also thought that he should stay as far away as possible.

'So,' said Scott Fink, 'who wants to stand with George Libby?'

He looked expectantly around the room.

Eric the writer nodded.

Amber the student looked at her boyfriend, Jarrod the political-science major. He asked to take a brochure with him. He said he would think it over and call Scott Fink.

Mike the lesbian said, 'Hell yes, I'm in.'

Demeter the hippie smiled at Scott Fink and nodded.

Javier the bike messenger wished them all luck and said that he was looking for something more radical.

Cornelius and Dorothy, the retired professors, said they would volunteer two hours a week. Jason Walker wondered if their schedule would coincide with the moment the juggernaut rolled through Chicago.

Gina Saraceno volunteered one day per week and evenings as time allowed.

Scott Fink looked at her gratefully. Then he turned to Jason Walker.

He wanted to help. He wanted to run.

'It's all, um, very compelling,' he said. 'It's kind of a tough time for me right now. I mean, I have time, but I'm struggling financially, so I feel like I should be looking for work.'

He felt a sharp elbow in his ribs. His girlfriend smiled sweetly.

'But, I guess this is more important, isn't it?' he said. 'So, sure, I'll help out. As time allows.'

Scott Fink thanked those who had declined to help, shaking their hands as they filed out the door. He closed the door and asked the volunteers to stay a moment. As they listened to the last footsteps thumping down the stairs, he spoke to them quietly.

'I've been involved in a lot of campaigns and a lot of actions. None have been more important than this. Now, I don't want to sound paranoid. I know I look like a hippie and you look like a room full of well-intentioned volunteers who want to work peaceably for change, but I've seen Quakers busted for holding prayer circles, and you never know who's really a friend. So let's keep this first names only. You all probably shouldn't hang out together or exchange phone numbers. I won't keep your names or numbers in writing here. You all have my phone number, and that's fine. But the less you write down, the better. Erase your call history once in a while.'

Cornelius looked at Scott Fink.

'Do you really think all this secrecy is necessary?'

'I hope not. But if we find out for sure that it is, it'll be too late to go back and do things differently.'

Cornelius, a slightly tired-looking man with patches of gray in his neatly trimmed hair, looked questioningly at his wife.

She nodded.

'Fair enough,' he said.

'Good man,' said Scott Fink. 'I forgot to tell you all that I do have a surefire method for finding spies. Let me go get my knife.'

He looked around at the seven astonished faces.

'Kidding, people, kidding.'

Jason Walker's heart had almost resumed beating again by the time Gina Saraceno started the car.

It was fully dark as they drove north on Lake Shore Drive. The park looked empty. White waves crashed on the revetments. Beyond that, the lake was black as a void.

Traffic was thick. Ahead of them, red brake lights pulsed on and off. Soon they were inching along.

'What's the deal?' asked Gina Saraceno irritably.

'It's got to be a festival, right?'

'Yeah, the glee club and a cappella extravaganza.'

They both laughed. They hadn't talked about the meeting. Gina Saraceno's involvement had made him nervous, and his own involvement made him doubly so. But if they didn't discuss it at his house, and if they didn't discuss it on the phone, maybe it could be their secret. It seemed a feeble hope. Of course, Chad Armstrong was interested in the Lebanese Cultural Center, not an aging radical's apartment in Hyde Park. As far as he knew.

'Gina, about tonight—'

'Oh, shit.'

They both saw the source of the slowdown. Blue-striped police cars and white Homeland Security vans, their flashers strobing, lined the hard shoulder. They narrowed the road to a V through which only two cars could pass at a time. Police officers were stopping cars and peering inside with long-handled flashlights. A garbage truck, parked just behind the checkpoint and perpendicular to the road, forced drivers to make a tight turn at slow speed once they'd been allowed to proceed.

'Beautiful,' said Gina Saraceno. 'Checkpoint. What were you saying?'

'Um . . .' he said.

He felt guilty, and stupid for feeling guilty. Obviously Homeland Security wasn't looking for George Libby campaign volunteers. He just wished they didn't have to go through the checkpoint. Checkpoints made him nervous. Who really knew what they were looking for? The last time he'd been close to a white van he'd been thrown inside it. He wanted to tell her about it.

'Just, you know,' he said, 'kind of a big night.'

If he told her, he'd have to tell her everything.

They inched forward. There was a weird electricity about the scene. Drivers gripped their steering wheels and stared ahead, tight-lipped.

'Look, Scott is a little melodramatic, but that's all. I think anyone who has been that political for their whole life probably gets a little paranoid.'

They had stopped. She turned her head to look at him.

'God,' she said, 'you don't think there was a spy in the room, do you?'

'Well, how would you know?'

She started laughing. The passenger in the car to their left turned to look.

'Stop laughing.'

'What, they've outlawed laughing now? That lady's going to bust me?'

She waved gaily at the staring passenger in the next car.

'Gina, just don't draw their attention.'

'Jason, honey, I think you need to relax. I know you're depressed because work's going badly. Who knows? Maybe you should go work for my uncle. The fresh air might cheer you up. Look, I'll help you unwind when we get home. Your place or mine?'

She put her hand on his knee.

He pushed it off.

She stared at him.

They were a half-dozen car lengths from the roadblock, but he could see the faces of the men searching the cars. They looked suspicious and unforgiving.

'Your place it is, then,' she said.

'Look, I'm sorry. I just—'

'Forget it.'

They were silent until it was their turn. The lights were blinding. It was as if a terrible accident had taken place.

Gina Saraceno rolled down her window.

'Hello, officer.'

The policeman said nothing. He shined the flashlight in her face. She scowled and faced forward.

The man trained his beam on the passenger seat. Jason Walker closed his eyes against the glare. His heart was pounding.

'Open your eyes, sir.'

He did, blinking.

The man stepped back, peering into the messy back seat. He thumped the trunk with the flat of his hand, making them both jump.

'Pop the trunk.'

She reached down and pulled the lever beside her seat. The trunk opened. The car bounced slightly on its suspension as the man shifted things around.

'What do you have back there?' whispered Jason Walker.

'Two terrorists and a machine gun,' whispered Gina Saraceno.

He shook his head. Didn't she see how serious this was?

The trunk slammed shut.

'Pull forward,' said the man.

After they turned around the garbage truck, they saw a half-dozen cars on the shoulder that had been pulled out of the line. Homeland Security officers controlled this scene. Two short, dark-skinned men were being loaded into a van. Others were being frisked against their cars. One car was being literally disassembled by a search team: its wheels had been removed and its seats rested a few yards away on the pavement. Barking German shepherds kept the suspects in line while smaller dogs crawled through the cars, sniffing, he guessed, for explosives.

Gina Saraceno dropped him off at his apartment building. He was upset that they were fighting, but in a way, it was good to be alone, too.

'It's been a wonderful evening,' she said.

'I'll call you tomorrow,' he said.

But she was already driving away.

Nine

Jason Walker found himself suddenly anxious to get back to work—his real work, editing and writing. He sent emails to some of the editors he'd worked with in the past year, asking if they had anything for him. He called the editors who he hadn't worked with for longer than that. Responses varied, but no one gasped in excitement that he was available. Most of the emails went unanswered. A couple of the people he phoned admitted that they weren't likely to have work for him. One said he might, another said she did. She was looking for someone to summarize other writers' reviews in two sentences for the arts listings. It would be a weekly deadline. The pay was pathetic. He said he'd take it.

After he hung up he wondered if she had deliberately quoted a low rate to scare him off. Perhaps she hadn't wanted him to take it. It was always easy to get an intern to do work like that. Well, he had surprised her. In his situation, even eighty dollars a week was something. With his new cooking skills, he could almost eat on that. He only hoped he wouldn't be cooking for one.

He decided to pay a personal visit to *Chicago Socialite*. There was another troubled relationship. He showered, shaved, and dressed as sharply as he felt able. As he headed out the door, on instinct he reached for his camera bag, as he normally would have, to take a few pictures once his errand was over. But then he remembered that he didn't feel like taking pictures anymore. He put the bag back on its hook in the front closet.

It was hot and humid with only a few white clouds drifting along in the sky. He walked to the Argyle station slowly, keeping to the shade wherever possible. He didn't want to be drenched in sweat when he arrived.

He got off the train in the Loop and walked to the beautifully restored Art Deco building that housed the *Chicago
Socialite* offices. Consulting the directory in the lobby, he
found the appropriate bank of elevators and pushed the call
button. Though he'd done a great deal of work for the magazine, he'd only been in the offices twice before. Freelancers
were cheap labor and considered a nuisance when they
showed up in person. Still, he wanted to make it harder for
his editor to say no.

The reception area looked more like a tastefully appointed
living room than the front room of a business. Fortunately,
there was a thin girl at a thin sliver of a desk just inside
the door. She looked six feet tall and seventeen years old.
Her bangs slashed across her face severely, and she had to
lean to her right to look at him with both eyes.

He asked for Lainie Verona. The girl narrowed her eyes
at him suspiciously, then tapped a button on her console
and whispered into a fiber-optic whisker that was suspended
below her lower lip.

'Please wait,' she said, pointing to an S-shaped chair.

Lainie Verona kept him waiting for twenty minutes. She
swept into the room and stood poised as if she were about
to sweep right out again.

'Hi Lainie, thanks for seeing me.'

'Jason, I'm glad you could stop by.'

She didn't seem all that glad. He glanced hopefully in
what he thought was the direction of her office.

'Do you have a moment?'

She stayed put. If she was going to sweep out of the
room again, she was going to do it without him.

'I do, just. What's this about?'

'Well,' he said, 'I'm very sorry about what happened a
few weeks ago. I didn't know that you were sending work,
and I was called out of town on short notice.'

'Nothing bad, I hope.'

'Nothing too bad. But I'm sorry I blew the deadline.'

'You couldn't check your email while you were away?'

He didn't want to make up a new lie, but he also didn't
want to tell her he'd been working for someone else.

'It was a difficult situation. But I hope we can continue our working relationship.'

She sighed and suddenly took an interest in the room's decor, as if she were seeing it for the first time.

'Our understanding,' she said, 'was that we could send you work at any time and expect a reasonably quick turnaround. If you were suddenly going to be unavailable, you should have let us know before you left.'

'I know,' he said. 'I'm sorry.'

'Well, I'm sorry, too. But we rely on professional behavior from our freelancers and contractors every bit as much as we do from our staff.'

Except for the writers, he said to himself.

'I understand.'

'I'm glad,' she said. 'I do wish you luck elsewhere.'

In fact he hadn't understood. He had thought she was merely admonishing him. But she was firing him. Before he knew it, he was riding the elevator downstairs. *Chicago Socialite* had been his fallback position. Now he was simply in free fall.

He called Gina Saraceno and left a message. He wanted to tell her what had happened but he didn't think she wanted more bad news from him at the moment. Instead he asked when they would be volunteering for George Libby. It was a transparent ploy to get back in her good graces, but it was also a no-fault chance for them to make up. He felt badly for the way he'd spoken to her, for being afraid. If he lost her, all he had left was his friendship with a Cubs fan and his forced allegiance to a government agent.

He went to the Lebanese Cultural Center again. He still hadn't decided if he was going to admit knowing Leo Haddad or not, but by going there he was able to entertain both notions. The man was friendly and erudite and, but for his over-formal English—he rarely used contractions—seemed very American. There had been moments when Jason Walker had forgotten his mission. At those times, Leo Haddad seemed only to be a new friend.

But the friendship had been one-way. Jason Walker had said he was looking for information and Leo Haddad helped provide it. He was a good conversationalist and yet he hadn't revealed anything about himself. The story of his origins could have been pure invention. It was easy to assume that Chad Armstrong was wrong, but what if Leo Haddad actually was a terrorist? What if he was planning to bomb a building full of innocent people? Jason Walker had no experience with men like that. Maybe they smiled and made small talk right up until the moment they pushed the button.

The thought that he might be protecting an actual terrorist made him angry. Angry at himself for not knowing, for his naïveté. But he couldn't condemn an innocent man to kidnapping and torture.

When he arrived at the center, Leo Haddad was playing chess with another man. Leo Haddad smiled at him and he went over.

'Mind if I watch?'

'Please. Perhaps you can teach us both something about this game.'

He sat down. The other chess player was short and, when he smiled, did so with only half of his face. Neither of the players needed any coaching. Not that he could have helped them anyway. He hadn't played chess since middle school.

The short man won the game.

'I would ask you to play,' said Leo Haddad, 'but we are playing best of three. I won the first. I hope you don't mind.'

Jason Walker assured them that he didn't mind.

Ahmad Saad came out of the back and saw him.

'Jason. Have you decided to become a member of the center?'

He said that he had.

'Wonderful. Come into my office, please.'

He followed the slightly pear-shaped man. They passed through a beaded curtain into the back. The office was immediately to the right. The restroom was several yards past it on the left. Evening light outlined an exit door directly ahead.

Ahmad Saad sat behind a desk and indicated that Jason Walker should sit in front of it. The small office was cluttered with a filing cabinet, a refrigerator, a hookah, stacks of Arabic-language newspapers, and several cases of bottled iced tea. The desk was covered with a mess of paperwork and ashtrays that needed to be emptied. The wall behind the desk was lined with floor-to-ceiling bookshelves. There were books in several languages, computer manuals, and dozens of cheap plastic binders. Were there guns behind the walls? Were there bombs under the floor? Would Ahmad Saad recruit him for a suicide mission?

'Yes, this is where it all happens,' said the director. 'The nerve center of the Lebanese Cultural Center. Very glamorous, indeed?'

Jason Walker smiled politely.

'In Lebanon, I was the grocery king. I had the largest grocery in Tyre. Western-style, with air conditioning, refrigeration, even freezers. But all to the glory of Allah, of course. Here I own one small store, a convenience market. But also to the glory of Allah.'

Again, Jason Walker smiled politely.

'Are you a Muslim?'

'No, I'm not anything.'

'You have become friends with Leo Haddad. A good man, but not a good Muslim. If you wish to learn anything about Islam while you are here, please consider me your willing teacher.'

'Thank you.'

'But you are welcome here under any circumstances.'

Ahmad Saad pulled a dirty blue vinyl binder off the shelf behind him. He opened it and leafed through to a half-filled page. He turned the binder around and slid it across the desk.

'Fill this out, please.'

Each member had written his name, address, and phone number, then dated the line and signed his name. Ahmad Saad had initialed the memberships that had been paid in full. After a moment's hesitation, Jason Walker filled out the first blank line.

'And one hundred dollars, please. Remember that you are also supporting an honorable charity.'

He handed over the hundred-dollar bill Chad Armstrong

had given him. Ahmad Saad took the money and put it inside a small cash box in a drawer of his desk. He initialed the membership book.

'Would you like a receipt?'

'It's not necessary.'

Ahmad Saad nodded.

'Then thank you. I hope you will consider this your home away from home. And please be certain to ask me if you should need anything.'

Jason Walker said that he would. They stood up and shook hands, and then he went back to the front. Leo Haddad had just won the third game and seemed to be giving his opponent a good-natured ribbing in Arabic. Without acknowledging Jason Walker, the man laughed, shook his head, and walked away.

'Jason, my friend, how are you? Would you like to play some chess?'

'Who was that?'

Leo Haddad deftly reset the board.

'I don't know him. He is just a man I see here sometimes. Would you like to play?'

'I'm not very good.'

'Nor am I. We will both try to become better together.'

It only took a few moves for Leo Haddad to establish himself as the superior player. While Jason Walker was trying to remember whether it was the bishop that moved diagonally, or the knight, Leo Haddad took two pawns and one bishop and put him in check. The game didn't last much longer than that.

They reset the pieces again.

'It wasn't fair of me,' said Leo Haddad. 'I should have let you play white.'

'I think I would have lost even if you let me play both sides.'

'Let me make it easier for you until you remember how to play. I will take one bishop, one knight, and one castle off the board.'

'Mine or yours?'

'Mine, until you beat me.'

Jason Walker played better in the second game. But even though he wanted to win, he was distracted. He needed to learn more about his opponent, not the game.

'How long did you say you've been in America?'

Leo Haddad was reaching for the chessboard. He paused. 'I do not remember telling you. But since the early nineties.'

Then he removed a white pawn from the board.

'But didn't you say that you came here because of the war?'

'I did tell you that. You asked how long I had been in America. Remember that we moved first to Canada. And that was in the eighties.'

'When the war was winding down.'

'It did not feel exactly like that to us. Many people continued to leave even after the war. Just because the war is over it does not mean that the city repairs itself.'

Jason Walker flushed. 'Of course not. I'm sorry.'

'And there is always Israel. To fight those whom they call terrorists, they bomb roads and bridges, schools and hospitals. To the people living in the south of Lebanon, America would at any time look more peaceful.'

'Even though the terrorists have begun to bomb us here.'

Leo Haddad gave him a sharp look.

'It is not the same thing. Unless you have grown up with guns firing, you do not know what it is like to live in terror.'

They played in silence for a while. The game became less friendly. Despite his generous handicap, Leo Haddad seemed determined to beat him as soundly as possible. Jason Walker was able to make the game last several moves longer than the first, but that was all.

'Another?' he suggested.

Leo Haddad shrugged indifferently but began resetting his pieces.

'I didn't mean to upset you.'

'I am not upset.'

'We just talk about me all the time. I thought I would like to get to know you better.'

'I am a simple man. I was born in a state, not a nation. Like so much of the Middle East, our boundaries were drawn by Europeans. But for some perverse reason I love my state as if it were a real nation.'

'But what do you do? What is your job?'

'I am between jobs right now. I do—how do you say it?—a little bit of this and a little bit of that.'

'What about your spare time? What are your hobbies?'

'I suppose that all my time is spare time right now. I come here and read the newspaper and play chess and talk to you.'

'But what do you do for money?'

'In Lebanon, it is very impolite to ask a man how much money he has. As it should be here.'

'I'm sorry,' said Jason Walker. Stop apologizing, he said to himself.

He lost another game and started setting up his pawns to lose a fourth. He thought he would try one more time.

'Where do you live?' he asked.

'Not far from here.'

It was time to stop asking questions. He cursed himself for being so clumsy. He had meant to create a friendly conversation and learn what he needed to know in that way. The direct questions had been off-putting.

The game was over. He was check-mated again.

Leo Haddad looked at his watch.

'I must go,' he said.

'Are you meeting someone?'

Leo Haddad ignored his question.

'I am sorry you had such bad luck at the game tonight. I am sure you will do better next time. If you like, I can lend you a book on chess.'

Now Jason Walker felt himself bristling.

'I'm quite capable of visiting the library.'

Leo Haddad merely nodded.

'Will I see you again soon?' asked Jason Walker.

'I am sure that you will.'

They said goodbye. Not wanting to follow the other man out the door, Jason Walker asked Ghassan for a cup of Lebanese coffee. He was growing to like it. He drank it slowly, savoring the rich taste, both sweet and bitter.

Leo Haddad was clearly put off by his questions. Was it

because he was simply a rude American? Or did Leo Haddad have something to hide?

Though it was several miles away, Jason Walker walked home that night. The strong coffee made him feel wide awake. As he walked, he weighed the possible outcomes of his actions. If he continued to protect Leo Haddad, he could be protecting a terrorist. And surely Homeland Security knew more about the man than he did. On the other hand, Homeland Security had known next to nothing about Jason Walker. But would an innocent man grow evasive when asked what he did for a living?

When he got home, he sat in front of the television with the phone in his hand. After a while he turned down the volume and dialed the number Chad Armstrong had given him. On the news he saw blurry video of rockets erupting skyward from parched brown hills.

There wasn't even a ring on the other end. A recorded message played, a woman's voice saying with professional detachment that he had reached the Acme Messenger Service. Then there was a beep.

He cleared his throat. There was still time to hang up. But of course, if Gina Saraceno had caller I.D., Homeland Security would have something even more sophisticated. It was too late.

'This is, um, Jason Walker,' he said. 'I'm calling for Chad Armstrong. I need to talk to him.'

Unsure if he should say anything else, he gave his phone number, needlessly, and hung up. He turned the television's volume back up and watched the news without seeing or hearing anything specific.

His phone rang five minutes later. He answered and heard a man's voice, sleepy and unfriendly.

'4141 North Clark Street, ten o'clock. Do you understand?'

'Ten o'clock tonight?' he asked.

'4141 North Clark Street, ten o'clock tonight.'

The man hung up.

He looked at the clock. He had one hour to get there.

Ten

Jason Walker felt tired. He considered hailing a cab but remembered a movie spy telling his girl that he never rode in cabs because it was like hiring a witness to identify you. So he walked to the train, rode three stops south, and then walked again. It was a Wrigleyville address. He wondered whether Chad Armstrong lived in the area or simply enjoyed its many bars.

As it turned out, 4141 North Clark Street was a two-story bachelor playground called Ballbreakers Billiards. After the quiet walk from the train it was like climbing inside a pinball machine. Loud electronic music failed to drown out the banks of blooping games salvaged from carnival midways. Televisions ringed the walls, showing everything from baseball games and auto racing to horror movies and vintage cartoons. A scantily clad cigarette girl weaved between knots of T-shirt-wearing, short-haired young men who tested their skill on skee-ball, pop-a-shot, and whack-a-mole.

In that crowd, it was easy not to be noticed. He made a slow circuit of the room. Passing a temporary bar in one corner, he turned down a promotional shot of beer-flavored vodka. But he did buy an oversized can of beer for three dollars from a bikini-clad girl stationed at an ice-filled trough. He didn't see Chad Armstrong.

Carpeted stairs led to something called 'Le Club.' For all he knew it was a replica tree fort, wallpapered with someone's father's *Playboy* magazines, but he climbed up anyway. He pushed through thick doors upholstered with green leather and brass tacks and found himself in yet another world. Men in their forties and fifties were smoking cigars, drinking Scotch, and shooting pool in a room that appeared to have been airlifted from the 1930s. He had no idea where to meet Chad Armstrong, but he decided to let Chad Armstrong find him. He didn't want to go back downstairs and risk being challenged to a skee-ball match in which the loser had to chug a can of beer.

He asked the hostess for a pool table. As he followed her through the smoky room, the jumbo can of beer, which he'd bought in order to fit in downstairs, suddenly seemed comical. He asked her to take it away and bring him a bourbon with plenty of ice. She smiled, amused, then racked the balls for him and took the beer away.

He had been given the last open table, which was against the far wall. He scanned the room. He still didn't see Chad Armstrong. He began to play.

He had only played pool a few times since being fired from *Billiards Journal*. Occasionally David Darling would decide it was time to humiliate the fans of a rival baseball team and would call on Jason Walker to do it. He wasn't good enough to beat even a serious amateur, but he could usually win against inebriated baseball fans who thought that brute force would increase their chance of pocketing balls. It helped that he knew a few trick shots and cheap hustles. Most of the professional players he had interviewed had spent some time on the road, and he had enjoyed asking them about the tricks of their trade.

The hostess had racked for eight-ball and he didn't bother changing it. He selected a cue stick, took several warm-up strokes, and broke the balls. It was a weak break, but somehow the three-ball dribbled into the corner pocket. He started shooting. At first he missed more shots than he made, but he closed out the rack by sinking three in a row.

A waitress brought his drink and a menu. She looked disappointed when he told her he would not be eating. There was still no sign of Chad Armstrong, so he kept playing. By the third rack he was finding his rhythm. A well-fed looking player at the adjacent table told him he was shooting 'lights out.' This was because he had made a rail-first combination shot. It was practically in the pocket already.

'They tell me you're a pool hustler, Fast Eddie,' said Chad Armstrong.

He looked up. The agent was sitting in a high chair against one wall, holding what looked like a gin and tonic. Jason Walker shot and missed. He had, for a moment, forgotten why he was there.

'Do you like to gamble, Eddie? Gamble money on pool games?' said Chad Armstrong.

It was a line from the movie version of *The Hustler*. Jason Walker was supposed to say, *Fats, let's you and I shoot a game of straight pool*. But he didn't feel like playing along.

'Hi, Chad.'

'You look like you're pretty familiar with the game.'

'I've played a couple of times.'

'Mind if I join in?'

He shrugged.

The government agent selected a stick from the wall, making a big deal out of checking it for warps. He rolled it on the table and then sighted down the shaft as if it were a rifle.

Jason Walker re-racked the balls. 'So, do you live around here?' he asked casually.

'No, I live at 333 North—whoops!'

Chad Armstrong covered his mouth and laughed as if he had been about to make a big mistake. It was annoying.

'It just seems like you like to meet in this neighborhood.'

'I don't work out of an office, Jason. Then again, I'm always at work. Maybe I was having a drink with some friends nearby. You're the one who called me at night. So I'm assuming it's urgent.'

They lagged for the break. Chad Armstrong's ball stopped about eight inches from the far cushion. Jason Walker's stopped four inches from it. He spotted the cue ball and broke hard. Two balls fell, one solid and one stripe.

'I met that guy. Leo Haddad.'

He lined up a shot on a solid and made it.

Chad Armstrong raised an eyebrow.

'Well, that was fast. You definitely hadn't seen him before?'

'No.'

He made a thin cut on another solid and the cue ball traveled the length of the table and back again, leaving him a poor shot.

'So how did it go?'

He concentrated on his next shot, a bank. He missed.

'Not too well, I don't think.'

Chad Armstrong made a hard shot and then missed an easy one.

'How so?'

'Well, I couldn't get anywhere.'

'What do you mean, you couldn't get anywhere?'

Jason Walker told him to wait a minute. It was tough to concentrate on the game and the conversation. And he suddenly wanted to win the game. He made three in a row and then scratched, giving up ball-in-hand.

'I think I'm in trouble,' said Chad Armstrong, surveying the table.

He put the ball down and shot straight into the side pocket. Then he tried a longer shot down the table. He made it but left the cue ball hanging in the jaws of the pocket. He couldn't shoot out. He made a desperation shot and his ball struck four rails but no balls.

'That's a foul,' said Jason Walker. 'Ball-in-hand.'

'You're the expert.'

He realized that of course the government agent knew that he'd been editor of *Billiards Journal*. With anyone else in the world he could play casual or fudge the facts. He set the ball and had an easy run-out. There were three striped balls still on the table.

Chad Armstrong put his cue down and picked up his drink.

'So you couldn't get anywhere.'

'Well, I tried to get to know him. He seemed like a nice guy, but if he's a terrorist like you say, I thought he was bound to make a mistake. So I asked him a bunch of questions.'

'What kind of questions?'

'What he does for a living, where he's from.'

'And he didn't say anything?'

'He seemed annoyed.'

Chad Armstrong's eyes flashed. He looked as if he wanted to throw his drink against the wall. Instead, he finished it, then banged it down on a nearby table.

'For the record,' he said, 'I didn't tell you to interview the fucker. I told you to try to make friends with him.'

'I tried to get to know him,' said Jason Walker defensively.

'You scared him off.'

'Look, that's how I make friends. I ask them what they do and where they're from.'

'Well, if your gargantuan social network is a sign of anything, I guess that works great.'

Jason Walker was fuming.

Chad Armstrong suddenly softened.

'Look, you blew it. People make mistakes. That's why pencils have erasers! Of course, we don't use pencils anymore. Never mind. I'm sure we can salvage this. Maybe the guy was just in a bad mood.'

'If you wanted a professional, you should have hired one.'

'I told you, we needed a real person for this job. Haddad would smell a professional.'

'Well he didn't seem to like the way I smelled, either. Look, I didn't ask for this job and I don't know how to do it. Meanwhile, I can't do my real job. I can't find work. The one steady gig I had was ruined when you guys kidnapped me.'

Chad Armstrong frowned.

'Keep your voice down,' he hissed. 'Look, if this is about money, if you need money—do you need money?'

'Of course I need money. You should know that. You stole my bank statements.'

'Then just ask for it.'

He reached into the pocket of his jeans and pulled out a large roll of cash.

'How much do you need?'

It was tempting. The rubber-banded roll looked as if it contained several thousand dollars in twenties.

'I don't want *your* money,' said Jason Walker.

Chad Armstrong shrugged. He put the money back in his pocket.

'Fair enough,' he said. 'I didn't have to offer. I was just trying to be nice. Look, sorry I got pissed off. You're right, this is your first time.'

He tapped the eight-ball on the table, then spun it idly, thinking.

'OK, new approach. You might be able to make up with Haddad, you might not. If he's suspicious, then there's no time to lose. You might not be able to keep hanging around the cultural center if he thinks you're a spy. Did you join? Pay your dues?'

Jason Walker nodded.

'They had you write something, right? You signed a roster.'

He nodded again.

'I need you to steal the membership roster. Probably any bad guys are using fake names, but we still need it. So go back tomorrow and take it.'

He wanted to punch Chad Armstrong or at least the wall. Instead he took a drink of his bourbon, draining it. His throat burned and he coughed despite the melting ice. A passing waitress happened to glance over as he set the glass down.

'You want another one?' she asked.

'A double, please,' he croaked.

'See, you are spy material,' said Chad Armstrong as she left.

'You said no—I wouldn't have to steal anything. No spy stuff. No breaking in.'

'I did say words to that effect, but that was before Haddad got cold feet. I need something from you. Look, I like you personally, but my boss, well, he's going to ask why we didn't get anything from you. He loves to send people to Camp X-Ray. But he loves sending them to Beirut even more. Hell, he sent *me* to Beirut once. But he let me come back.'

'I've never stolen anything in my life!'

'Walk in, pick your spot, grab it, and walk out. Have a taxi waiting for you outside. It's not in a safe, is it?'

He shook his head.

'Well, then.'

'But most of the people in the book are innocent. Maybe all of them.'

'Let us worry about who's innocent,' said Chad Armstrong. 'You steal the roster and bring it to us, or you're going somewhere that really sucks. Now, what do you say we play a few more games? I haven't played pool in a long time, either. It's really fun.'

Jason Walker was shaking. He didn't want to play pool. He wondered what would happen if he hit Chad Armstrong with a pool cue. Not that he could do it. He'd never stolen anything, and he'd never been in a fight, either.

He laid his cue across the table, crosswise, so it rested on the cushions.

'I think I'm done playing. But I'll bet you a hundred bucks you can't roll the cue ball under this stick.'

Chad Armstrong smiled and started to say something. Then he picked up the cue ball. He rolled it along the length of the cue, from cushion to cushion. He tapped the ball against the wood.

'I can't,' he said. 'No one can. The ball's too big.'

'I can do it,' said Jason Walker.

'Without touching the cue?'

'Without touching the cue.'

The government agent scrutinized the set-up again. He frowned and shook his head. 'Five hundred bucks says you can't.'

'You're on.'

Jason Walker picked up the cue ball and moved to the end of the table. He crouched down and rolled the cue ball on the floor, under the length of the table.

Chad Armstrong watched the ball roll out and rebound off his shoe. He laughed.

'That's bullshit! Total bullshit! A dirty trick.'

'You should know all about dirty tricks.'

'Hey, I didn't say I wouldn't pay up. I just said it's a dirty trick.'

He pulled out his bankroll again and peeled off twenty-five twenties.

'You know,' he said, 'that's a smart way of doing it. I could pay you like that every time. No one would ever know. I could just be some sucker and you could be some pool hustler.'

Jason Walker stared at the money in his hand.

'This isn't payment.'

'Exactly. You won a bet.'

He considered giving it back. He put it in his pocket. He had felt for a moment as if he had won a small victory. Now he felt even worse than before.

They put their cues back on the wall rack and finished their drinks.

'Go ahead and leave first,' said Chad Armstrong. 'I don't want to leave together. I'll get the bill.'

Jason Walker left. He walked all the way home. He had a lot to think about.

There was a voicemail from Gina Saraceno waiting for him.

'Hi Jason, it's Gina. I have the feeling that you don't really want to do any campaign work but that you don't want me to be mad at you, so you're asking to come along. I'm not mad at you, so you don't have to come. Well, I'm mad, but I'll get over it, even if you don't come help me hand out brochures. But if you really do want to come—and I'm pretty sure you don't—that's all right, I guess. I'll be standing in Daley Plaza from eleven to two, trying to hit the lunchtime crowd. So, I'll either see you there or I won't.'

He listened to the message several times before he finally deleted it. She still sounded angry. Her voice wasn't warm and playful like it usually was. But of course she had described the situation exactly right. He didn't want to go. He had only asked her in the hope of getting back in her good graces.

But despite it all, he would go. He needed her.

He woke the next morning feeling tired and groggy. He had stayed up late, drinking and watching the news. Citing 'a pattern of suspicious incidents across the country,' Homeland

Security was tightening security near the water supplies of large cities. There had been video of National Guardsmen patrolling the reservoir in Central Park. In Chicago, the pumping station of the Water Tower, which also housed a restaurant, a theater, and a tourist information center, had been closed to the public until further notice. A rural sheriff complained that he lacked the resources to adequately protect his small town.

Thinking that a walk would clear his head, Jason Walker crossed the street into the park, walked under Lake Shore Drive, and followed the bike path north to Foster Beach. Only a few people were using the beach. An elderly man dozed in a lawn chair, his leathery chest facing the rising sun. An intense-looking Chinese girl practiced tai chi just feet from the bubbling surf. And a half-dozen children frolicked in the water under the watchful eyes of a lifeguard, who pushed and pulled gently on her oars to keep her place in the current.

It would be nice to just sail away, he thought. Only he didn't know how to sail a boat and he didn't know where he could land.

As he reentered his building, the mail carrier was just locking up the mailboxes. He opened his box and was surprised to find a dozen envelopes. There were several credit-card come-ons, several advertising circulars, and a half-dozen bills: rent, electric, telephone, cable, and two credit cards. In the elevator, he broke the flaps open with his thumb. In his apartment, he spread them out on the table and added them up. He booted up his computer and checked his bank balance. The debits were larger than the credits, even with his gambling winnings.

He showered, shaved, and dressed. He walked to a nearby restaurant to eat breakfast, then crossed the street to the bank. He deposited the check from *Philadelphia Magazine*. Then he took the train downtown. He felt like screaming the whole way.

Daley Plaza was crowded. At one end, a farmer's market had been set up and office workers browsed flowers, fruits, and vegetables to take home at the end of the day. Nearer the towering brown Daley Center, a children's choir sang inspirational songs promising fulfillment and justice. Tourist children scrambled up the incline at the base of the huge Picasso sculpture, sliding down on their bottoms with seeming disappointment that the ride wasn't farther or faster.

Gina Saraceno was already at work. Professionally dressed in a white blouse, checked skirt, and high heels, she smiled widely at passersby as she tried to thrust leaflets into their hands.

'Help bring democracy to America,' she said. 'Tell the president to call an election. Vote Libby!'

She hadn't seen him, so he watched for a while. She approached perhaps twenty people. Most of them ignored her. One or two seemed angry at her. Only one person took a brochure, a young skateboarder who might not have been old enough to vote.

Jason Walker sighed, then forced a smile on to his face and approached her. Her own smile was warmer than he had expected, but still restrained.

'So,' she said. 'You're here.'

'I'm ready to join the Libby Lobby,' he said.

'Well, all right then.'

She put a small stack of brochures in his hand.

'Relentless. Professional. Cheerful.'

'Got it,' he said, then added, '*Honey.*'

It didn't work. She flashed a brief smile and turned to the oncoming stream of passersby.

'If they count the votes, then your vote counts,' she declared. 'Vote George Libby.'

He turned the other way, to catch people coming from the other direction. He took a deep breath. A wide-bottomed woman was waddling toward him. She wore red, white, and blue shorts and an *America First* T-shirt.

'I agree with you, lady,' he said. 'America first. Let's fix America and then worry about the rest of the world.'

He tried to hand her a brochure. She swatted at his hand indignantly. He may as well have tried to pinch her ample bosom.

'Thanks for stopping,' he said.

A husky construction worker bore down next.

'If they let you vote, vote Libby,' said Jason Walker. 'Let's bring them all home.'

The man spat on the ground, catching a string of saliva on his own stubbly chin. He wiped it off with the back of his hand.

'Terrorist,' he said.

The three hours of pamphleteering seemed to energize Gina Saraceno. Though the pedestrian traffic had slowed, she wondered aloud whether they should keep going. For his part, Jason Walker was ready for a drink. He was amazed and gratified when she agreed.

They walked a short distance to Cardozo's Pub, an underground bar frequented by governmental workers. In the mid-afternoon it was all but deserted. They ordered beers at the bar and sat down to compare notes. Gina Saraceno's pleasure at the work they'd done seemed to have diminished her earlier pique.

'I think I handed out fifty brochures,' she said. 'I know that's not a lot, but just think, people are doing this in every major city.'

'How many of those people do you think will support you?'

'Us,' she chided. 'Support *us*.'

'How many of them will support us?'

'Well, I only gave them to people who seemed interested—'

'Or who didn't spit on us.'

'—*who seemed interested*. I have no idea how many of those people will support us.'

'Maybe they support us already. In which case, what's the point? Even back when there were elections, it seemed like both parties spent all their energy going after the five percent who couldn't make up their minds. You—I mean, we—are going to need a lot more than five percent. The president's approval rating is back up to ninety percent, just like it was right after September 11.'

Gina Saraceno took a long drink of her beer. She set the glass down on the table and smiled at it.

'I know what you're doing, Jason. You're trying to ruin my good mood. And I know why you're doing it. It's not because you don't like me, or because you want me to feel as if I'm wasting my time. It's because it's your nature to assume the worst possible outcome. But that's OK. I forgive you. I know that you're helpless against your own nature.'

He had handed out only seventeen brochures. The people who took them looked as if they would indeed side with anyone who stood against the president. They also looked like the sort of people who would never influence anyone else or be taken seriously themselves. They were hippies, punks, and skateboarders. Even if Gina Saraceno's efforts had been duplicated in twenty cities that day, and were repeated every day for a year, he couldn't imagine the result creating a groundswell. It would be a ripple, nothing more.

Public sentiment was not moved by pamphleteers on the sidewalk, he mused. If he had the courage to check the trash cans on nearby corners—or if trash cans were still allowed within two hundred yards of government buildings after the Austin, Texas bombing—he was certain that most of their efforts would lie within them.

Opinions changed either by slow degrees, which meant opposition might mature in the fourth or fifth term of the president—if 'term' were still even a concept—or they changed because of violent events. The slow accumulation of greenhouse gas had not led to improved fuel efficiency, but a meteor strike would flood the aid agencies with volunteers and donations. Just as airplanes toppling buildings, poisoned water supplies, and plots to blow up the St. Louis Arch prompted people who had never left their hometowns to send their sons and daughters to the dusty birthplaces of terrorism with rifles in their arms.

Gina Saraceno was still smiling at him, daring him to puncture her idealism.

'I'm also helpless against you,' he said. 'Sweetheart.'

'Sweetheart.'

They clinked their glasses and ordered more beers.

They said goodbye an hour later, having made plans to spend the following night together. He rode the train home and, drowsy from drinking beer on a hot afternoon, took a nap. He woke up feeling a half-step behind his own thoughts. He washed his face and ordered Vietnamese food from a restaurant on Argyle Street. While he slurped his noodles, he watched the TV news. Fox News 2, a new channel, had a program called 'In the Field.' From a studio draped with camouflage netting, the host interviewed battlefield commanders, quizzing them about recent offensives and tactical maneuvers. The soldiers refused to answer many of the questions, saying that the answers were 'privileged information.' The host, a civilian, said that he 'understood the protocol.' The soldiers were more forthcoming when discussing 'neutralized targets.'

When he was done eating, he threw his food containers in the trash and left the building to go catch the bus. Schatzi sent him off with a door-rattling volley of barks.

He walked into the Lebanese Cultural Center feeling he'd already been caught. He expected every face to turn toward him accusingly. But he was met by the same indifference he'd grown used to. One or two men nodded to him, but that was all.

Leo Haddad wasn't there. Ghassan wasn't, either, so he poured a coffee from the urn and bought a pastry from the cooler, leaving his money in the honor jar. He took a table near the back, opened a book, and pretended to read.

The center was more crowded than usual. He didn't know why. Normally he would have assumed that a lecture had been scheduled, but the calendar—posted near the bulletin board—was blank.

The bells on the front door clunked and Ahmad Saad came in. He said a friendly hello as he walked to his office. Jason Walker had chosen a table that gave him a view down the back hall. He watched as Ahmad Saad walked through the beaded curtain, opened his office door, and went in.

He cursed silently. If he had moved more quickly he would have been done already.

Ahmad Saad came back out almost immediately. He poured himself a cup of tea and returned to his office.

Jason Walker sipped his coffee slowly. When it was cold he poured another. The center hummed with comings and goings, greetings and farewells. That was the one thing he liked. It made him feel anonymous.

Ahmad Saad came out to the front seemingly every twenty minutes for more tea. Jason Walker watched carefully, waiting for him to go to the toilet. But Ahmad Saad kept going back to his office.

He kept drinking coffee. He used the toilet several times. He would have to be able to run if necessary. He scanned the room for Leo Haddad. Sometimes he forgot to pretend to read and sat staring for five minutes without turning a page.

The center stayed open until ten o'clock. He began to wonder if the director would hold out that long.

Ahmad Saad came out and poured another cup of tea. But this time he took the tea to his office and then came out again. He turned right, toward the back of the building, where the toilet was.

Jason Walker's heart started hammering. As casually as he could, he slipped his shoulder bag on and strolled into the back. He resisted the temptation to look behind him to see if anyone was watching. He passed through the beaded curtain, opened the office door, and walked in. Pulling the office door closed, he stepped quickly behind the director's desk. He scanned the shelves for the blue vinyl membership binder. Was it on the middle shelf or the one above it?

He heard a flush. He heard running water.

He saw the binder. Feeling as if he was wearing mittens, he pulled the binder off the shelf and practically leapt to the door.

In the hall, he saw the toilet door open. He hadn't had time to put the binder in his bag. Panicking, he tossed the notebook back into the room, where it landed on the cluttered desk.

He stood awkwardly in the door as Ahmad Saad came out of the toilet, hands not quite dry, and saw him.

'Ah, there you are,' said Jason Walker.

'And there are you,' said Ahmad Saad, sounding somewhat puzzled.

'I, um, I was wondering if you have Arabic classes.'

'Have you finally decided to learn to speak and write properly?'

'Well, I'm still, you know, mulling it over.'

'We don't have classes here. But I'm sure you can't have missed the large flyers up front, advertising that very service. You can take classes either through a mosque, or something secular, if you prefer.'

'I'm afraid you overestimate my powers of observation,' said Jason Walker.

They made a little more small talk and then he left the center, defeated. Leo Haddad was on his way in. They greeted each other politely but neither of them stopped.

He waited for the bus in a daze. Then, sitting by the window, he watched the familiar blocks and buildings pass behind his reflection as if making a farewell. His career as an informant was finished. He'd botched the task. He'd exposed himself. He was no longer useful to Chad Armstrong. And being no longer useful, he had nothing to bargain with to keep himself from being sent to Beirut or Guantanamo. He had no idea which was worse.

When he got home he called the Acme Messenger Service and waited for the return call. There was no reason not to get it over with. But the phone didn't ring.

He tried to sleep.

Eleven

The next morning he was waiting outside the center when it opened. There had been no return call, so Chad Armstrong still didn't know what had happened. And Jason Walker had managed somehow, despite the emotional swings brought on by sleeplessness, to convince himself that maybe, given the clutter of Ahmad Saad's office, Ahmad Saad had not in fact realized that the membership roster had been left on his desk.

Convince was too strong a word, but he had decided to try again anyway.

Ghassan opened the doors and, if he was surprised to see Jason Walker, he didn't let on. Two old men were also waiting. They asked Ghassan to make them coffee and then took the steaming cups outside.

Jason Walker also asked for coffee. After he had made it, Ghassan took a push broom and went outside to sweep the sidewalk.

He was alone in the building. At least, it seemed reasonably certain that he was. Ahmad Saad was a businessman, so it seemed unlikely that he was hiding in the back.

He hurried back to the office and knocked twice, just to be sure. No one answered. He opened the door. The office was dark. He turned on the light and found the office just as he had left it the night before. Thankfully, the notebook was still on the desk. He had been right after all. Ahmad Saad hadn't even noticed it.

Hurriedly, he put the blue notebook in his shoulder bag, turned off the light, and peered around the edge of the door before leaving the office. He could see Ghassan outside, sweeping vigorously while the two old men held their hands over their coffee cups to keep the dust out.

He turned right and walked down the dark hall, past the toilet, to the rear exit. As he pushed the bar to open the door, he was certain that this was the last time he would ever see the Lebanese Cultural Center.

The bright sunlight was disorienting. When he could see again, he realized that he was looking at Leo Haddad. A very large man was standing to his right. With a staggering half-turn to his left, he saw that direction blocked by a large man, too.

'Who are you working for?' demanded Leo Haddad. 'Why do you want to steal the names of innocent people?'

Jason Walker looked up and down the alley. He half-expected vans to screech around the corners and skid to a halt, with government agents piling out to rescue him. But the alley was quiet in the morning sun. A car honked on the street in front of the building. A fly buzzed over the lid of a dumpster.

'Who are you spying for?'

'I'm not a spy.'

'Then why did you take the notebook? Are you going to send a Christmas card to everyone on that list?'

His head swam. His escape routes were blocked. Except one. Surprising both Leo Haddad and himself, he wrenched open the door to the cultural center and ran back inside. He ran down the hall and through the main room. He stumbled into a chair and threw it down behind him.

The door slammed. Footsteps pounded down the hallway. Leo Haddad and the two men were running after him. His shoulder bag bounced on his hip.

When he threw open the front door it knocked the broom out of Ghassan's hand. The big man's mouth fell open. On the corner, a southbound Kedzie bus was pulling out of the stop. Jason Walker lurched right and ran. He pounded on the door as the bus picked up speed, shouting for the driver to stop.

The driver shook his head with a satisfied smirk.

'Jason!' shouted Leo Haddad.

He plunged into traffic amid a cacophony of honking horns and screeching brakes. He saw a look of terror on the face of a diminutive woman who stopped just in time to avoid killing him. His pursuers were slowed by the chaos. They weren't in fear for their lives.

On the corner, a woman wearing a headscarf pushed a double stroller. He ran past her on to a side street lined with neatly kept three-flats. He ran down a narrow sidewalk past one building and into a small, paved back yard. He pushed open a tall wooden gate and crossed the alley, climbed a short chain-link fence, and stopped behind a small apartment building. A dumpster was enclosed by a slat fence. He lifted the latch and slipped inside. He closed the gate.

It was quiet for a moment. Then the gate across the alley opened and someone came out, panting.

He held his breath.

The footfalls were quick but indecisive. They ran one way, stopped, then ran another. They stopped again and circled. Someone cursed in Arabic. The footfalls moved slowly away.

He exhaled. It was then that he noticed the papery wasps' nest daubed into a corner of the enclosure. Several wasps made exploratory flights in his direction, but he held perfectly still. When one landed on his arm, he killed it with a quick flick of his wrist against the slats that sounded deafening to him in the quiet alley. The other wasps kept their distance.

He waited fifteen minutes and then climbed on a crosspiece and peered over the top of the fence. He didn't see anyone. He reached over the top and undid the latch. He eased the door open.

A narrow sidewalk led between the apartment building and its neighbor, and he followed it through to the sidewalk of the next street. Under the circumstances, the day seemed disturbingly normal. A child rode her bicycle. A driver reversed into a parking space. An ice-cream truck tootled its way along the street.

He walked quickly, kind of a stiff-legged run, his eyes roving left and right, back and front. After a few blocks he saw a taxi letting an old woman off at her house. He ran to it and breathlessly asked if he could get in. The driver nodded and he was in the back seat before the woman had collected her shopping bags.

The door shut. The air inside was cool. He panted in relief.

The taxi didn't move.

He realized he hadn't told the driver where to go. Of course he shouldn't even be taking a taxi. He had just created a witness. But he didn't have to take the taxi home, either.

On impulse he told the driver to take him to Clark and Division. It was a busy intersection far from his home. And on the off chance he was still being followed, it would be easy to disappear into a crowd there.

The driver nodded and put his car in gear. His medallion identified him as Mansoor Musharraf. It sounded like a Pakistani name. The man looked Pakistani, wearing a small round hat and a full beard. Things had been rough for Pakistanis ever since Osama bin Laden's compound had been discovered inside their country.

As they picked up speed, Jason Walker finally started to relax. But it seemed more likely than ever that Leo Haddad was more than he seemed. In the first place, he had been waiting. He knew what Jason Walker had done. If the center's affairs were truly innocent, there would have been no reason to suspect they were of interest. But more than that, there was something about Leo Haddad's manner. In all their conversations he had seemed to be nothing more than a well-informed, generous man who loved the country he'd left. This morning he'd spoken with authority, like someone used to being in command. And he'd had two men with him. Men who looked like soldiers.

Jason Walker took the binder out of his bag and opened it. The scribbled, handwritten pages he'd seen before were gone, replaced by a neat computer printout. He had no idea whether the names had been changed. But either yesterday was coincidentally the day the records had been modernized or they had known he was coming back and swapped out the real roster.

He looked for his own name under the recent entries and

didn't find it. For all he knew, the names had been copied from the phone book.

He slumped against the seat and let the binder fall to the floor. Once again he had nothing. But at least it was a nothing he could show to Chad Armstrong.

The driver let him off on the southwest corner of the five-way intersection, in front of a health-food store. He crossed to the northeast corner and ducked into a bookstore, then walked out an entrance on the other side, on Broadway. He went back to the intersection, crossed, and walked north on Clark. He went into a vertical mall called the Century Shopping Centre. Its concourse climbed up around a square atrium, meaning that he could look down and see whether anyone was coming up behind him.

No one was. At least not Leo Haddad and his helpers. He was safe for the moment.

But what did he do now? He didn't know. The street outside the mall was full of malevolent possibilities. Despite his ride in the taxi, his pulse was pounding so hard that he thought a headache might be coming on.

He followed the concourse to the top of the mall, to the movie theater. At the ticket office he chose the first thing showing, a movie with a foreign-sounding title that he'd never heard of. He bought a bottle of water at the concession stand and followed the ticket-taker's pointed finger. He walked through a door into the cool, enveloping darkness of the theater. It was nearly empty. He climbed the stairs to the top and sat in the back row with the wall behind him so he could not be surprised. He fell into his seat.

It was fifteen minutes before he could turn his attention to the screen. But half an hour after that he still wasn't sure he understood the story. It was set in some dusty country in the Middle East, in both an apartment in a city and a house in a village. It moved slowly. In the city, a young boy wrote letters that he never mailed. In the desert, a young girl wrote in a secret diary and talked to her pet spider. At first he thought that they were writing to each other. But he could discern no logical connection between them. He couldn't understand the movie at all. Was that because it was in some kind of art-film code? Or was the story plainly apparent and his mind wasn't working correctly? The latter was a possibility he couldn't rule out. Appearance and reality had become unwired.

At some point he fell asleep. He woke in an empty theater, the lights raised, an usher picking up popcorn cups below him. Embarrassed, he hurried out, then ducked into the next theater before anyone saw him. Again, he climbed the stairs to the back row. This film was an erotic thriller. There was a dogged American agent, a beautiful Asian dancer, a villainous Russian with a blond ponytail and a beard. After making love to her, the American asked the Asian to hide a computer drive for him, knowing that she would betray him to the Russian. The computer drive held false information.

He stayed awake. The air conditioning made him shiver. When he got hungry, he went to the concession stand and bought a candy bar and some coffee. Fortunately no one asked to see his ticket and he was allowed back into the theaters. He chose yet another movie, this time hardly paying attention. He had to decide what to do. He had to get the notebook to Chad Armstrong. But he couldn't decide whether or not to tell him that it was a fake. Chad Armstrong would find out anyway, but it would take him time. Then again, what did it matter? It wasn't as if Jason Walker was going on the run. He wanted more than anything to leave Chicago, but he had nowhere to go and was certain they would find him anyway.

He debated calling Chad Armstrong and asking him to meet at the theater. He thought he might need protection on his way home. Then he decided that he was being paranoid and left the theater.

He emerged blinking his eyes at the dim evening light. The passersby and the street traffic all looked normal. But the crowded sidewalk made him nervous. There were too many people. He felt as if he couldn't see. Reluctantly, he crossed the intersection to Broadway and waited for a bus.

The bus let him off at Argyle Street. He stopped at Tank Noodles for a quick dinner and then walked east toward

Marine Drive. Half the shops were shuttered for the night, and the others advertised their wares—noodles, groceries, music and video—with garish neon signs. On the north side of the street, Chicago police frisked two black teenagers against the hood of a car. They were looking for drugs, not bombs.

He walked backward up the sidewalk in front of his building, then practically ran through the vestibule once the guard buzzed him in. He waited for an elevator that he could ride alone.

As he exited the elevator car on his floor, he saw that the stairwell door was cracked. It wasn't opening or closing.

He whirled to jump in the car again but the elevator doors thumped shut. Two men rushed out of the stairwell and dragged him inside to the landing. One of the men held him in a full-nelson while the other one leaned against the door. In fluorescent light turned green by the chartreuse paint on the walls, he recognized the two big men he'd seen in the alley that morning.

'Wait,' he said feebly.

'You got the wrong guy,' said one of the men, grinning.

He sounded like an Arab imitating John Wayne. The other man laughed.

They frog-marched him down thirteen flights of stairs to the ground floor and pushed him out the service entrance into a small, sputtering blue car.

Leo Haddad was waiting in the back seat.

'You see,' he said, 'you wrote down your address in our membership book.'

Twelve

They took his shoulder bag and fastened his hands behind him with plastic ties. The ties were the same kind that Homeland Security used when detaining large groups of people and were available at any hardware store. Once again he had a mask pulled over his head. This time it was a beige, flowered pillowcase through which he could discern dark shapes. One of the big men pushed him down and he knelt on the tiny floorboards, his head in the musty seat cushion, between the legs of Leo Haddad and the other man.

The front door slammed and the car's tires popped gravel in the alley. Once again he was taken for a long, disorienting ride. His captors didn't speak. Instead they listened to the radio news, an upbeat blend of national affairs, sports, and human-interest stories. There was bad and good news about global warming. In Florida, the decision had been made to declare hurricane-ravaged Key West off-limits to overnight stays for the next year. In California, unexpected rains had produced a bumper crop of tomatoes.

He counted rights and lefts, confident that they were heading north to Rogers Park, until he suddenly wondered if he'd counted an extra left at the very beginning. They could be anywhere. He gave up. The pillowcase smelled like lavender.

Eventually the car stopped. He was helped out of it and up a flight of creaking wooden stairs. As they climbed, he heard pans clattering and smelled grilling meat. He thought he detected a trace of cumin. Despite everything it made his stomach grumble.

A door opened and he allowed himself to be led inside, stepping gingerly as if he might fall into a hole. He thought that it must be an apartment over a restaurant. He walked over linoleum on to carpet and made a right turn. A door closed and the hood came off. He was in a small room with one of the big men. The room was almost empty, as if it was unused or as if the apartment was between tenants. A bare mattress and a box-spring sat atop a metal bed frame on gold-colored ball rollers. Next to the bed was a four-drawer dresser with veneer chipped off in places to reveal sand-colored particle board. In the middle of the room were a cardboard card table and two metal folding chairs. The room's only window was covered with an American flag.

'Sit,' said the man.

He sat.

The man left the room and closed the door behind him.

He waited. He wondered if they would torture him. He had no intention of giving them any reason to do so.

After about fifteen minutes the door opened and Leo Haddad came in holding a large tray. On the tray were plates with silver steam covers. He set the food down on the card table and lifted the covers. It was a feast of Lebanese food.

'Please, eat.'

Despite his sudden hunger, Jason Walker eyed the food suspiciously.

'The food is fine. I will share it with you.'

Leo Haddad filled a plate with food and began eating. After a few minutes Jason Walker did the same. The food was delicious—even better, he had to grudgingly admit, than his mother's. They ate in silence, making a little small talk about the food. Leo Haddad seemed even hungrier than he did. Jason Walker wondered if he had spent the afternoon in his car at the service entrance.

When they were done, Leo Haddad took the tray to the door and gave it to someone waiting outside. He said a few things in Arabic. Then he came back in.

'They will bring us coffee and something sweet. Was it good?'

Jason Walker nodded.

'Yes, I think so, too.'

Leo Haddad sat down and rubbed his chin.

'When I was a child,' he said, 'I lived in Beirut. As you did—or as you say you did. I should not say "in Beirut." That would imply that I lived in Ras Beirut or on Rue Hamra, in the beautiful part of the city. As you know, that city has a complicated history. It is claimed, in some sense, by both the East and the West. However, the Christians claimed Beirut more fervently, and so I lived in a part of Beirut where the movie stars did not lie on comfortable chairs next to swimming pools. I was a Muslim, so I lived in a slum.'

Jason Walker thought of his own childhood. He remembered swimming in the aquamarine water of the pool at his father's hotel. The men and women on the chaise longues surrounding the pool had looked like movie stars.

'Of course, I did not know it was a slum,' continued Leo Haddad. 'Just as a child must be told by adults the difference between a flower and a weed, or a butterfly and a moth, I learned this later. To me it was simply my home, and I was happy there. I accepted as normal the difficulty of finding clean water and the smell of human feces. I loved to go to the beach and swim in the ocean. We were not allowed on the truly beautiful beaches, of course, but to me any beach was beautiful. I did not notice the litter. Like any child, I looked for shells and the small sea animals that lived in them. I dreamed that I was a pearl diver, but though I dove and dove to the bottom, I never found any pearls.

'When the fighting began, I was a boy, maybe just a few years older than you were. My father wanted to leave, of course, but it was difficult. We had very little family anywhere else, and very little money with which to go to them. He made plans and begged us to be patient.'

The door opened and one of the men brought in a tray with coffee and spongy, honeyed pastries. Jason Walker waited for Leo Haddad to take a sip and a bite before he followed suit. Then Leo Haddad went on with his story.

'The thing about a city under siege is that normal life must somehow go on. People must cook, eat, bathe, sleep, make love, play games, and all the rest. It is not like a movie where men shoot their guns until everyone is dead. A bomb explodes and you are terrified. There is shooting and your mother gathers you and your brothers and sisters in a closet and you wait for it to stop. You are terrified, of course, but you are also a child. When there has been no shooting for several days you want to play. Your mother understands better than you do that the shooting can start again at any time, but just as you are only a child, she is only a mother. Children are more energetic than any soldiers. She must sometimes relent to your demands. You go outside.'

Leo Haddad smiled a bittersweet smile. He drank his coffee.

'It was on just such a day, a day free from fighting, that I made my way to the beach with my brother. There weren't many people there, and we felt that all the sand, all the water, were ours. The sky was an infinite blue. Then in the sky we saw two trails of smoke. Incoming missiles. They exploded somewhere in the city. We smiled at each other, as one always does when one finds that the missile has landed elsewhere.

'I should have told you about my father's shop. It was a poor shop, very small. He sold whatever he could turn for a profit: cigarettes, tea, candy, sandals, rugs, radios, tinned food, newspapers, magazines. He had so little of any of them, but he would stand outside the shop, smiling, and take your arm and lead you in to show you what he had. He was very good at reminding you of what you had forgotten you wanted. He was a Muslim, yes, but he saw how the Maronites did not allow their religion to keep them poor. Perhaps secretly he wished he was one of them. He was not a very good Muslim, but a Jewish missile killed him anyway. When my brother and I returned home we passed by my father's shop to see if he had any sweets for us. But the building in which his store had been was gone. I couldn't even see where his shop had been. Men from the neighborhood were digging frantically through the rubble to find the people trapped inside. When they found my father, he was white with dust and still as death. As they lifted him on to a blanket to carry him to our home, pieces of his afternoon newspaper fell from his fingers. There was a humorous column which he had loved to read. I often wonder whether the man who fired the missile was a good Jew, or whether he was just going along with his fellows. My father lived with his fellows, I suppose, because he didn't know anything else.'

Jason Walker lifted his pastry to his mouth but set it down again. The honey on his lips was suddenly too sweet.

'Because my father died, his sister finally sent money to the rest of us and we were able to leave. I believe my mother paid some bribes, but I was never told all the details. I thought our lives had ended. But, as I have told you before, we made our way to Canada and then to America. My mother had a cousin in Chicago who was a successful businessman. He first owned dollar stores, then laundromats, then grocery stores and a gas station. My brothers and sisters and I all worked for this man, who we called our uncle, after school and on weekends and once we had left school. I was fortunate enough to attend the University of Illinois, the only one in my family to do so. And, like my brothers and sisters, I am a citizen here.'

'You're a citizen!' Jason Walker couldn't believe it.

'Yes. I renounced my Lebanese citizenship.'

'But you told me you loved Lebanon.'

'Have you never ended a relationship with a woman you still loved?'

He thought of Gina Saraceno. He'd been tempted to break things off with her, for her own safety. But citizenship would also help someone like Leo Haddad to move undetected.

'Is that why you became a terrorist? Because an Israeli missile killed your father?'

Leo Haddad shook his head.

'I am not a terrorist. I understand that your ride here may have been terrifying, but that was for all our safety. It is best if you do not know where you are right now. Have you heard me preach hatred?'

He waited for an answer.

Jason Walker shook his head.

'Have I hurt you, even though you tried to betray us? No, I am making you my guest. I am feeding you the same food I eat, the best I have to offer. You think of me as a Muslim. You are not a Muslim, are you? I know you said you are not anything, in that American way, but I mean that your parents were not followers of Islam, were they?'

'No.'

'And I remember that you told me that your father was French. Perhaps a dark-skinned man, Mediterranean. But your mother was Lebanese. She was a Maronite? Her father was your father's prosperous business partner.'

'Yes, I think so. She didn't pray.'

'She was not very religious.'

'No.'

'Just as you are not. Just as I am not very religious, and neither was my father. You see, to Americans these differences are hard to understand. In these days, a Protestant does not hate a Catholic so much. You see the civil war between Shiites and Sunnis in Iraq, you see what happened in Lebanon. You forget that many of us are like you. For many of us, religion is a custom, a convenience.

'I consider myself now a citizen of the world. My life experiences, my education, they have helped me to see things differently. What I hate—what I fight—is fear. Fear and ignorance and oppression. I saw my country, a fractured, polyglot dream of a nation, fall into anarchy. I have watched other countries fall under the rule of military despots. It is not so unusual. But one cannot run forever. And America is my new home. I consider myself a patriot. I plan no acts of violence, but already the president scoffs at the constitution. If resistance is outlawed, I will fight in the resistance. All I am doing now is preparing.'

'How are you preparing?'

Leo Haddad smiled.

'You are a spy for the government,' he said, 'but you are clearly not a professional. I have seen professionals. I think they are threatening you, just as they are threatening me.'

'Then what do you want with me?'

'I want you to join our struggle, Jason.'

He might have expected any other sentence more.

'You want me to *what*?'

'If I am correct, and they are holding something over you, then I don't know why you would in any case want to help them. Am I correct?'

Jason Walker weighed his answers. Leo Haddad watched him carefully.

'You must realize that spies are more like criminals than police, Jason. If you borrow money from a criminal, do you think the debt is ever repaid?'

'I don't know.'

'You are acting out of a sense of self-preservation. That is natural. But you are someone who believes that rules are to be followed. But what are the rules? No one knows what they are. You cannot expect dishonorable men to honor agreements. Your only course is to fight those who oppress you.'

'What do you want me to do?'

'I want you to tell me about the men who asked you to steal the notebook. How they contacted you, how they coerced you, what they look like and where you meet. I want you to give them false information that I will provide.'

'You want me to be a double agent.'

'I suppose that is the word. Most double agents operate for financial gain, however. I will offer you nothing. Do they pay you?'

Again he didn't answer. He felt uncomfortable under Leo Haddad's intense stare. He had no idea why he should trust a man he hardly knew. Of course, he didn't trust Chad Armstrong, either.

'Are you an honorable man, Leo?' he asked.

'I think so.'

'Can you prove it to me?'

'In time.'

'You want me to just trust you?'

Leo Haddad sipped his coffee and grimaced. It had grown cold.

'We are not strangers,' he said. 'For a while I thought I was making a friend, until I discovered that you were speaking under false pretenses. But I have spoken the truth in all our meetings.'

'Leaving a few things out.'

'The rejoinder I could make would insult both our intelligences.'

Jason Walker took a big gulp of his own cold coffee. He wanted more. He wanted whiskey. The worst part was that everything Leo Haddad said made perfect sense. But he didn't want to fight for anyone. He hadn't wanted to do Chad Armstrong's bidding and now he didn't want to take sides with Leo Haddad and his shadowy group. He wanted to be left alone to take pictures. But not of buildings. Not anymore.

'I don't have any useful information,' he said.

'I believe otherwise,' said Leo Haddad.

'What if I refuse? Will you still feed me and treat me as a guest?

'You may do as you wish, with nothing to fear from me. It will be a great inconvenience to both of us, however. I will be forced to leave Chicago, and you will never learn about your Lebanese heritage.'

If Chad Armstrong's word wasn't binding, perhaps Leo Haddad's wasn't either. There was no point in treating his own word any differently. It was the easiest way out of a bad situation.

'I'll help you,' said Jason Walker.

Leo Haddad smiled. 'Good, good. I know this is a difficult decision, but you have decided wisely.'

He thought that he might be free now to go home, but he was wrong. Leo Haddad ordered more coffee. After the coffee came a hookah and several cushions, which were arranged on the floor.

'Let us be more comfortable. Do you smoke?'

'Cigarettes, once in a while.'

'You will enjoy this. The tobacco tastes like apples.'

Broken pieces of wood charcoal glowed in the hookah's bowl. Under them were damp pieces of what looked like old-fashioned chewing tobacco. Four corded pipe stems snaked out of a silver throat plugged into a painted, beaded, water-filled glass jug. He took one of the pipe stems and puffed dubiously. It was actually quite pleasant. The smoke was cool and mild, and the nicotine only tickled his brain. Cigarettes had a much more overwhelming effect on him.

Pleasantly ensconced, Jason Walker found himself subjected to another interrogation. It was much friendlier than the one in Egypt had been, but no less thorough. Leo Haddad questioned him long into the night, always smiling, but always wanting to go over the smallest details again and again. When and where had he met Chad Armstrong? What did Chad Armstrong look like? Did it seem as if he did anything to alter his appearance? Were the roots of his hair darker than the rest? What was his manner of speech? When Jason Walker's attention or energy seemed to flag, Leo Haddad ordered more coffee or food, or re-lit the hookah.

He tried to seem friendly and cooperative without giving away any information of real value, although he hadn't been lying when he said he didn't think he had any information of value. Several times Leo Haddad seemed frustrated but the moments quickly passed. It was impossible to tell what he was thinking.

Finally, when Jason Walker was so tired he stumbled over his words, Leo Haddad stopped.

'I think that's enough,' he said. 'I will have my men drive you home. I apologize that we must follow some of the same security measures.'

'The same security measures' meant the lavender-smelling pillowcase but not the plastic ties. Leo Haddad's trust was not complete. He would accept Jason Walker's help but would not reveal the apartment's location.

They guided him down the wooden steps once again. The restaurant's kitchen was quiet except for the whir of a large extraction fan. The drive home was more direct but included enough random turns that he once again lost his way. For all he knew, the house where they talked had been across the alley from the Lebanese Cultural Center.

The car stopped in front of the Argyle El station and he got out. One of the men handed him his shoulder bag and then the car drove off. The blue binder was in the bag. Leo

Haddad had told him to deliver it to Chad Armstrong as if nothing had happened.

He walked home, crossing the street once to avoid a large group of loud young Asian men. He crossed again to avoid a Homeland Security van that was parked in front of a fire hydrant.

Chad Armstrong had told him to put the binder in a plain manila envelope addressed to general delivery and to drop it in the mailbox in front of his building. He had the envelope ready in his bag, so he completed the operation before going inside. Once inside, he dialed the Acme Messenger Service and left a message for Chad Armstrong saying that the drop had been made. Was he a spy now? Surely he was no longer just an informant.

Then he checked his voicemail. Gina Saraceno was very angry.

'So I'm lying here in my least comfortable bra and panties, drinking a glass of wine, waiting for some hot make-up sex, *honey*, and then I have another glass of wine, and another, and then I wake up and realize I drank two-thirds of the bottle by myself and I've been asleep for two hours and I'm still alone. This better be another fabulous out-of-town assignment, or at the very minimum, your only friend David dropped by on the spur of the moment to take you out and get you drunk. And if that's the case, I want photographic evidence.'

She had cursed as she hung up. The words were classic Gina Saraceno, funny and tough, but he thought he heard a tremor in her voice. If he had been speaking to her, there would have been a tremor in his own. He didn't know how to explain away their missed date without telling the truth. Another lie seemed preposterous. Yet he wanted more than anything to keep her out of danger.

That wasn't quite true. He wanted more than anything to be with Gina Saraceno. But he didn't want to do anything that jeopardized their future together.

It was nearly 4 a.m. Unable to sleep, Jason Walker sat at the window, his unwatched television a dyspeptic flicker on the glass. He watched the mailbox, wondering who would open it and remove the envelope. He watched as dawn turned blue then gray then yellow, bringing the green leaves of the trees slowly back into color. People jogged, bicycled, and walked their dogs, but no one stopped at the mailbox. The sun was high off the horizon when a mail truck pulled to the curb and the driver got out carrying a white plastic tub. He unlatched the mailbox, swapped his empty tub for the full one, and carried the full one to his truck. From the way his lips were pursed he appeared to be whistling.

Jason Walker stumbled to the couch and fell asleep.

Schatzi was barking. The phone was ringing. A double ring. The intercom. The phone stopped ringing. Schatzi kept barking. The phone started ringing again. He staggered to the table and answered it. Gina Saraceno. He buzzed her up.

He barely had time to splash water on his face and gargle mouthwash before she was thumping the door impatiently. Loudly, as if enjoying the way that it wound up the dog. He glanced at the clock. Just after noon. His head throbbed as if he had a hangover.

She swept in as if on a mission. She asked to use the toilet. He waited, standing up in the living room, scratching his head. When it seemed she'd been gone too long he went to look. She was in his bedroom, sniffing the sheets.

'All right, I admit it,' she said. 'I came by unannounced so I could spy on you. I thought the door would be answered by a sleazy blonde or that, at a minimum, the sheets would look like you had an oil-wrestling contest in them.'

'I didn't sleep with anyone.'

'Based on the evidence, I think I'm willing to concede that. But you stood me up. Did you get another last-minute assignment?'

'No, I . . . .'

'You what?'

His mind went blank.

'I was abducted by some men from the Lebanese Cultural

Center who thought I was spying on them,' he said. 'They wanted me to tell them everything about who I was working for. They didn't let me go until three in the morning.'

Gina Saraceno stared at him. Then the corners of her mouth curled.

'You forgot, didn't you?'

'Forgot what?'

'You forgot our date last night. You know, the only thing more preposterous than the story you just told me would have been if you told me you forgot, which I take it is the truth. Do you want me to forgive you?'

'Of course, but—'

'Then get on your knees and bark like a dog.'

'What?'

Schatzi was still barking furiously.

'Never mind,' said Gina Saraceno. 'I guess that's covered.'

She sat down on the couch while he stood there dumb-founded. Of course she wouldn't believe him. Would he have believed her if she said the same thing? If he was going to tell her the truth he would have to lay the ground-work. He went into the kitchen and poured two glasses of water. He went back into the living room and handed one of them to her, then sat down next to her.

'Am I losing my mind, or are you losing yours?' she asked.

'I'm losing mine.'

'Are you stressed about work?'

'Yes.'

'You've still got some of the money from that Philadelphia thing, don't you? Hey, when is that coming out?'

'I don't know.'

'But they did pay you, right? I saw the check lying around.'

'Yes.'

'Isn't that kind of unusual? Don't they usually pay on publication?'

'Usually,' he said. 'But remember that the editor is my friend. He probably just told them to cut the check.'

'Lucky you. When they kill stories, what do they pay? Like half?'

'Sometimes only twenty-five percent.'

'Oh.'

She sipped water.

'Well, I'm looking forward to reading it. Maybe you should call them and ask what the schedule is.'

'That's a good idea,' he said without enthusiasm.

Schatzi finally stopped barking.

'Have you handed out any more flyers for George Libby?' he asked.

'Not yet. Listen, I keep making these speeches about how I don't put up with any shit, but then I keep putting up with your shit. I don't know why, but I guess I like having you around, honey. Can you promise me something?'

He looked at her, unsure he could promise anything.

'Could you try to be less of a flake?'

He could, and told her so.

'OK then. Now, I'm not sure I'm in the mood for make-up sex anymore, but what say you give me an apology backrub? We can see where things go from there.'

They went to his bedroom and stripped down to their underwear. She was not wearing her pretty-but-uncomfortable bra and panties from the night before. He rubbed her back and shoulders for a long time. Once in a while he kissed her neck and let his fingers wander below her waist, but she didn't respond except to murmur noncommittally. After an hour or so they fell asleep.

She left in the late afternoon, groggily explaining that she had to help her mother cook dinner for old family friends. She made him swear to come to a meeting at Scott Fink's house the following night. He swore, hoping he wouldn't be made a liar once again.

The moment he closed the door, the phone rang. It was almost as if someone had been watching and waiting for her to leave.

It was Chad Armstrong.

'Hey, buddy,' he said. 'Got your message. Up for a ballgame tonight? My treat.'

Thirteen

David Darling's hatred of the White Sox was equal to his love for the Cubs. Despite the White Sox's superior play in recent years, he refused to say anything good about the team. If pressed, he grudgingly conceded that they had been 'lucky.' He especially hated their ballpark, U.S. Cellular Field. He hated the video screens, the loud music, and the fireworks that erupted from the scoreboard when the home team hit a home run. He called it 'Nuremberg' and had forbidden Jason Walker, who didn't care one way or the other, ever to go there.

Chad Armstrong had obtained what he called 'world-class seats.'

The air hung muggy and still as Jason Walker trudged from the 35th Street station toward the stadium. Where Wrigley Field was nestled comfortably in its neighborhood of three-flats, bars, and restaurants, U.S. Cellular Field squatted amidst its parking lots like a fortress on a plain. It was massive. In no mood for entertainment, he found himself angry at the spectacle of it. The blazing lights, the noise of the crowd, and the smell of grilling food assaulted his senses, and he wanted nothing so much as to sit quietly in a dark room at home.

He gave his name at the ticket office and was given a ticket, which was scanned as he passed through the gate. There was a special promotion that night: every tenth fan received a free pat-down, courtesy of Homeland Security. He was number ten. The check was cursory. Even the agent's hands felt bored.

Inside the stadium, the scale was just as massive. Broad concourses, soaring ceilings, and a stadium that seemed to fall away below as he emerged on the upper deck.

He was late. The announcer was already introducing the players. He consulted his ticket stub and wandered about until he found the right seating area. He thought that Chad Armstrong wouldn't want him to ask an usher for help. The usher might remember him.

Their seats were in the very front. Chad Armstrong was already there, typing furiously on a small electronic device with his thumbs. When he saw Jason Walker, he tapped it once more and shoved it in his pocket.

'Not bad, huh?' he said. 'The seats. Can't go lower level, of course. Too many cameras.'

Jason Walker just stared at him. He didn't have the same ability to make facile small talk.

The announcer asked the crowd to please rise for the singing of the national anthem.

'Let's go get a beer,' said Chad Armstrong.

He rose and walked away without looking back. Jason Walker followed him. Chad Armstrong stopped inside the concourse. The crowd sang along lustily as a local pop diva trilled and swooped her way through the first verse.

'The roster's a fake,' said Chad Armstrong.

'How do you know?'

'I know. I have people who do things with computers. They told me.'

'Well, I can't do anything about that,' said Jason Walker. 'I did what you asked me to do. I can't do any more than that.'

'Look, I don't blame you, but it does mean we're even more short on results than I thought we were. I need you to go back. Try to make friends with Leo Haddad again.'

Jason Walker thought that he should seem frightened.

'I can't go back!' he said. 'That's crazy! They have to know I was the one who took the notebook.'

'I know that. I want you to look a little clueless. Shouldn't be too hard. I'm hoping our man Haddad will make contact and try to turn you as a double agent. If he does, appear reluctant but then go along with it. I'll give you some meaningless but important-sounding information to feed to him.

Then, once you have his trust, you can provide some really useful information to *me*.'

'What if he doesn't try to turn me into a double agent?'

Chad Armstrong shrugged. 'No idea. Look, I'm good at my job, but I'm not a psychic. Who knows how terrorists' minds work?'

'But what if they, I don't know, what if they abduct me? What if they want the notebook back?'

'They won't. It's a fake, remember? If you had gotten useful information, then they might be pissed off at you. But you didn't get anything useful. So if they're smart, they'll try to figure out how they can use you.'

Chad Armstrong gave him an appraising look.

'You're not already working for them, are you, Jason?'

'Of course not!'

As soon as he said it, he was sure he sounded too vehement. The wrong note in his voice would be as good as a confession.

But Chad Armstrong nodded amiably.

'No, I know. Of course not. Hey, let's get back to the game.'

He wanted to leave but Chad Armstrong insisted they stay. He said that baseball was baseball regardless of the circumstances. It would be criminal to waste good seats. They bought beer and hot dogs and returned to the upper deck, where the White Sox had taken a two-run lead in the bottom of the first inning. The second run had scored on a suicide squeeze, their neighbors informed them. Chad Armstrong took the news with an equal measure of excitement and disappointment.

'I can't believe we missed that!' he said. 'I guess that's what happens when you mix work and pleasure.'

Jason Walker allowed Chad Armstrong to buy him beer after beer but felt guilty with each mouthful he swallowed. The agent's sunny disposition would have made anyone around them think that he was just another fan in love with his winning team. But in the seventh inning, when a television cameraman swung his lens toward their section, inciting the fans to wave to the viewers at home, Chad

Armstrong suddenly jerked his arm and dumped his entire beer over the woman to his immediate left. He apologized profusely as he helped her blot it with paper napkins, his back now square to the camera.

It was quick thinking, Jason Walker had to grudgingly admit. But it seemed somehow in keeping with the agent's character that the woman was buxom and wearing a white T-shirt and shorts.

They said goodbye outside the stadium. Chad Armstrong had a car. Thankfully, he didn't offer a ride. But he had one more surprise.

'Oh, by the way, I was surprised to hear that you've gotten politically involved,' he said casually. 'I thought you said you weren't a political kind of guy.'

'I said I wasn't the kind of guy who bombed buildings.'

Chad Armstrong winced. He glanced right and left.

'Hey, keep it down. Just making small talk. It's because of her, right? Gina? You see, that's the difference between East and West. With us, it's all about getting laid before we die. With them, it's all about getting laid in paradise, after they die. That's why they're in such a hurry to get it over with. You know, Mormons have it worked out so they can do it now and later. That's why they're such cheerful sons-of-bitches.'

'It doesn't have anything to do with what you want me to do.'

'No, of course not. If you want to hassle people on public sidewalks and try to enlist them in a hopeless cause, you're within your rights. For now. But it is interesting. I'd be curious to see what kind of people are campaigning for George Libby. Besides you and your girlfriend, of course. Think you could take a few notes next time you get together? Tomorrow night, right?'

Jason Walker didn't say anything.

'I mean, I could always ask your girlfriend Gina to help out. I'm sure she'd be interested to learn about your other project.'

'What do you want?'

'Names, faces, addresses, phone numbers, juicy quotes. You know, anything that seems important. No need to type it up or anything. I've got a girl who can do that. So you're on board?'

He nodded grimly.

Chad Armstrong slapped him on the back.

'Good boy.'

They walked away from each other, Jason Walker trudging along the crowded sidewalk toward the train station, Chad Armstrong weaving among knots of people toward the parking lots. The agent didn't look back once.

The next night Scott Fink served homemade hummus that was dry and chunky. Some of the chickpeas were still wholly intact, and he hadn't used any salt. The bowl was ringed by toasted pita bread, stale stone-ground crackers, slightly limp carrots, and even a few blue-corn tortilla chips. Scott Fink apparently catered by cleaning out the refrigerator. They drank bitterly strong iced tea and tart lemonade out of pint glasses that had apparently been filched from a pub serving a lot of Midwestern microbrews.

Eric the writer was there, as were Mike the lesbian, Demeter the beautiful hippie, and Dorothy the retired professor. Dorothy said that Cornelius was feeling 'psychic fatigue' and therefore needed to rest. Amber and Jarrod the students were absent. Perhaps they were still studying the brochure they had taken.

Scott Fink was talking about the need to get the media involved. Evil it might be, he said, but it was still a necessary evil. A political movement could grow in the dark, but it couldn't flower without the bright lights of television and radio. Troubled by the metaphor, Jason Walker wondered if he should volunteer to write the press releases.

Worried about his ability to remember names and faces, he pulled a reporters' notebook out of his bag and started jotting things down. Even radical groups kept minutes, he reasoned.

'What are you doing?' said Scott Fink.

'Just taking notes. I work best on paper.'

'No notes, no records,' said Scott Fink emphatically.

'But how will we remember what we talked about?'

Scott Fink tapped his forehead. 'We'll remember. I know you probably think I'm being paranoid, but these are evil times, Jason.'

Everyone was watching him, waiting for his reply. Was he the dissident of the dissident group?

Shrugging, he tore off the sheet he had written on and handed it to Scott Fink. He put the notebook away. Scott Fink made a show of lighting the paper and letting it burn in a tarnished brass tray filled with the ashes of incense cones.

'Thanks, man,' he said.

'I understand,' said Jason Walker.

The meeting dragged on. It was decided that campaigning should be carried out in front of a local television station. Even a lazy news crew might turn on their camera, went the reasoning. But there was debate about whether they should carry placards, which might alienate some people, and whether they should wear suits and ties.

Hungry, Jason Walker picked at the hummus. He thought that, even if Leo Haddad's group were terrorists, they had the better food. Then he felt sick and angry with himself. It was nothing to be glib about.

It was decided. Both placards and suits. The day after tomorrow.

Gina Saraceno and Jason Walker drove to the Woodlawn Tap in Hyde Park. Gio Saraceno had been a regular there, loving the bar for its unusual blend of patrons. Close to the University of Chicago, it drew everyone from beer-guzzling undergraduates to whiskey-sipping professors, with a liberal sprinkling of freelance intellectuals.

It was crowded. They ordered beers from a barman who looked like a smooth-faced Samuel Beckett and then found an open piece of wall to lean against.

During the meeting, while Jason Walker had been inwardly bemoaning the quality of the food, Gina Saraceno had been intently focused on the discussion. Now she looked happy and refreshed.

'You're in a good mood,' he said.

'You know, I am. I'm kind of frustrated with my boyfriend, but I'm in a good mood anyway.'

'So you're thinking about forgiving him?'

'I'm considering it. I hope he doesn't get ahead of himself. But I'm in a good mood because, well—it seems stupid.'

'You really like volunteering.'

'I do. This is going to sound corny, but it makes me feel closer to my dad. Most teenagers are cynics and most twenty-year-olds are idealists, but I think I got cynical in grade school. Maybe it's because I had my dad to be the idealist for me. And kids can't help but think their parents are getting it wrong. But I think I'm starting to understand what he liked about what he did.'

'You share his love of lost causes.'

'See? I'm in such a good mood that I'm going to let that one go. That's not it at all. I hate losing. I hate that people don't seem to see what's happening. But I think I might have hated myself a little bit, all those years I didn't do anything. If you do all you can, at least you have a clean conscience. That's something.'

'That makes it sound selfish.'

'Maybe it is. But I don't believe in selflessness. See? I'm still cynical. I think even Mahatma Gandhi and Mother Teresa did what they did because it gave them a good feeling inside. Nothing wrong with that. True selflessness would be to do something for other people even though it was hard and you didn't like it. But there's nothing wrong with a little self-interest when you're a do-gooder. If it makes you feel good to try to make peoples' lives better, it sure beats the other way of doing things.'

'But your opinion of how to make their lives better is still just that: your opinion.'

She laughed and tipped her beer back.

'Look, just because we're surrounded by undergraduates doesn't mean I'm going to let you engage in tail-chasing moral relativism all night. I think that's something my dad might have said. As you get older you become more aware of how complicated everything is, but you also don't feel the need to chase logic down every rabbit hole. If other people have a different opinion, let them work for it. Most people are carried along by the inertia of the majority opinion.'

At the bar, a white-bearded man in a Greek fisherman's cap was in a heated but friendly-seeming argument with a young man with blue hair and a pierced nose. They took turns flipping through a shelf-worn paperback and pointing to specific passages. He couldn't hear what they were saying.

Jason Walker had never really questioned anything before. While others his age were starting bands, traveling, volunteering for charity, or even just doing too many drugs, he had spent time in the darkroom, trying to make his precisely focused pictures come out even more clearly. His father had been a man of unambiguous opinions, and Jason Walker believed that he, too, knew the way the world worked. But he had come to his own opinions quickly. And he had never been called upon to defend them.

Watching the two men arguing at the bar, he envied them both for their conviction, even though he had no idea what their disagreement was or what their opinions were. If only he had a little bit of time. Time to think without everyone asking something of him.

Gina Saraceno was smiling at him, raising her eyebrows and rotating her empty beer glass.

'Earth to Jason. Earth to Jason. What is the frequency?'

'What?'

'Do you want another beer?'

'Sure,' he said.

She started to walk to the bar, then stopped.

'Are you OK?' she asked. 'You look like someone killed your dog.'

Maybe she was right. Maybe standing up for something, however hopeless, was the only way to feel good about yourself. But the closer he got to anything good, the more danger good was in.

'I'm fine,' he lied, 'just a little bit tired.'

They went back to her apartment. Both of them sleepy from beer, they climbed into bed and made love tenderly, almost without moving. She fell asleep in his arms. When her breathing was deep and regular, he rolled her on to her side and slithered his arm out from under her body. In the near dark, he felt inside his bag for his pen and notebook. He took them into the bathroom and closed the door. The string for the fluorescent bulb was thin and elastic and bounced out of his hand after he pulled it. The bulb tapped and winked on and he winced.

He sat down on the toilet and began to write down everything he remembered from the meeting at Scott Fink's house.

Fourteen

In the morning, Gina Saraceno went to work and Jason Walker rode the bus and train north. He bought breakfast at the red-vinyl diner and read the newspaper, then walked home. Schatzi didn't bark, so he assumed that Richard Zim was at home. He considered complaining to his neighbor about the noise but decided against it. He knew nothing would happen. And having both an angry dog and an angry neighbor seemed worse than just an angry dog.

He had not checked his emails for several days. He turned on his computer, not expecting to find anything, but he was surprised. There was a short note from Lainie Verona informing him that she needed the two attached pieces copy-edited in three days. There was no warmth of reconciliation in her words, leading him to believe that his replacement was either busy or unacceptable. He had no way of knowing whether he was in Lainie Verona's good graces again, but despite everything, he needed the work.

He checked the date on the message. It had been sent three days ago. She had asked for the work to be completed by midday. It was ten o'clock.

He made coffee and turned on all the lights, then got to work. Both stories were articles about fashion, which made it more difficult for him to be certain about matters of style. He knew the difference between an A-line skirt and a V-neck sweater, but that was all. His own sartorial style ran toward subdued, solid colors, although he did own several shirts that were conservatively striped. He relied heavily on manufacturers' websites as he wrestled 'The Old New You: Taste Tips from the Elderly' and 'Monochrome Glory: No-Brainer Accessorizing' into conformity. He was done by one o'clock. He sent the edited stories attached to an email thanking Lainie Verona for thinking of him.

As much as he hated the stories he'd worked on, he'd enjoyed working. It had been three hours of blissful escape from his problems. If he weren't a plague-bringer, he thought, he would enjoy employing his skills on a more worthy enterprise, perhaps a political magazine.

That night he went back to the Lebanese Cultural Center. Leo Haddad was playing chess but this time he interrupted his game. He seemed surprised and upset to see Jason Walker. They unfolded two chairs and sat near the darkened stage in the back. Leo Haddad didn't suggest coffee and pastries.

'Jason,' he said, 'what are you doing here? Surely it's not safe for you to be seen here right now. Your handler wanted you to steal the notebook as a last act, knowing we would identify you as the thief.'

'He told me to come back. He thinks you'll try to turn me into a double agent.'

Leo Haddad seemed almost startled. Then he smiled a sly smile.

'This Chad Armstrong is a smart man. He is almost ahead of us, but not quite.'

It occurred to Jason Walker that if Chad Armstrong could predict Leo Haddad's behavior, he might also know what the man was really up to. But there was nothing to do now but play along. He tried to smile.

'Not quite,' he agreed.

'But now I know for certain that I can trust you, Jason. This is a wonderful opportunity, even better than what I had hoped for. If he believes that you have gained my trust and that I believe you are working for me, then he will accept what you tell him more readily.'

'But what do you want to know from him? If you're just preparing for the worst-case scenario, then why do you need to actively deceive a government agent?'

'These men are also preparing, Jason. Many things are already happening. If we are to protect ourselves, we need to know what they know and what they are doing. If we wait until they come for us, all will be lost. Do you see?'

He said that he did.

'Good. Now, what I need first is a photo of Chad Armstrong. That is the hardest part for us: knowing who is watching. Can you provide this?'

He didn't own a very powerful telephoto lens. When he photographed buildings he preferred to focus on the mass of the structure rather than individual ornaments. In fact, he often used a medium-format camera with a fixed lens. In order to hide and shoot a quality headshot of Chad Armstrong he would need a 300mm lens or even longer, the kind used by birders and sports photographers.

He shook his head. 'Not unless you have a spy camera. Something tiny that I can hide.'

Leo Haddad seemed amused.

'I don't have a spy camera,' he said.

'It's too risky otherwise.'

'A photograph would be best, but it still would be immensely helpful if I could simply see the man. Can you tell me the next time you are to meet? I will arrive before you and conceal myself.'

'Our meetings are always arranged just a few hours before they happen. I get a phone call telling me where to go.'

'And when you get this phone call, call me. If I can arrive an hour earlier than you, we should be safe. Otherwise I will not come. Wait here.'

Leo Haddad passed through the beaded curtain into the back. He emerged five minutes later holding a cheap-looking cell phone.

'Use this,' he said. 'It is disposable. It has two hours of calling time prepaid. I have another phone like it. I used my phone to call yours just now, so in order to reach me, all you have to do is to return the call. But let us try not to say important things over the phone. Consider that all conversations may be monitored.'

'Even this one?'

'It is possible, although I doubt that they would send a van to listen when they have sent you. Besides, we take at least rudimentary precautions here. It is possible to buy a simple frequency scrambler on the World Wide Web.'

'What do you want me to tell him? The false information?'

'I am not sure. I need more time to decide. I will call you and we will meet. And since we are now allowed to be seen with one another, can I offer you coffee and a game of chess?'

When he got home, Jason Walker returned Gina Saraceno's call. She had left a message asking whether he would be campaigning with her tomorrow.

'Where were you, Jason?' she asked.

'Out.'

'Just out?'

'Taking a walk by the lake.'

'After dark? Isn't that kind of stupid?'

'Well, I survived. Besides, the police clear it at eleven with spotlights and loudspeakers.'

'As long as they didn't arrest you. We need bodies tomorrow. We're going to look like the lunatic fringe if we show up with three people.'

'I'll be there.'

'And can you bring anyone else? Do you think your friend David would come?'

He couldn't imagine anything more unlikely.

'I don't know,' he said. 'Maybe.'

'Can you call him? Promise you'll at least ask.'

'I promise.'

'I can see you crossing your fingers.'

He uncrossed them.

'Uncrossed. I'll call him. But it's a long shot.'

'Well,' she said, 'that fits.'

They said goodbye. Jason Walker looked at the glowing green numbers of the clock on his stove. It was almost eleven thirty. But David Darling would be up. He didn't start work until late in the morning, and often worked into the evening.

David Darling answered his cell phone on the seventh

ring. It sounded as if he were at the semifinals of a shouting contest.

'David, it's Jason.'

'Who?'

'Jason.'

'Jason! It's David.'

Perhaps it was a drinking contest instead.

'Where are you?'

There was a pause, as if David Darling were looking around.

'Um, the Irish Oak? I dunno, one of the fake pubs. What's up?'

'I need a favor.'

'Did I see the paper? No.'

'*Favor*. Can you come downtown tomorrow and hand out brochures for George Libby?'

There was another pause. Processing.

'Jason, it sounded like you asked if I would campaign for George Libby tomorrow.'

'That's right. Are you in?'

'Fucking hilarious. Come off it, Jason.'

'I'm serious. Don't you think there should be an election?'

'Of course, but what are you gonna do? You can't fight city hall.'

'Well, we're going to be there. In front of the ABC studios at noon.'

'You're going to do this in front of a TV station?'

'Yes.'

'Well, maybe I'll see you on TV then. Look, gotta run.'

He clicked off.

Jason Walker thrashed restlessly in bed that night. Of all the strange things he had done lately, none of them had been in public.

At first the passersby on the sidewalk seemed quizzical or bemused. Some shook their heads and kept walking. Several stopped and leaned against lampposts or buildings to watch the tiny spectacle.

There were eight of them: Scott, Demeter, Eric, Mike,

Dorothy, Cornelius, and Gina Saraceno and Jason Walker. They were all dressed as if they were going to job interviews, wearing bright red, white, and blue *VOTE LIBBY* badges on their lapels, holding thick stacks of brochures in their left hands. They smiled, greeted passersby, and offered the campaign literature in an exhaustively discussed, non-threatening manner. Stairs led down from El tracks on the corner, and led up from the subway almost in front of them, so a steady stream of pedestrians stumbled into their trap. But an equal number saw them coming and crossed to the other side of the street to avoid them.

The ABC-7 State Street Studio faced on to the sidewalk, providing the cheery hosts a colorful background against which to chat and read the news. Tourists from downstate, from Iowa, Indiana, Wisconsin, and Michigan, routinely pressed their noses to the glass or waved hand-lettered signs with greetings to their friends at home. There were only a handful of them there for the midday news, but they regarded the Libby Lobby with annoyance. The serious-minded campaigners were party-crashers.

Television monitors faced the sidewalk and showed the live feed. This allowed the sign-wavers to know when they were on the air. When the studio was inaugurated, the station had followed the protocol set by the flagship station in New York City, using the human backdrop for the morning and midday news but not for the evening and nighttime news. The nighttime news was more serious, less likely to feature a hot-dog-eating contest. But then the rules changed. The human backdrop could be used for the five and six o'clock news, too. Only the ten o'clock news was still deemed serious enough to not use it. Either that, Jason Walker mused, or there weren't enough people on the sidewalk at that hour to make it look good.

He watched the monitors. The group's hope was that the hosts would be forced to acknowledge them. A single sentence would give them the momentary attention of nearly a million households. Even better would be a news producer's decision to send out a reporter and a camera crew. But they had been outside for twenty minutes and the cameras had not shown the sidewalk. It was almost time for the sports segment.

And then the police showed up.

There had been a foot patrolman watching them for ten minutes, but he had looked bored, and Jason Walker hadn't seen him radio for reinforcements. Now there was a sudden whoop of a siren followed by several deep horn blasts. Two patrol cars glided to a stop, followed a moment later by a paddy wagon.

Suddenly the crowd was interested. As a half-dozen policemen climbed from their vehicles, pedestrians began to stop, wondering if there was going to be a confrontation. Several of them appeared to be hoping for one. But the policemen climbed the curb and stopped to watch, too. One of them leaned against the paddy wagon. Several others folded their arms. Their faces were blank.

Scott Fink raised his voice. He was saying the same things he had been saying, but now his words carried down the block.

'George Libby supports the idea of a democratic election,' he said. 'I support George Libby!'

Gina Saraceno strolled toward a tourist couple, smiling.

'Even if you don't support him,' she said, 'George Libby supports your right to vote. Tell the president you want to vote—even if you want to vote for him.'

The couple waved her away, embarrassed. She tried politely to press the brochure into their hands, but they lurched to the side as if afraid to touch her. The woman waved her hand as if shooing a fly. They quickened their pace.

In just a matter of minutes the crowd seemed to have grown fourfold. Jason Walker found it hard to think. So many people were looking at him. He couldn't come up with anything to say, so he just smiled as broadly as he could and aimed his brochures in the general direction of the few people who walked through.

He was ashamed to find himself thinking that if anything happened to the group, he would be all right because he was working for Chad Armstrong. Unless Chad Armstrong thought that he was working for Leo Haddad.

David Darling was standing on the edge of the crowd. Jason Walker actually blinked twice and rubbed his eyes. He couldn't believe it. His apolitical friend had come to support him. It cheered him immensely. He smiled.

But David Darling's smile was weak. He stayed where he was. Jason Walker saw fear in his eyes. Whatever he had planned to do, he had changed his mind.

The crowd grew. A man wearing a T-shirt that depicted a pit bull driving a race car started to heckle them.

'Traitors!' he shouted. 'You give aid and comfort to the terrorists! Support the president!'

A white van stopped at the end of the block, blocking the crosswalk. Two men wearing black slacks and black windbreakers got out and took their time walking toward the scene. One of them was speaking into a thin cell phone.

Eric the writer seemed visibly nervous. Demeter the hippie smiled a beatific smile, as if saying she would suffer this foolishness even though it didn't really concern her. Dorothy and Cornelius were stoic. They had actually handed out more brochures than anyone. He thought he remembered Scott Fink saying that, when they were teenagers, the couple had marched with Martin Luther King in Birmingham.

He walked over to David Darling.

'I was surprised to see you here,' he said.

'I was surprised to see *you*.'

David Darling seemed acutely aware that the people standing on either side of him were listening. Jason Walker decided to retreat.

'Well, hope you have a good afternoon.'

As he walked away, his friend made a strange gesture with his hands. Like a strangled wave, maybe it was meant to shoo him away. Or maybe it was meant as an apology. The next time he looked, David Darling was gone.

A bright light bobbed toward them. A news crew had come out of the studio. They headed for Gina Saraceno but Scott Fink cut them off. It looked as if the reporter had not been ready to come on shift. He had a dab of shaving cream in his ear and his make-up was lighter on one side of his face. Jason Walker recognized him as Kent Rocklin, part of the nightly news team.

The crowd on the sidewalk seemed to press even closer.

'Hi, Kent Rocklin, ABC-7 News Chicago. Can I get your name, sir?'

'Scott Fink. Nice to meet you, Kent.'

'What are you protesting here today?'

'We're not protesting. We're campaigning. Our candidate is George Libby, and we believe he deserves a chance to be elected president.'

Kent Rocklin furrowed his brow so perfectly that he must have practiced it in the mirror. Jason Walker couldn't stop staring at the shaving cream in his ear. It was the only detail of the whole surreal encounter that seemed real.

'But isn't that a kind of protest?' said the reporter.

In their last meeting, Scott Fink had stressed the need to avoid seeming angry. To avoid terms that alienated people, like *protest*.

'We prefer to think of it as showing support for our candidate. We'd like to encourage the president to show Americans that democracy begins at home.'

'What is your candidate's platform?'

'America first. He wants to bring our troops home and concentrate on building bridges to other countries, not bombs to drop on them.'

'But what about the problem of terrorism? He'd rather fight them here than there?'

'George Libby believes that we're creating more terrorists every day,' Scott Fink said matter-of-factly. 'We've tried fighting terror with violence. He believes it's time to try fighting it with peace.'

He never knew exactly what happened next.

There was a blur and then Scott Fink staggered. There was a tiny *crink* of shattering glass and the light on the television camera lurched skyward.

'Fuck!' said the cameraman.

'What?' said Kent Rocklin, already moving for the safety of the building.

Scott Fink went down on one knee, holding his head. He lifted his hand and looked at it. His fingers were covered in blood.

He saw movement out of the corner of his eye. Eric was being shaken like a doll by two construction workers. Demeter stood frozen, her mouth hanging open. Dorothy and Cornelius were actually moving toward the construction workers, telling them to stop.

Gina Saraceno was arguing with a red-faced woman who looked as if she was about to start throwing punches.

'Scott, are you OK?' he said.

Scott Fink shook his head. 'Yeah,' he said. 'Head wounds bleed a lot.'

Jason Walker looked at the police. They seemed to be weighing up the situation. He ran to Gina Saraceno and pulled her away from the red-faced woman. She whirled, arm pulled back as if she were about to throw a punch herself.

'It's me, Gina.'

'You're lucky it's you,' she said.

But she seemed shaken.

One of the construction workers punched Eric. He took two steps on rubbery legs and fell, skinning his cheek on the sidewalk. The other construction worker was engaged in a shouting match with Dorothy and Cornelius.

'Why on earth did you hit that young man?' demanded an outraged Dorothy.

'Love it or leave it, lady,' said the construction worker.

As if from nowhere, a skinny young man with a pink Mohawk weaved through the bodies and hit the second construction worker in the head with a bicycle lock. The burly man staggered but didn't fall. He raised his hands uncertainly, ready to defend against another blow. But the young man with the pink Mohawk ran away through the crowd.

It was becoming a brawl. The police waded in, nightsticks swinging. They weren't issuing any orders.

This time it was Gina Saraceno who pulled Jason Walker by the arm, trying to escape the melee. He saw the cameraman panning wildly, trying to record the scene. But the camera lens was shattered.

They pressed up against the thick window of the sidewalk studio. The anchors gaped at the scene outside. One of them was talking, perhaps narrating what he saw for the viewers at home. The monitors facing the sidewalk showed only the anchors.

The sidewalk became a surging mass of bodies. Some people seemed to be running into the melee. Most people were running away. A man wearing glasses tripped over them, fell, climbed to his feet, apologized, and ran on. Another man was thrown so hard against the window that the glass thrummed.

A policeman appeared in front of them. He looked at their hands. They looked down and saw that they were still holding stacks of brochures.

'Turn around!' barked the policeman.

They turned around.

'Hands on the glass! Feet apart!'

They complied. The policeman poked their hands with his nightstick and the brochures fell to the pavement. Jason Walker was searched first, quickly, the strange intimacy of the policeman's gestures well practiced. His hands were forced down behind him and zipped together with plastic ties. Then Gina Saraceno was searched and her hands fastened together, too.

The fighting was over as quickly as it had begun. The policeman marched them across the sidewalk and into the paddy wagon. Dorothy and Cornelius were already in the back, sitting on a metal bench with their hands tied behind them. Cornelius's white hair was tinged pink on top and he was breathing heavily. Dorothy, stricken, could do nothing to help him. Demeter was inside, too. Then Scott Fink was hoisted up and thrown on the floor. He kicked and cursed at the policemen until one of them casually kicked Scott Fink's legs out of the way and slammed the door. In the light from the small portholes in the back door Jason Walker saw red welts on Scott Fink's face and arms.

The van pulled away. The construction workers were not with them, nor was the young man with the pink Mohawk.

'Where's Eric? Eric's not here,' said Demeter. She was trembling. 'Is he OK? Did anyone see him?'

Scott Fink was trying to get up on the bench. It wasn't easy. He had been thrown in on his stomach. He got to his knees, then the van turned and he fell against Gina Saraceno's legs. No one could reach out a hand to steady him.

'Eric's going to be riding in an ambulance,' said Scott Fink.

He spat blood on to the floor of the van and then heaved himself up on to the bench.

It occurred to Jason Walker that Scott Fink was a lot tougher than he looked.

'How did this happen, Scott?' said Dorothy.

'Someone didn't want us to look good on television,' said Scott Fink.

'Who did it?' asked Demeter. 'Was it those construction guys?'

'Who knows? Maybe they were just hobbyists. Somebody threw something. Maybe somebody on a Homeland Security payroll, maybe not. For all we know, it was that punker kid with the U-lock.'

He stomped the floor so hard the paddy wagon wobbled.

'God *damn* it!' he shouted.

They rode the rest of the way in silence. It was a short ride. When they reached the police station the men and women were separated. Jason Walker was photographed and had his particulars entered into a computer. His fingerprints were scanned and his finger was pricked for a blood sample. His wallet, belt, and shoelaces were removed and he was searched again. Then he, Scott Fink, and Cornelius were ushered into a large cell that had several dozen other men already inside. Most of the men ignored them. Several looked them up and down with interest.

They helped Cornelius to a bench and stood protectively in front of him. Jason Walker was sure Cornelius needed a doctor. He was just as sure Cornelius wouldn't get one.

'Why are we in here together?' questioned Jason Walker. 'And with everybody else? Don't they want to interrogate us?'

Scott Fink looked at him.

'What for? They don't want to learn anything from us. They already got what they needed: bad news.'

Scott Fink was right. Their stay in jail was brief. By late afternoon they were all crowded together in front of a judge. Their names were called one by one, but they were all charged with the same thing: creating a public disturbance and resisting arrest. The judge set bail and a date for their hearings. The judge looked bored. Bail was five thousand dollars each. They could leave if they posted one-tenth that amount in cash. Conveniently, there was an automatic teller machine in the building.

Jason Walker's bank card had a daily withdrawal limit of four hundred dollars. He couldn't remember the PIN for his credit card because he had never used it to withdraw cash. Fortunately, Gina Saraceno had a bank card and three credit cards. She withdrew enough money for both of them.

'I'll pay you back, Gina,' he said.

'Jason, honestly, that's the last thing I'm worried about right now,' she said. 'Let's get out of here.'

There were television cameras waiting outside the police station. Reporters shouted questions.

'Was your protest a planned act of civil disobedience?'

'Will today's events help or hurt your cause?'

'Does George Libby know that you were arrested today? Does he have a comment?'

Scott Fink answered their questions wearily. They were not protesters and they had not resisted arrest. Violence never helped anything. He regretted that some onlookers were unable to express themselves peacefully. He had not had a chance to speak with George Libby. He imagined that George Libby would share his distress at today's events. He thanked the reporters and apologized for not taking any more questions, but several of their comrades had been injured.

Scott Fink shepherded the group to the curb.

'Damn it, shouldn't have said *comrades*,' he muttered.

They hailed a cab. The group agreed that Dorothy and Cornelius should go first. Scott Fink urged Cornelius to go to a hospital. They hailed another cab. Scott Fink told Jason Walker and Gina Saraceno to take it. He and Demeter were going to Cook County General Hospital to look for Eric. The police wouldn't confirm where he was, but that seemed the most likely place.

'Sorry about all this,' said Scott Fink gloomily.

'Hey, you got conked on the head,' said Gina Saraceno. 'I'm sorry we couldn't catch the asshole who did it.'

They closed the door and the cab sped away.

'Where are you going?' asked the driver. His name was Ahmad Haddad. A common enough name, but startling.

'Are you Lebanese?' asked Jason Walker.

The driver squinted at them in the rear-view mirror.

'Yes. Why do you ask?'

'Your last name. I'm Lebanese, too.'

The driver watched the road.

'Then that explains why I am picking you up at the police station.'

Gina Saraceno slumped against Jason Walker.

'I don't know about you,' she said, 'but I could use a drink.'

Fifteen

They asked Ahmad Haddad to take them to the nearest bar. It was a short trip. The first bar had police cruisers lined up two deep at the curb in front. They told Ahmad Haddad to keep driving. They ended up at the South Loop Club, which was slowly filling with a mixture of regulars, students, and after-work drinkers. They took seats at the bar. Gina Saraceno ordered a martini, 'and another one after that.' Jason Walker ordered bourbon and cola. It was easier to drink whiskey quickly if it was suspended in soda pop, he'd discovered.

There was a television directly in front of them, hanging over the bar. It was tuned to channel seven. The news was starting.

Graying anchor Joel Devonshire faced the camera without the usual twinkle in his eye.

'Good evening. Our first story tonight is local—so local that it took place outside our very own State Street Sidewalk Studio.'

Videotape showed Scott Fink and Gina Saraceno offering flyers to passersby. Jason Walker thought he glimpsed himself in the corner of the frame, his back to the camera. Joel Devonshire continued in voiceover.

'Starting shortly before noon today, a group of protesters organized informally on behalf of would-be presidential candidate George Libby was seen buttonholing pedestrians and distributing what they called "campaign literature."'

Kent Rocklin held his microphone up for Scott Fink.

'We sent reporter Kent Rocklin out to speak with the group's self-styled leader, a man who goes by the name of Scott Fink. A subsequent Internet search revealed that Fink has a long history of supporting unpopular causes, from stronger unions for transit workers to subsidies for alternative sources of fuel. As you'll see here, the interview had hardly begun when Rocklin's cameraman was attacked. Fortunately, nearby police were able to quickly subdue the resisters and restore order.'

The audio on the videotape finally came up.

Scott Fink said, 'George Libby believes that we're creating more terrorists every day.'

His next line was missing. The glass of the camera lens starred jaggedly and the camera reared back as its operator startled. Buildings swayed and lurched in the sky and then the angle changed to that of a camera inside the studio that had been turned to point out at the sidewalk.

The young man with the Mohawk hit the construction worker with the bicycle lock. A frightened man was thrown against the window. Jason Walker and Gina Saraceno stood against the glass, unaware of the camera recording them, as they were searched and zip-tied.

'They edited it,' whispered Gina Saraceno.

The producer cut back to Joel Devonshire in the studio.

'Despite the terrifying melee that suddenly erupted around the lunchtime crowd, police spokeswoman Jacqueline Torres assured us that no one was seriously hurt. All eight protesters were arrested and are still being held at the First District Police Station at this hour.'

The producer changed cameras again, and Joel Devonshire swiveled in his seat.

'We'll have more details as they emerge. And tonight at ten: who is George Libby, and what does he want? A special in-depth report.'

Yet another camera revealed Joel Devonshire's co-anchor, Linda Liu, sitting beside him.

'Scary stuff, Joel,' she said.

'We're used to reporting the news, but we never like to be a part of it,' he said.

'I'm just glad the window didn't break.'

Their report moved on to happier news. The drinks arrived. Gina Saraceno tilted her glass back thirstily. 'Scott seemed to think that the attack was a set-up, that someone started it on purpose to make us look bad. Do you think someone would actually do that? We're the most harmless bunch of people. Why would they need to make us look like we weren't? Who would even be paying attention to us?'

He had to say he had no idea.

They spent the night together in Gina Saraceno's bed, neither of them sleeping well. They lay holding one another, occasionally breaking the silence when remembering a new fragment of the day's events. Gina Saraceno had called Scott Fink and learned that Eric the writer was indeed in Cook County Hospital. He had sustained a mild concussion, a broken nose, three fractured ribs, a torn knee ligament, and various scrapes and bruises. They hadn't watched the ten o'clock news, fearing to see more omissions and creative editing.

In the morning, they ate breakfast with Maria Saraceno. Then Gina Saraceno went to work and Jason Walker rode the bus and train home. There were three emails from *Chicago Socialite* waiting for him. The first two were from an assistant editor. They had articles attached and instructions that he copyedit the articles. The third had been sent early that morning and was from Lainie Verona herself.

> *We are withdrawing the previous two articles. We will mail full payment for any outstanding invoices today.* Chicago Socialite *has a strict code of conduct and involvement in any police matter by employees or contractors may be cause for termination of services, at the employer's discretion. We are exercising that discretion now.*

It was bizarre. As a lowly copyeditor, Jason Walker's name didn't even appear on the masthead of the magazine. It was exceedingly unlikely that anyone would draw a connection between Jason Walker, the Libby Lobby, and *Chicago*

Socialite. And even if they did, it was exceedingly unlikely that anyone would care.

He pounded the keyboard in disgust, then instantly regretted it when a key popped off. It was the *J*. He was unable to reattach it.

He had wondered if there might be a message from David Darling, too, but there was no word from his friend.

He spent a little while writing notes on what had happened the day before. He added them to what he had already written about the meetings at Scott Fink's house. He considered various options for hiding them: his underwear drawer; an empty can in the pantry; under the mattress. None of them were any good. He had seen spies in movies get much more creative than that, hiding contraband by taping it underneath drawers, folding it into the space behind light switches, burying it under coffee grounds.

But who would be looking for the notes? He was making them on the orders of the only people likely to conduct a thorough search of his apartment. Gina Saraceno, as far as he knew, would never paw through his possessions.

He decided that the best hiding place was in plain sight. There was a stack of miscellaneous paper on his table, from bills awaiting payment to advertising circulars. It looked so boring, he was certain no one would lift the top page. He lifted the top page and put his notes underneath, then tidied the stack.

That night he went to the Lebanese Cultural Center. He didn't see Leo Haddad. He asked Ahmad Saad if he had seen Leo Haddad.

'I believe he is three doors down,' said Ahmad Saad, 'dining at Fragrant Cedars of Lebanon.'

It was the restaurant where Jason Walker had stopped before his first visit to the center. He hadn't noticed the unlikely name. Now that he did, he wondered if the space had previously sold candles and incense and the restaurant had simply not bothered to change the name.

Leo Haddad was eating a falafel wrap. He raised an eyebrow at Jason Walker.

'How are you feeling today?' he said.

'I'm fine.'

'I think that your life is very complicated.'

'What do you mean, Leo?'

'Besides being a double agent, you still find time to promote the cause of George Libby. I feel a bit like a man who finds that his wife has a wandering eye.'

Jason Walker stood, unsure what to say.

'Are you opposed to George Libby?' he asked.

'Not at all.'

Leo Haddad chuckled.

'I am sorry. Perhaps now is not the time for me to tease you. Please sit.'

He pulled out a chair and sat down.

'Would you like some food?'

'I'm not hungry.'

'Coffee, perhaps?'

Jason Walker pulled a napkin out of the dispenser and bunched it in his fingers.

'You saw what happened?'

Leo Haddad nodded.

'The men in the crowd—the ones who probably started it—they looked normal. Just normal, ignorant people. Do you think the government would have paid someone to throw something?'

Leo Haddad patted his lips with a napkin. He sipped his water.

'Look at the two of us. Anyone who walked in here would not think twice about us. Two friends, they would think. Two friends eating dinner. They would have no idea of our complicated lives.'

'You think they did?'

'I do not know. But it is certainly possible. The public approves of the president. But the more power a man has, the more he is concerned by dissent. That is partly why I choose to do my work in secret.'

Jason Walker was suddenly very tired. He hailed a waiter and ordered coffee. It came instantly. It tasted like instant coffee.

'I should have warned you,' said Leo Haddad, smiling at his frown.

'Do you still want me to work for you?'

'Very much.'

'What do you want me to do?'

'Have you seen Chad Armstrong since we last talked?'

He shook his head.

'Wait another day or two, then call him and tell him we have met twice. Tell him that, as he suspected, I asked you to become my agent. Tell him I offered to pay you. Do you have money to show him?'

'No.'

Leo Haddad opened his wallet and removed some folded bills. He slid them across the table.

'I don't want your money.'

'Consider this a loan. Or a stage prop. It will make our ruse look more convincing.'

Leo Haddad's hand was still on the table. The money was under his palm. Jason Walker put his hand on Leo Haddad's. Leo Haddad withdrew his hand, leaving the money.

He put it in his pocket.

'Tell him that I asked what is known about me and my organization,' said Leo Haddad. 'Tell him that I took you into the basement of the Lebanese Cultural Center and showed you a small cache of weapons: some rifles, a pistol, a rocket launcher. Tell him that you saw canisters of gas, and gas masks, armored vests, and balaclavas.'

'Do you have these things?'

'Some of them. Chad Armstrong will certainly suspect even more.'

'I didn't even know there was a basement at the cultural center.'

'There is not a basement. If they break in, it will be very frustrating for them.'

'Won't they know there's no basement? I could find that out at City Hall, and I wouldn't even have to work for Homeland Security.'

'Tell them it was dug by hand, without a permit. They will like that detail.'

Jason Walker shook his head in amazement.

'What else should I tell him?'

Leo Haddad smiled.

'That is all for now. We need to build our story slowly. To say too much more would be suspicious. And now, you must excuse me, but I am meeting a friend.'

They said goodbye. Jason Walker walked to the bus stop. Standing in a doorway, he eased the money out of his pocket and counted it. He was holding five hundred dollars in well-worn twenties.

The bus came and he got on.

He stepped out of the elevator car. Schatzi was woofing furiously. Even from around the corner he could hear the door booming like a drum as the dog threw herself against it. When he saw his door he stopped. Someone had written on it in black marker: *IF YOU DONT LIKE IT HERE THEN LEAVE!*

Schatzi threw herself against the door so hard that he expected the door to splinter and the dog to come tumbling out. He unlocked his own door and went inside.

One of his neighbors had recognized him.

He wadded a bunch of paper towels and wetted them at the faucet, then grabbed the bottle of dish soap. He squirted soap on the graffito and then rubbed it with the paper towels. The letters smeared a little and lightened almost imperceptibly. He tried again with almost no improvement.

In his bathroom he soaked a sponge and took the scouring powder from under the sink. That combination worked much better. When he was done, the white paint was worn through to a pale blue coat underneath it, but it was almost impossible to read what had been written there. He closed the door and locked it. Schatzi was still trying to break down the door.

There were two messages on his voicemail. One was from Gina Saraceno, sounding subdued, saying she just wanted to talk. One contained just a few seconds of static before the hang-up. He wished that he had bothered to buy a phone with caller ID.

He pressed *69 to call back the caller. The line rang.

After the tenth ring it went silent. He couldn't imagine an explanation for that.

He called Gina Saraceno.

'Hi.'

'Hi.'

'It's late.'

'Sorry.'

'Where were you?'

'Out walking.'

'You do that a lot, don't you?'

'There's a lot to think about.'

'Listen, I don't feel like being alone,' she said. 'Do you?'

'No,' he admitted.

But he didn't feel like a long trip by train and bus. She may have heard it in his voice.

'I'll come to you,' she said. 'We can go out for a drink and go back to your place.'

He suddenly noticed the newspaper lying folded on his table. He must have carried it in that morning and set it down without even thinking about it. On the front page, in the lower right-hand corner, the headline read:

LIBBY CONDEMNS TREATMENT OF PROTESTERS

Self-declared presidential candidate George Libby condemned in 'the strongest possible terms' the arrests of eight protesters outside the Sidewalk Studio of ABC-7 TV Chicago yesterday. Speaking from what he called a 'campaign stop' in Albuquerque, New Mexico, Libby referred to the group as 'campaign workers' and said that they were 'exercising their rights and duties as American citizens'. Dubbed the 'State Street Eight' by a rival newspaper, the group's protest turned suddenly violent and required six uniformed police patrol officers to restore peace.

'Jason? Are you there?'

'Yes, sorry. There's an article in the paper. I just saw it.'

'I know. If you read to the end you'll learn that one of

the construction workers was hospitalized and that one of the quote-unquote protesters was the aggressor.'

'This is unbelievable.'

'Look, do you want me to come or not?'

'Come.'

'See you in half an hour.'

Gina Saraceno buzzed up from the lobby and he went down and got in her car. They drove to the nearby neighborhood of Andersonville and, after a fifteen-minute search, found a legal parking spot.

'I don't want to give them any more ammo,' she said. 'I can see the headline now: "Militant Libby Activist Steals Handicapped Parking Space from Quadruple-Amputee War Veteran."'

On the way he had told her about his graffitoed door. She wasn't impressed. Someone had thrown tomatoes at her house.

'Canned tomatoes,' she added. 'They broke my mom's window. Fortunately for me, she's a good commie and replaced the glass with a sign that says "I Support the Commander-in-Thief."'

They walked down a dark sidewalk between sturdy tree trunks and brick two-flats. Cicadas cycled through their metallic robot whine. Air conditioners whirred. Alcohol-emboldened voices poured out of a window. A party. It was humid, but the warmth was leaving the air. Summer was almost over.

They poked their heads inside the Hopleaf, but even standing room was in short supply. The situation was the same at Simon's Tavern. They gave up and turned into Charlie's Ale House, an over-proportioned pub that had sprung up several years ago to cash in on the neighborhood's growing popularity. Large television screens showed the wrap-ups of the day's sporting events: baseball, tennis, and golf.

Young men and women drank flavored martinis and picked at mountains of nachos and buffalo wings. The stereo played a song from the 1960s that had once been an anthem of protest but had more recently been used to sell cars. A hostess in a tight, midriff-baring top took them with a gleaming smile to their seats. She assured them that a waitress would come to their table as soon as was humanly possible.

The menus were thick and heavy as wooden tablets. They flipped the pages, whose corners were crimped with gold foil, scanning them without appetite.

'Forget the food,' said Gina Saraceno. 'I'm drinking.'

At a nearby table three men were laughing boisterously. Then one of the men rose from his stool and turned toward them, heading for the toilets.

It was Chad Armstrong.

Jason Walker saw him first. As the agent neared the table his laughing face recomposed itself, as if it were taking him some time to recognize Jason Walker. His face froze in a lopsided grin.

Quickly, Jason Walker averted his gaze. He thought that it would be best to pretend not to know Chad Armstrong. But Gina Saraceno had noticed his quick glance away. Her eyes moved from Jason Walker's face to Chad Armstrong, who was now passing their table.

Chad Armstrong was either keenly aware of the subtle glances that had just been exchanged by the couple or he was drunk. He stopped.

'Jason!' he said.

He put his hand out. When Jason Walker took it, he was pulled in for a half-hug and a manly thump on the back.

'How's it going?'

Chad Armstrong was smiling broadly. He did look drunk. His eyes flashed.

'Good,' said Jason Walker. 'Good to see you.'

'Aren't you going to introduce me to your special lady?'

Gina Saraceno shot him a curious look.

'This is my girlfriend, Gina. Gina, this is—'

This was who? Chad Armstrong? Joe Smith? John Doe? The government agent smiled broadly and put out his hand.

'Chad Armstrong. Great to meet you.'

'Nice to meet you,' said Gina Saraceno.

'I didn't get your last name?'

'Saraceno.'

'Wow! Cool name. Italian?'

'So how do you two know each other?'

Gina Saraceno was looking at Jason Walker, but Chad Armstrong answered.

'Actually, I'm a friend of Jason's from college. I feel terrible running into you like this, Jason. I would have called to let you know I was coming to town, but I'm only here for two nights, and I didn't even think I'd have a chance to get out.'

'That's all right,' said Jason Walker.

'What do you do?' asked Gina Saraceno.

'I'm the editor of *Philadelphia Magazine*.'

Gina Saraceno brightened.

'You're the one who gave Jason that big assignment, to write about the Liberty Bell.'

Chad Armstrong smiled even more broadly.

'That's me.'

'So when is it going to run?'

'It's hard to say. We commission a lot of things in advance because of our schedule, but we have to allow room for breaking news and stuff like that.'

'Well, it sounds as if this is news. If you wait much longer, the story might be over.'

Chad Armstrong turned to Jason Walker.

'Are you sure she's your girlfriend? She sounds more like your agent.'

'I just hope you don't kill it,' said Gina Saraceno.

'I can't even imagine we'd kill anything of Jason's. Listen, I'd love to stay and buy you guys a drink, but I was actually on my way out. Those guys I'm with are—' he hesitated for what seemed to Jason Walker like an endless moment '— reporters, a couple of reporters I'm kind of having a get-to-know-you session with. Kind of informal job interviews. I told them to take me to some "real Chicago" places to see if they know their stuff.'

Gina Saraceno looked around at the oversized in-authenticity surrounding them.

'Don't hire them,' she said.

Chad Armstrong looked confused.

'Well, we'll see.'

'Why don't you hire Jason?'

'I tried to hire Jason, but he didn't want to move. Something about a special lady. At least that's what he called her.'

Gina Saraceno gave Jason Walker an incredulous stare.

Chad Armstrong winked.

'Sorry, Jason. Gotta run.' He walked double-time toward the toilets.

'"Special lady?"'

'That's just a Chad thing. From college. You know I'd never . . . "honey", maybe. But "special lady?" Never.'

A waitress came to their table. She took their orders and then gathered up the menus that covered the tabletop.

As she walked away, Gina Saraceno looked at Jason Walker and shook her head.

'I just don't see you guys hanging out. That guy's so smarmy.'

Chad Armstrong had come out of the toilets and was walking by their table. He turned and gave them an on-the-fly wave and smile.

When he turned away again Gina Saraceno covered her mouth.

'I can't believe I said that right when he was walking by.'

'I'm sure he didn't hear you.'

Chad Armstrong said something to his companions. They nodded. One at a time, they stole glances at Jason Walker and Gina Saraceno. Then they rose, left some bills on the table, and followed Chad Armstrong out the front door.

Jason Walker wondered who they were. They weren't informants—they didn't look browbeaten. Maybe they were Homeland Security agents, too. The three of them together looked like software salesmen or car-rental agents.

At the door, Chad Armstrong gave one last wave and then he was gone.

'So what was he like in college?'

'I'm not sure. Different, I guess.'

'What did the two of you do together?'

'You know, the usual stuff guys in college do.'

The noise of the room seemed suddenly deafening. The lights burned painfully bright. He excused himself and left the table. Shaking his head to clear it, he stumbled against a chair and found himself apologizing to an angry, thin-faced blonde. Finally he reached the toilet. Mercifully, it was empty.

Steadying himself against the sink, he stared at his own reflection. It was like looking at a stranger. Did he look Lebanese? Maybe his skin was darker than he'd always thought.

He splashed water on his face and ratcheted paper towels out of the dispenser. He held them against his skin, breathing deeply. He had to tell Gina Saraceno what was happening. But it was harder now. She would want to know why he had lied for so long, why he hadn't trusted her sooner. And she was different from him. She would want him to do something. The 'right' thing. If he knew what that was, he might do it. She would think the right thing was to put his ordeal down in writing and send it to the newspapers. Or to tell his congressman. She would laugh at Chad Armstrong's threat to send him to Lebanon.

The paper towels smelled vaguely fishy, like lake water. He crumpled them and threw them in the trash. He wasn't ready to go back outside yet. He unzipped his pants and stood in front of a urinal, an excuse to stand there if someone came in. There was a chalkboard screwed to the wall over the urinals. Patrons could write graffiti without marring the carefully rusticated walls.

There was something written there already.

Beirut, Lebanon, it said. *Paradise on earth.*

His stomach lurched and he vomited into the urinal.

The next ninety minutes were agony. He felt as if he had the flu. And Gina Saraceno knew something was wrong, he could tell. But he did his best to smile and laugh and drank two drinks while he waited for her to say she was ready to call it a night. At long last, she did.

They went back to his apartment. Schatzi was silent, a sign that his neighbor was home for the night. While Gina Saraceno brushed her teeth and put on her pajamas—they each had a drawer in each other's dresser—he guzzled a whiskey, an antacid, and then another whiskey. She asked if they could trade backrubs. She looked beautiful in her pink satin shorts and top, her face scrubbed and her hair brushed and pulled back in a stretchy band. She was even wearing the pink fluffy slippers he'd gotten her as a joke but that had surprisingly turned into her favorites. He wanted nothing more than to burrow into the mattress and feel her fingertips kneading his spine until he fell asleep.

Instead he told her that he was feeling feverish and needed to sleep alone on the couch. He had no idea whether she believed him.

The next day dawned dark and never got lighter. Clouds hung low and black and rain fell in a fine drizzle. He woke to the sound of Gina Saraceno singing a sad song in the kitchen as she made coffee and toast. He stared out at the sky until the coffee was ready, then went into the kitchen and poured himself a cup. The radio was on low, the news no more than a mumble. His eyes were scratchy and his head felt packed with wool.

The newspaper thumped against his door and Schatzi gave a few half-hearted barks before Richard Zim quieted her. Jason Walker opened the front door and retrieved the paper, checking the door's exterior for fresh writing as he did so. But there was nothing.

He sat down at the table and unfolded the newspaper. On the lower right-hand corner of the front page, the headline read: *LIBBY COMING TO CHICAGO.*

Sixteen

Before leaving for work, Gina Saraceno called Scott Fink. As she suspected, there would be a meeting that night to discuss George Libby's impending arrival. The newspaper had reported:

> *One day after a Chicago protest in his name turned violent, Libby announced that he will visit the city to meet with supporters and foes alike. 'I have complete faith in the men and women of my campaign organization,' he told reporters, 'just as I have faith in the men and women of law enforcement. I want to hear what everyone has to say. Hopefully, we can clear the air.'*

'I know he has to talk like that,' said Gina Saraceno, 'but it kind of bugs me. He's coming down hard on the war on terror, so why can't he come down hard on the cops?'

'Maybe he will,' said Jason Walker. 'After he talks to you guys.'

'Talks to *us*. He's going to have to meet with all of us, even the reluctant recruits like you.'

After she left he watched television, hoping to learn more about George Libby's forthcoming trip. The article hadn't said when he was coming. The candidate himself had said only that he was 'reviewing his schedule' and that he planned to come 'as soon as possible.'

On a headline news channel he saw a thirty-second clip that showed George Libby saying the same things he'd been quoted as saying in the newspaper. On camera, George Libby was even more unprepossessing than he had been in his photo on the cover of *Mother Jones*. Physically, he looked less like a furniture-company CEO and more like a furniture salesman. When he spoke, though, he looked his questioners in the eye and answered them directly. His voice was clear and strong.

The next headline snippet arrived on the screen with the noise of a landing fighter jet. In downstate Illinois, a small boy was trapped in a well, prompting an outpouring of community support. Jason Walker turned the television off.

Chad Armstrong's threat the night before had been frightening. His behavior had been infuriating. The performance he'd put on for Gina Saraceno—his brazen lies, his cocky insinuations—all indicated he believed that Jason Walker's life was merely a game. He wondered if what Leo Haddad had said was true; that no promises would be kept. He wondered if, knowing what he knew, he was more likely to end up in Guantanamo than he was to be left alone when it all was over.

And when would it all be over? How would he know?

He dialed the Acme Messenger Service. He heard the woman's recorded voice. He left a message saying that he needed to meet with Chad Armstrong. The return call came fifteen minutes later. The caller sounded like the same woman who had recorded the outgoing message.

'Lincoln Park, between Montrose and Wilson, east of Lake Shore Drive. On top of the hill,' she said. 'Eight o'clock tonight. Do you understand?'

It took him a moment to process the directions. The meeting place was less than half a mile from his building.

'Do you understand?'

The woman on the phone sounded as if she was tired of repeating herself to people who didn't understand.

'Yes, I understand.'

She hung up.

He took the cell phone that Leo Haddad had given him and went outside the building. The drizzle was so fine and so slow that it felt as if the tiny droplets were suspended in the air and he was walking into them. It was just cool enough to feel clammy. He wished he had thought to bring an umbrella.

He went across the street into the park and then into the field house. In the gym, a half-dozen middle-aged black men were playing a game of basketball. He climbed on to the bleachers to watch. Besides the basketball players, he was the only one in the gym. Their shouts and the squeaks from their shoes made enough noise to cover his conversation. He didn't want to call from his apartment for fear that the rooms, not just the phone, were bugged. And he didn't want to call from the sidewalk in case a surveillance van was parked down the street.

He turned on the phone and found Leo Haddad's number in the call register. He pressed call.

'Hello, how are you?' said Leo Haddad.

'Fine, thanks.'

He guessed that Leo Haddad didn't want to use their names while they talked.

'Do you have news for me?'

'Yes. I'm meeting our mutual friend tonight at eight o'clock. Between Montrose and Wilson in the park. On the hill.'

'I do not know that place, but I am sure I can find it. If you do not see me, do not worry.'

'I won't.'

'Goodbye, then.'

'Goodbye.'

They clicked off. He climbed down from the bleachers and pushed through the gym's back doors into the parking lot. The mist made him feel as if he was covered in sweat. Hunching his shoulders, he walked east, toward the lake.

The timing would be tricky. The meeting at Scott Fink's house was at seven. Even if he caught a cab right away, it would take him at least half an hour to make it to the meeting with Chad Armstrong. It would be best to skip the meeting entirely, but that could make Gina Saraceno even more suspicious. And he couldn't use work as an excuse. He had to think of a way to get away quickly.

The clouds lowered. He kept walking.

Scott Fink looked happy and energetic, not at all like a man who'd taken a blow to the head and been thrown in jail for his trouble. His small living room was full: Mike, Demeter, Cornelius, and Dorothy were all there, as were a few others. Amber and Jarrod had returned. And there were three new faces: Parminder, a student; Roy, a cook at a vegetarian cafe; and Manny, a therapist. The bad publicity hadn't scared everyone off. A few minutes after the hour, the intercom buzzed again and Eric limped up the stairs.

His appearance caused a commotion. Pale and still visibly bruised, he was offered the most comfortable chair, then given a footrest once he had lowered himself into it. He was offered a drink, an aspirin, a plate of hot food.

Eric seemed embarrassed by the attention and insisted that the meeting start. Jason Walker glanced at his watch. He had ten minutes before he had to go. He leaned close to Gina Saraceno's ear.

'I think I'm getting sick,' he said.

Her look told him that it was bad timing to be sick just then.

'I'll give it a few more minutes,' he said, 'but I may have to go. I feel nauseated.'

'Jason,' she whispered, 'I'm sorry you don't feel well, but I don't want to leave.'

'It's all right. I'll take a cab.'

'That's going to cost like fifty bucks to your place.'

She seemed to be reconsidering.

'I know this meeting is important,' he said. 'I don't want you to miss it. Let's just see. Maybe my stomach will calm down.'

Scott Fink started the meeting.

'A lot has happened and there's a lot to talk about, but obviously we're all here tonight because of one piece of news: George Libby is coming to Chicago. This afternoon I spoke with his national coordinator and confirmed this. They haven't told the papers yet, but they're planning to be here three days from now. Libby's going to meet with us and the police, and he's going to have a press conference and a town hall meeting.'

Scott Fink laughed.

'He'll probably eat at some local restaurants and kiss

some babies, too, because he is a presidential candidate, after all.'

This prompted cheers and chants of 'Libby, Libby!' It was as if the fear and trauma of the attack had combined with excitement at Libby's coming to produce an adrenaline rush.

He had to go. He whispered in Gina Saraceno's ear and then made his apologies to Scott Fink and the group. He tried to look sick. His girlfriend seemed anxious for the meeting to continue.

He left the building and jogged to the nearest busy street. Even then it took ten minutes to find a cab. While the cab driver motored up Lake Shore Drive at an unhurried pace, he realized that the windshield wipers weren't going. The rain had finally stopped.

It was fifteen minutes after eight when he reached the park. It was crowded. On the brightly lit soccer field, two teams of men—Mexicans, he thought—played a heated game. They wore bright, silky uniforms with patches from local sponsors sewn on. On the sidelines were their families, men, women, and children, plus ice-cream vendors, hecklers, and curious passersby. Children played their own games with small balls under gnarled trees, and substitutes warmed up by jogging double-time with their knees high in the air.

Children played on the slopes of the big hill, too, but someone stood alone on top.

Chad Armstrong.

He started to climb up.

It was dusk. The clouds had parted overhead, leaving the sky a deep, cobalt blue. Over the lake the retreating clouds were black and lit by intermittent flashes of lightning. The rumble of thunder could just be heard over the shouts and cheers of the game.

Chad Armstrong was wearing a black, belted overcoat. The wind tousled his normally spiky, gelled hair. Standing against the stormy sky he looked like a character in a movie.

Jason Walker was panting just a little as he reached the top.

'I have to tell you, this is a bummer,' said Chad Armstrong. 'I like to meet my informants up here sometimes because it's so spooky and dramatic. You know, two guys alone on a hill with night falling. It has a way of making people wonder what I'm thinking, whether anything bad's about to go down.'

He waved his arm dismissively at the soccer game below.

'And then look at this. A soccer game. Little kids, ice cream, and everything. It kind of steals my thunder.'

In the distance, thunder boomed.

Chad Armstrong giggled. 'Now that's just stupid.'

'He did what you said he would,' said Jason Walker. 'He said he knows that I'm working for you, but that I should help him instead.'

The other man seemed suddenly very focused.

'He did?'

Jason Walker nodded.

'How did it go down?'

Jason Walker told him, an abbreviated version. He left out the more honest-seeming things that Leo Haddad had said. He also left out his own agreement to pass false information to Chad Armstrong.

'So you agreed?'

'Yes.'

'You think he bought it?'

'I think so.'

'Did he want information from you? Of course he did. What'd he want?'

'I told him I didn't know much, that you were very secretive. He wanted a picture of you. I told him I had no idea how to get one.'

Chad Armstrong scanned the park. Jason Walker felt a chill of fear, as if the agent knew what he was thinking.

'Did he show you anything? Did he take you into his confidence?'

'He took me into the basement of the cultural center. There was a trap door. He showed me some guns and a rocket launcher. They had gas, too, and gas masks and other things.'

'The basement?'

'It was more like a hole. Something they dug themselves. We climbed down a ladder.'

'How big was it?'

'About ten feet square, barely deep enough to stand up in.'

'What about this trap door? Where is it?'

'It's in the director's office. Ahmad Saad's office.'

'Where specifically?'

'It's . . . under the desk. He had to push the desk out of the way to open the trap door.'

'Who did? Ahmad Saad?'

'No, Leo Haddad.'

'Was there anyone else there with you?'

'No.'

Finally, Chad Armstrong quizzed him about the weapons. Jason Walker hoped he remembered what Leo Haddad had told him.

The questioning went on for five or ten minutes. Having been interrogated several times before, he was better prepared. He realized now that it was best to invent as few details as possible, to answer the question asked and no more. And when he did have to make something up, it was very important to remember what he had said.

But there was one question he was completely unprepared for.

'What did he say he wants?'

'Leo Haddad?'

'Terrorists want something. They want Israel out of the West Bank, they want America to stop bombing Venezuela, they want us to stop killing them so they can do a better job killing each other, like in Baghdad.'

'I thought you knew.'

'I don't. Enlighten me.'

Jason Walker didn't know what to say.

'I mean, if he recruited you, he must have told you what he wants, right? What his group is fighting for.'

'But if you don't know, how do you know he's dangerous?'

'I said we were pretty sure the group was planning some-thing big. I didn't say we knew why they were doing it. So why are they doing it?'

'He didn't say he was planning anything. He said that he wanted to protect people from fascism. He called himself a patriot.'

'A patriot?' Chad Armstrong snorted. 'Well, don't feel bad if he didn't show you the bombs. These guys aren't stupid. They're not going to take a new recruit into their confidence. It's totally possible that he's just playing the game, pretending to bring you on board, hoping you'll have some information. That doesn't make you feel bad, does it?'

'No.'

'You wouldn't expect him to drive you out to wherever and show you the storage unit where they're keeping the fertilizer.'

Below them, a brother and sister ran hard and joyfully, playing tag on the steep slope of the hill. First the girl slipped and fell, then the boy did. They sprang to their feet laughing, their cheeks flushed and their eyes bright and shining.

'Look, I know Leo Haddad is really charismatic,' said Chad Armstrong. 'And I can be kind of a dick. But you have to remember that this isn't some spy novel you read when you were thirteen. We're watching him for one reason: because we believe he has the ability and the intent to harm American civilians. Because we believe that he wants to bomb a building. Soon. And that's why we can't screw around. You're doing good work, but I'm worried about the timing. If Haddad doesn't give up some good information soon, we're going to have to bring him in and do it the old-fashioned way.'

'Do you mean taking him to Egypt?'

Chad Armstrong grinned.

'Egypt? Egypt is for pussies. No offense.'

It was dark. What few stars there were in the Chicago sky twinkled in the smoggy firmament. What grass there was on the soccer field glowed green under the lights. Midfield and the penalty areas were nothing but brown dirt.

The agent took two steps and stopped.

'I saw you on TV, by the way. I don't know what you

see in Libby. He's unelectable. People are afraid. And when they're afraid, they won't retreat. Are you still taking notes?'

'Yes.'

'Good boy. We'll talk about those soon. Go see Haddad tomorrow, maybe the day after tomorrow, too. Keep in touch. If he doesn't spill anything, we're going to change our approach.'

'If you're so sure he's going to bomb a building, why don't you take him in now?'

'If we move now, we might catch one or two terrorists. If we wait longer, we might catch a whole rats' nest. Of course, if we wait too long, kaboom.'

Chad Armstrong turned and walked down the north side of the hill. He followed a curving path under some trees, then disappeared when the path went under an overpass.

Jason Walker turned and watched the game. To the south, the skyscrapers of downtown Chicago pricked the sky. The John Hancock Center had always been a favorite of his, and he was not alone. Chicagoans loved its graceful muscularity, the way it tapered as it rose to its squared-off top. Called 'Big John,' the black steel skyscraper was ornamented only with criss-crossing braces that formed gigantic Xs.

Above him, airplanes descended in parallel lines toward O'Hare. He imagined watching one veer left, dropping at terrible speed until it disappeared into the side of the Hancock in a thin burst of explosions. He didn't have to imagine the rest. He had seen all that before.

Shaken, he started down the hill. The vision was wrong, he knew. Chad Armstrong had said nothing about a plane. But what if he was wrong about Leo Haddad? He hadn't seen proof of anything.

He walked north, following the path that Chad Armstrong had taken. It would lead him home eventually. He passed under the dark underpass and felt a momentary fear. Dark and dripping, it was an ideal spot for a mugger to wait. Something had seeped through the stone and concrete over the years, forming hundreds of tiny, milky stalactites.

Coming out the other side, the path swung east toward the lake, skirting a parking lot. After about thirty yards he saw a car idling with its lights off. The car was blue and its motor stuttered. In the cab, a red dot glowed hotter and then dimmed. The driver was smoking.

Cautiously, he walked closer. He could barely make out the driver's features. But he knew it was Leo Haddad.

'Nice work,' said Leo Haddad. 'I saw him. First on the hill and then, fortunately, he walked right past my car. This guy is very high-up. It's worrisome, but knowledge is power, right?'

'What are you planning?'

'We are planning to defend ourselves if necessary. Did Chad Armstrong warn you about something specific? Of course he did. Probably he told you that we are planning to bomb a school bus.'

'A building. A skyscraper.'

Leo Haddad exhaled smoke. He put his cigarette out in the car's ashtray, then slid the ashtray closed.

'If you don't want to hurt anyone, why are they after you?' asked Jason Walker.

'Jason, to this government, ideas are more explosive than bombs,' said Leo Haddad. 'Listen: we will fight. We have guns. We will be a resistance. It is my sincerest hope that that day does not come to pass, but I fear it will. We may be past the tipping point.'

Leo Haddad climbed out of his car. He closed the door to shut off the dome light.

'I know that you are not sure who to trust. But you have thrown your lot in with us, and so you are in danger, too. More danger than you were in before. Things may happen quickly. If anything should go wrong, if they come for you, and you can escape, go to the Greyhound bus station in Gary, Indiana. Make certain you are not followed. We will look for you there.'

Leo Haddad held out his hand.

'Be careful.'

Jason Walker took the man's hand and shook it. He only hoped he knew how to be careful.

Seventeen

When he got home he checked his messages. The first one was from David Darling, trying too hard to be cheerful.

'Jason, David. David, Jason. Nice to meet you again. Hey, I feel kind of weird about the thing the other day. I wasn't really up for joining your group, but I thought I'd stop by anyway to say hey. But then I got a little weirded out by everything. Cops, TV cameras—not really my scene. Anyway, I watched a lot of the stuff on TV. Pretty . . . freaky. I'm sorry I didn't call sooner. I hope you're OK. Hell, I hope you're out of jail! I assume you are because I was waiting for you to make your one phone call and borrow some bail money but you never called. Uh, at any rate, before your robot butler cuts me off in mid-sentence, do you want to go to a Cubs game tomorrow night? Seeing as how they just edged out Pittsburgh for the worst-record-in-baseball honors, I was able to get a couple of really great tickets for practically—'

The sixty-second time limit cut him off. The second message was from Gina Saraceno. She sounded distant.

'Well, I'm calling to see how your tummy is doing, but either you're not answering your phone or this is another one of your mysterious absences. I'd be tempted to think that you're one of those charming serial killers I've heard about—you know, the well-scrubbed boy next door—except you're not all that charming. Hope you're OK. Call me.'

He punched the buttons quickly and misdialed. He got it right the second time. The call went to her voicemail. He hung up.

He went outside and got a cab. He gave the driver Gina Saraceno's address.

The cab let him off directly in front of her building. His two cab rides that night had cost him a small fortune—close to a hundred dollars.

Gina Saraceno's front door, painted bright yellow, was recessed under her mother's porch in a shady, plant-lined nook. He went down the narrow concrete steps and rapped on the door. He heard steps approaching inside, then watched the tiny gleam in the peephole wink out for a moment.

The door opened. She was wearing sweatpants that had been cut to make shorts and a University of Illinois T-shirt.

'You made a quick recovery,' she said.

'I don't want you to be mad at me.'

She sighed, turned around, and walked back into her living room. He followed her, shutting the door after himself.

'I thought I knew you,' she said. 'I thought you were a sweet, uncomplicated guy. But there's something going on. You're never at home when I call, you're making weird excuses for things, and then there's your weird friend the other night.'

'Chad? What about him?'

She laughed. It sounded more like a sob. She threw her arms up in the air.

'I don't know what's wrong with me. I checked up on you.'

She picked up a magazine from her table. She held it out for him to see. It was *Philadelphia Magazine*.

'Where did you get that?' he asked.

'Borders. Does it matter?'

'Were you looking for my article?'

'No. You told me it hadn't come out yet, and I believed you. But there was something creepy about that guy, so I was looking for him on the masthead. And he's not there. Anywhere. He's not on their website, either. But it doesn't make sense. They paid you for an article. Who is he, Jason?'

She was still holding out the magazine. He took it and opened it to the masthead. There were dozens of names, from editor-in-chief and publisher to editorial assistant and circulation manager.

He couldn't tell her. He had to protect her. He had to protect their relationship.

'Jesus Christ, Gina!' he shouted.

She looked shocked.

'I don't know why he's not on the masthead. All I know is that he called me and gave me an assignment and I did it and they paid me for it. I met with him in his office. Maybe he uses a different name for professional purposes, I don't know.'

'Jason—'

'And as for everything else, I don't know what to tell you. I'm not avoiding you. Sometimes I leave the house, it's true. Do you want me to sit by the phone for you?'

He saw uncertainty in her eyes. He thought she was thinking that she'd read everything wrong, that she'd pushed too hard. Embarrassment and contrition were welling up in her. Hating himself, he turned the screws one last time.

'Are you looking for a way out of our relationship?'

'No!' she said. She grabbed a tissue and blotted the corners of her eyes. 'Wow. I've never seen you like this.'

He glared at her.

'I feel really stupid,' she said. 'Can we start over? Like a month ago?'

'I'm tired of feeling like you think I'm a liar,' he said.

'I think I'm stressed,' she said. 'That's definitely it. Stress. Look, I'm going to apologize: I'm sorry. I'm really, really sorry.'

He didn't say anything.

She forced a smile.

'I have a good idea: let's cook.'

She opened a bottle of wine and poured two glasses. She turned on the light in her tiny kitchen and took vegetables out of baskets and the refrigerator. She looked at him, standing still in the living room, his heart breaking.

'Please,' she said.

He went to her. She gave him a knife. He kissed her,

then began cutting the things she told him to. In near-silence they prepared a simple pasta fresca, then sat down at the table.

Gina Saraceno poured more wine.

'I'm just so pissed off,' she said. 'I can't believe what they did to us. You know, I've always been very opinionated about everything, but politics has always seemed like kind of a game to me. Sometimes your guy wins, sometimes theirs does, a lot of what all of them do is silly and a waste of time. I understand now how people are radicalized.'

Jason Walker said that he did, too.

After dinner they left the dishes on the table and went straight to the bedroom. For a long time they kissed deeply, standing up, their greedy hands racing over each other's body and clothes. When they made love it was with urgent intensity. Gina Saraceno cried a little, locking her arms behind his back and pulling him to her chest so tightly that it was hard to breathe.

Afterward, she apologized again.

'I guess I feel like so many things are spiraling out of control, maybe I wanted to control you,' she said. 'Do you forgive me?'

Jason Walker said that of course he did.

The next morning he called David Darling and said that he would like to go to the Cubs game. His friend seemed relieved. It was an afternoon game, he said, so he could take off work.

The sky was blue and sunny and the air was cool and dry. The stadium was only half full. Even the most ardent fantasists had now conceded that the Cubs would once again fail to play in the postseason. And even though the Cubs opened the game by taking a two-run lead, the atmosphere was subdued. Chicago's summers were so short that many Chicagoans began mourning even before the leaves turned brown.

He had thought that David Darling would talk more about

'the thing the other day,' but his friend didn't expand upon his halting apology of the previous night. Instead he talked about the Cubs' need for starting pitching; the need for a left-fielder who could hit for power; and the rookie second-baseman's mental lapses. He shared his relief that many of the women in the stands had not opted to cover their tank-tops with windbreakers.

Jason Walker didn't mind. He was just grateful for a few hours where he knew the score and the rules of the game.

In the bottom of the seventh inning, the Cubs' star first baseman fouled a ball straight back into the stands. It struck the press box above them, rebounded, and seemed to hang in the air for a moment before it fell toward the seats just behind them.

Five men all went for the ball at once, one of them leaping across the lap of his startled wife. Another, lunging forward, tripped and landed hard across several rows of plastic seat backs. As the men tried for the ball, the women and children got out of their way. Suddenly it was down to two men, each with a hand on the ball. One of them was off-balance and fell. The man with the ball jumped up, triumphant, showing his souvenir to the whole stadium. The other man slumped to a sitting position, holding his wrist and grimacing. The second man was later helped off by an usher, his wrist already starting to swell.

'Now, if we saw that kind of effort on the field,' said David Darling, 'we'd be in first place.'

After the game Jason Walker called Gina Saraceno and told her in an offhand fashion that he was going to see a movie that night. Then he read several reviews so he would be able to discuss it intelligently if she asked his opinion. Given enough time, he thought, he might become a competent liar.

He called Leo Haddad on the cell phone and asked if they could meet. Leo Haddad agreed and gave him the address of a coffee shop close to the Lebanese Cultural Center. When he arrived, Leo Haddad was drinking a tall confection topped with whipped cream and cocoa powder.

'Now you know that I am not an extremist,' he said. 'Surely there is a fatwa against such Western decadence.'

'Is it good?' asked Jason Walker.

'It is not bad. It tastes something like a milkshake.'

'I have to ask you something.'

'Very good. I have something to ask of you, as well.'

'I want to help you, but I need you to give me some proof that you're not really a terrorist.'

Leo Haddad pushed his drink aside. 'This is troubling you.'

'Yes.'

'Let us walk while I try to answer your question.'

They left the coffee shop and walked down a residential street into the neighborhood. It was very quiet. Air conditioners had been turned off, perhaps for the rest of the season. When a jet overhead broke the silence, its contrails burning in the setting sun, it sounded impossibly loud.

They looked into front rooms lit with televisions' electronic fire.

'Are you capable of an act of violence? Could you kill a man?' asked Leo Haddad.

'I don't think so.'

'You doubt it.'

'Yes.'

'But you could not say with certainty.'

'Well, in self-defense, that's different. I mean, if it's my life or some other guy's, I guess I could probably do it as a last resort. I can say with absolute certainty that I would never hurt innocent people.'

'Do you think that self-defense is always a matter of a man holding a knife to your throat? Do you always know who is innocent and who is guilty?'

'No, but those are two different—'

Leo Haddad opened his palms.

'I am not trying to use logic to defend violent acts. I ask you merely to consider that we do not always know what we are capable of, just as we do not always know what threats we will face or how we will attempt to combat those threats. For myself, I hope to never take another man's life, or a woman's, or a child's. But to give you my word would be to lie to you.'

He turned into an alley.

'We are almost there.'

Jason Walker followed Leo Haddad down an alley, across a street, and into another alley. They came to the back of a restaurant. He smelled good food and heard voices in the kitchen. They climbed wooden stairs to the second floor. The door was fitted with a push-button combination lock. Leo Haddad entered a four-digit code and opened the door.

'I cannot promise you what will happen in the future,' he said, 'but to earn your trust, I will keep no secrets.'

They went into the apartment, through a kitchen and down a hall. Off the hall was the room where Jason Walker had been brought the night Leo Haddad and his men abducted him. They went into another room, another bedroom with a bare mattress. Leo Haddad opened the closet. It was very shallow and appeared to have been freshly painted. He pulled out the shelves and leaned them against the wall. There was a keyhole where the middle shelf had been. He took a key from his pocket and turned it in the lock. The back of the closet opened like a door.

Leo Haddad stepped out of the way.

'So you can see,' he said. 'Here is our armory.'

There were several hunting rifles, a half-dozen pistols, perhaps twenty boxes of various sizes of ammunition. There were black gloves and balaclavas and military surplus gas masks hanging on hooks. There was a box of hand grenades.

'Most of those make smoke,' said Leo Haddad. 'But one or two of them make proper explosions.'

He picked up a binder and handed it to Jason Walker.

'This is why we are preparing.'

The binder was full of newspaper articles, the majority of them from the *Chicago Clarion*, but many torn from other newspapers as well, all of them taped to white pieces of paper. The articles started several years earlier and detailed a steady erosion of civil liberties: suspected terrorists named 'enemy combatants'; enemy combatants tried without the protection of U.S. law; changing precedents in U.S. law; the president's declaration of martial law.

There were fewer articles from the present year.

'The newspapers do not report as much as they once did,' said Leo Haddad, reading the look on his face.

'Newspaper articles and guns. It doesn't add up.'

'It is all I can show you. You wish to see what is in my heart. How can I show you that?'

Jason Walker closed the notebook. If Leo Haddad and his men were truly terrorists bent on striking against innocent Chicagoans, the articles made an odd rationale. The persecuted people in the articles included Muslims and other people of Middle Eastern descent, but they also included university professors, environmental activists, and Quakers. Guns or no, it was hardly a portrait of a death-to-America jihadist group.

'I have shown you everything,' said Leo Haddad. 'What do you decide?'

Even with the weapons, there was no way this group could bring down a skyscraper. He tried to think what Gina Saraceno would tell him if he brought her into his confidence. *Trust your gut*, probably.

'OK,' he said.

'I am glad,' said Leo Haddad. 'I am also glad that you are not easily swayed. We need skeptics, men with critical minds.'

He took the notebook and put it back in the closet. He closed the door and began putting the shelves back in place.

'Jason, did you give Chad Armstrong the information we agreed upon?'

'Yes.'

'And he believed you, or appeared to believe you?'

'Yes.'

'I'm sure that he asked you many more questions as well. What you told him is not so far from the truth, as you have seen. If you want someone to believe your lie it must be believable. We will gradually begin to lead him astray with greater falsehood, while learning more about the way his people work. I hope to use this information in our own defense, and to aid other like-minded groups. But now I have something to ask of you. I want you to meet with Chad Armstrong again. And when he leaves I want you to follow him. We need to discover where he works.'

Giving Chad Armstrong false information was one thing, thought Jason Walker. Following him was another. He couldn't imagine doing it without being caught.

'But I don't have any idea how to follow someone. I don't even have a car.'

Leo Haddad nodded.

'It is a risk, but a risk worth taking. Chad Armstrong has met with you many times. He is likely to be complacent. You must try this for us. You will, won't you?'

He thought he would shake his head, but instead he found himself nodding yes.

Eighteen

When he got home that night, Jason Walker dialed the Acme Messenger Service and left a message requesting a meeting. Usually the callbacks were quick, within ten or fifteen minutes. After twenty minutes passed, he turned on the television. He flicked through the news channels looking for word of George Libby. Instead there was an update on the 'St. Louis Six,' as they were now being called. A trial date had not been set, but Homeland Security officials had called a press conference to announce new evidence in the case. Grainy security-camera footage showed three of the men riding the tram to the top of the arch. All three had cameras and were busily snapping photos.

'Although innocent enough on its own,' said the Homeland Security spokesman, 'this new piece of evidence fits with the others we've gathered to complete the puzzle, showing a picture of radicals who in cold blood were researching and planning the horrific destruction of American life and an American symbol. We salute the vigilance and the diligence of the field agents who were able to stop this heinous plot before it came to fruition.'

After an hour, the phone finally rang. He was almost asleep. The sleepy-sounding man told him to go to the public library at noon the following day. The fiction collection. Did he understand? Yes, he understood. The man hung up.

He fell asleep.

Even the main branch of the Chicago Public Library was not immune to the budget cuts that had pruned away at 'non-essential' city services. 'The country is on a war footing,' the president was fond of saying. 'We must be willing to make every sacrifice to vanquish our foes.' The hulking brick building, built in the postmodernist style that Jason Walker abhorred, had seen its staff cut, its hours reduced, and its light bulbs rationed. Librarians had not been allowed to purchase new books for two years. Occasionally, human-interest newspaper articles showed that librarians and other staff had responded to the purchasing freeze by donating their own books to the library. Invariably, the authors of these articles heralded the librarians' patriotic spirit. As he approached the building on foot, Jason Walker wondered if that was the librarians' sentiment or the newspaper editors'.

The Harold Washington Library Center, named for Chicago's first African-American mayor, was open from noon to 6 p.m. on Mondays, Tuesdays, Thursdays, and Fridays, and from ten to four on Saturdays. On Wednesdays and Sundays it was closed. As he muscled open the massive brass door and made his way inside, Jason Walker had the feeling that the library was still closed but someone had forgotten to lock up.

The ground-level lobby was dimly lit. A coffee shop had a metal gate drawn across the entrance with a sign reading *Closed Until Further Notice*. Another room, the 'Popular Library,' was closed without even that much information. The escalator leading to the stacks wasn't running, so he tramped up all three flights. On the third floor, out-of-order signs topped many of the computer terminals, and he could see only a few library workers staffing the check-in and check-out desks. Despite the fact that the library had only been open for a few minutes, several homeless men were already inside, reading out-of-date newspapers in the periodicals section.

He consulted a directory and began climbing escalators to the seventh floor. He wasn't sure whether the escalators were broken or simply turned off to save power. Every so often he found a flight of steps that was moving.

The fiction section covered nearly the whole floor. He wished the voice on the telephone had specified the letter of the alphabet where Chad Armstrong would be lurking. After a few minutes of fruitless loitering, he began a methodical search. He walked to the north corner of the east wall and began making his way south, carefully peering down every row. The floor was spookily empty.

He jumped. In a quiet alcove, the body of a man was slumped inside a carrel. Then he saw the man's chest rise and fall. His desert camouflage jacket and pungent body odor indicated that he was homeless. How had he arrived here and fallen asleep so soon? Or had he been overlooked and locked in to spend the night?

Collecting himself, Jason Walker resumed his slow search. He reached the southeast corner and started north again. Then he saw Chad Armstrong, halfway down a row of shelves, rubbing his eyes and paging through a book. His mouth was slightly open. He didn't see or hear Jason Walker.

The cocky young agent didn't look like someone who oversaw torture and interrogation in foreign lands. He looked like an ordinary man. A slightly hungover ordinary man.

Jason Walker slipped out of sight behind the end of the shelves. He didn't want to talk to Chad Armstrong. For a moment he didn't care whether or not Leo Haddad was who he said he was. He wanted to help Leo Haddad. He wanted to hurt Chad Armstrong.

Carefully, he crept into the next aisle and bent his knees until he could see Chad Armstrong through a gap in the shelving. The agent turned a page and read some more. Then his gaze drifted above the book and into space. He stayed like that for a few minutes, apparently daydreaming. Then he turned and walked away, dropping the book on the floor.

It was surprisingly easy to follow him. While Chad Armstrong marched up the middle aisle and then back down again, Jason Walker kept pace parallel to him, several steps behind and well out of sight. There were no patrons around for him to bump into, or who would stare at him and give him away.

After two back-and-forth marches, Chad Armstrong sighed in exasperation and slumped into a chair at a table covered with unshelved books. Jason Walker worked his way around the periphery of the floor and crept down the escalator to the sixth floor. He kept going all the way down to the first floor. The only way down from the third floor to the first was via the broken-down escalators or a single elevator car. Behind a dusty, half-stocked brochure spinner, he found a perfect vantage point to watch both.

Chad Armstrong's tenacity surprised him. The agent waited nearly an hour before he finally came clumping down the steps of the frozen escalator. Jason Walker had assumed that Chad Armstrong would have been more impatient. But this was his job, after all, and he would be obligated to assume that his informant's information was important.

Jason Walker wondered what Chad Armstrong was thinking now.

The spiked blond head didn't turn left toward the State Street doors. It turned right, down a hallway leading to the Van Buren doors. As soon as Chad Armstrong was out of sight, Jason Walker ran to the hallway and peered around the corner. He waited until Chad Armstrong had turned out of sight, then ran down the hallway to the end. He turned left and found himself at the Van Buren doors. He opened one and peered out, then stepped out on to the sidewalk.

Chad Armstrong was gone.

He looked left and right frantically. He ran to the El platform stairs and looked up them. He backed up and tried to see on to the platform, but his view was blocked.

Stupid, he thought, worrying about whether to chase him on foot or in a car.

There was a car parked on the south side of the library, provided for him by Leo Haddad. Unless Chad Armstrong suddenly appeared and reversed direction, the car was already useless. The whole chase was useless.

Then he saw Chad Armstrong. On foot, on the north side of Van Buren, moving west. How had he gotten so far so fast?

Jason Walker broke into a run, keeping to his side of the street, where the stanchions of the El tracks and the cars on the street gave him some cover. He was winded after half a block. After another half-block he was able to slow to a fast walk.

Chad Armstrong turned right on Dearborn Street. Jason Walker crossed the street and followed, holding back about fifty yards. The street here was narrow and walled in by old high-rises. The one on the left, the Monadnock, had in its time been the tallest building built with load-bearing walls. At ground level, they were nearly eight feet thick. He told himself he was not on an architectural tour.

Chad Armstrong turned left on Jackson Boulevard. Once again, Jason Walker ran to the corner and peered around it. Once again, he couldn't see his quarry. Cautiously, he came around the corner. There was a coffee shop on his left. Glare on the glass made it hard to see in, but he thought he saw the agent standing in line, with his back to the window. He couldn't chance a better look. He backed up to the corner and waited.

He kept waiting. Apparently Chad Armstrong had not taken his coffee to go. It occurred to him that the shops in the Monadnock also had interior entrances. Quickly, he retraced his steps and went in through a Dearborn Street entrance. As he remembered, a hall ran down the center of the building, meaning the shops and restaurants could be entered from inside or out. He walked to the north end of the building. There was a window in the door of the coffee shop. He peered through. He could see only part of the room, several customers he didn't recognize.

His heart pounded. Chad Armstrong could have strolled out the door while he was running around the building. He had to find out now.

He eased the door open and stepped inside. The sales counter and espresso machines provided some cover. Pretending to examine the pastries in a refrigerated display case, he edged into the shop. He scanned the room with his peripheral vision. He didn't see Chad Armstrong.

Wait—*there*, he thought, reading the newspaper.

A tuft of blond hair peeked over a newspaper.

'May I help you?' boomed a voice.

A clerk, tall, tattooed, and unshaven, was smiling at him.

He smiled stupidly and shook his head. He didn't want to risk Chad Armstrong recognizing his voice. He opened the door and rushed out.

'Weird dude,' he heard the clerk say as the door closed.

He walked double-time down the hall, back out on to the street, and ran to the corner. He peered around. He could only assume that Chad Armstrong had not suddenly thrown down his newspaper and run out the door.

Finally he came out. He had the newspaper, the *Wall Street Journal*, tucked under his arm. Yawning, he rolled his neck. Then he started walking west on Jackson.

When Chad Armstrong had first turned north on Dearborn, Jason Walker had wondered whether he was returning to an office at the Federal Center. It would make sense that a Homeland Security agent might work there. It would have made less sense for a secret agent, even one who was hungover, to schedule a meeting so close to his workplace. But with the new security restrictions that applied to all government buildings, Jason Walker wouldn't have been able to follow him inside without showing an I.D. and some proof that he had a reason to enter.

So this was better. Jackson was crowded with workers returning to their offices at the end of their lunch hours. He felt less risk of being discovered here.

On LaSalle Street, they passed the Chicago Board of Trade. Immediately north were the Federal Reserve Bank and the Bank of America. As usual, National Guardsmen were stationed at the intersection to protect the financial institutions from terrorist attack. Besides bollards and crash barricades, there were sandbags sheltering machine-gun emplacements.

Chad Armstrong passed through the soldiers as if he didn't see them. He turned right on Wells Street, where the El tracks curved north to create the western edge of the Loop. A southbound Brown Line train thunk-thunked around the corner, its wheels squealing and sparking on the tracks.

The Quincy station was immediately ahead. Chad

Armstrong was walking directly toward the stairs leading up to the tracks.

He began closing the distance.

Suddenly Chad Armstrong stopped and turned around.

Jason Walker turned around, too. His heart pounding, he began walking back the way he'd come. When he reached the corner, he chanced a look back. Chad Armstrong wasn't in sight. What was he doing? He'd acted like a man who had forgotten something. Or a man who'd realized he was being followed.

He waited by the corner, watching the sidewalk.

Chad Armstrong came out of a shop, carrying a plastic shopping bag with several small objects inside. He went up the stairs to the train.

Jason Walker followed slowly. He waited outside the turnstiles until a train came into the station, then swiped his pass and hurried through. It was a Pink Line train. Chad Armstrong was standing several cars to the right, waiting for the doors to open.

When the doors opened, Jason Walker jogged into the car directly in front of him. The doors closed and the train pulled out of the station.

The car was half-full. Nobody appeared to notice that the man who stood nervously by the door was involved in a chase. The train traveled the short distance to the Washington stop. When the doors opened he stayed inside, watching. The turnstiles were directly in front of him, so he had a clear view. But Chad Armstrong didn't get off the train. The doors closed again.

The train was slowing for its turn west when he realized that, because he was in the middle of the train, when Chad Armstrong got off, the agent would need to walk back toward him to exit the station. If he waited inside the car until Chad Armstrong passed by, the doors might close before he could safely get off.

He needed to leave the train behind Chad Armstrong. But how could he do that? If he went to the last car of the train, Chad Armstrong would still be coming toward him. And he couldn't pass through Chad Armstrong's car.

He had an idea. There were emergency exit doors, never locked, at the end of every car. Heading toward Chad Armstrong's car, ignoring the sign that read *AUTHORIZED PERSONNEL ONLY*, he pushed the door open. He stood between two cars, the wind and noise momentarily disorienting him. The train was crossing the Chicago River where it split in two, east toward the lake and northwest toward the suburbs.

He entered the next car. The train was already slowing down for the Clinton station. He hoped Chad Armstrong wasn't getting off yet. When the doors opened, he watched with relief. Hardly anyone got off.

It was a long way to the next station. He went through the car to the next one. At the far end, he peered through the window. There was Chad Armstrong, sitting in the handicapped seat, peeling back the plastic wrap on a sandwich.

There was a small, sideways-facing seat right next to the emergency door. Jason Walker sat down. Through the window to his right he could just see Chad Armstrong chewing in profile.

As the train slowed for the Ashland station, Chad Armstrong suddenly stood up. He dropped the uneaten half of his sandwich in his shopping bag.

Jason Walker took a deep breath. When the doors opened, he pushed through the first emergency door, heading into the car that Chad Armstrong had just left. But the second door, the door into the car, was stuck. He pushed as hard as he could.

'*Stand clear of the doors, the doors are closing,*' said the recorded voice.

He threw his shoulder against the door and it opened. He stumbled into the car, stepped on the foot of an indignant middle-aged woman, and scrambled for the side doors as they began sliding shut. He slipped out just in time to see Chad Armstrong moving through the turnstile, his back squarely to Jason Walker.

Allowing himself two seconds to feel relieved, he started off once again.

It was an area of warehouses, condominiums, nightclubs,

and restaurants. The nightlife was still closed for the day, and graffiti-scrawled panel trucks double-parked with impunity. There was almost no foot traffic, so Jason Walker let Chad Armstrong get much farther ahead, nearly a whole block.

They didn't go far. After several blocks and two turns Chad Armstrong walked through an open gate in a chain-link fence, through a nearly empty parking lot, and through a smoked-glass door. The building he'd entered was low and squat, just two stories, but looked recently built. It was made of gray cinder blocks and, though it had glass bricks set in at irregular intervals, had no windows. A small sign on the building read: *COMMUNICATION CONSULTANTS, INCORPORATED*.

They had probably laughed about that name, he thought. A joke among spies.

Chad Armstrong came back outside. He jogged to a sport-utility vehicle, climbed in, and started the engine.

Jason Walker turned and ran back to the corner he had just turned. It was an intersection of two one-way streets. Unless Chad Armstrong was going to drive against traffic, he would be driving by in a moment.

He kept going, running as fast as he could. It was a side street between two warehouses, the sidewalk cracked with weeds, with no doors to run into, no alleys or alcoves in which to hide. He'd never make the next intersection in time. And even if he could, Chad Armstrong would still see him.

He threw himself down, his face to the wall, amid soggy fast-food bags and pebbles of bottle glass. He lay carelessly, as if he were sleeping or passed out drunk. It was all he could do.

The big car rolled around the corner and crept down the street. Chad Armstrong could have been talking on the phone or rummaging in the glove compartment. Or maybe he was staring at the back of the prostrate man, thinking the man looked familiar.

After coming to a complete stop at the next stop sign, the car sped away with a throaty roar of its engine.

Jason Walker counted to twenty and then sat up. He did his best to brush the dirt off his clothes. There was a small piece of glass embedded in his palm, but it hadn't cut the skin.

He walked back to the El station.

When he got home he had two messages waiting for him, both from Gina Saraceno. He dialed her work number.

'Jason, honey, I'm glad you called. Scott gave me the schedule for tomorrow.'

With everything that had been happening, he had almost forgotten that George Libby was coming to Chicago the following day.

'Oh, good,' he said.

'Try putting an exclamation point on the end of that. Anyway, he's getting into town in the morning, and Scott is going to meet him at the bus station.'

'He's riding the bus? Can't he afford to fly?'

'It's so he can meet regular people. I think it's a great move. I mean, personally, I wouldn't ride Greyhound, but, then again, I don't have a camera crew following me. So Scott is going to meet him and they're going straight to the police department for a meeting with the chief. And here's another great idea, and it involves you: Libby's going to campaign with us at the State Street Studio of ABC-7 news.'

'What?'

'He wants to show everyone that we're lovers, not fighters. And after he talks with the police, they're going to have an extra incentive to keep things orderly.'

His stomach lurched as he remembered the melee the last time.

'That doesn't sound like a great idea to me.'

'It's going to be safe, believe me,' said Gina Saraceno. 'And it's only for an hour. Then, lunch. Then, we all get to meet with Libby for an hour at Scott's house. The next morning, Libby's going to have a town hall meeting at one of the city colleges, and in the afternoon, he's going to wrap it all up with a press conference. I'm sure he'll kiss some babies on the way to the bus station, though.'

Jason Walker tried to think of a good excuse not to go.

'You don't want to do it, do you?' said Gina Saraceno.

'Well, after what happened, we can't afford not to do it. So you're coming, buster. If you're sore at me afterward I'll give you a backrub. Deal?'

'Deal,' he said.

When they were done talking, he took the cell phone Leo Haddad had given him and started to dial. Then he remembered that someone could be listening. He canceled the call and left the building.

The field house across the street was quiet, so he walked down Argyle Street until he came to a bustling Vietnamese grocery store. He went inside and pretended to look at colorful cans of exotic fruit. There was enough noise, he thought, to confuse a listening device if one happened to be pointed at him. He took out the phone and dialed again.

'Hello, how are you?' said Leo Haddad.

'I'm fine,' said Jason Walker. 'I found out where our friend works.'

'This is excellent news. We will visit him tomorrow morning.'

Visit him? It didn't make sense. Unless it was some oblique way of saying something else. Or unless he was kidding.

'Can you meet me in the morning at six o'clock? At our usual place. We won't have time for a game of chess, but we can drink a cup of excellent coffee together.'

Once again he wished for an excuse not to go.

Once again he found himself agreeing.

'Deal,' he said.

Nineteen

He was at the bus stop by five fifteen, but waited for what seemed like forever before an 81 bus finally rolled up. He arrived at the cultural center ten minutes late. Leo Haddad was sitting on a chair just inside the door, waiting. Seeing Jason Walker, he sprang up, unlocked the door, and ushered him inside.

'The van is waiting for us out back,' he said.

He locked the door behind them and hurried through the darkened room toward the hallway in back.

'Where are we going?' asked Jason Walker.

'To see where our mutual friend works.'

'Why don't I just write down the address for you?'

Leo Haddad stopped, turned, and came back.

'Jason, I want you to come with us.'

'Why? What's going on?'

'We are already running late. I would prefer it if we could talk in the van.'

Jason Walker's scalp prickled. But why had he followed Chad Armstrong if not to help Leo Haddad?

He followed. They walked down the back hallway, which was nearly pitch black, and out the back door. A white van with tinted windows was idling just outside. On the side was painted *Heartland Surveying Company*. The rear bumper had a 'Support the Troops' bumper sticker and the rear window had a decal for the Police Benevolent and Protective Association of Illinois. The van was scratched and dented, but perhaps that made it more authentic.

Leo Haddad opened the side door. Sitting in the front seats were the two men who had abducted Jason Walker before.

He hesitated.

'You are among friends now, Jason,' said Leo Haddad. 'That is Marid, and that is Abdul. You have been their passenger before, but this time it is different.'

The men grinned.

Leo Haddad climbed into the van. Jason Walker climbed in after him and pulled the door closed.

Marid put the van in gear and started driving.

'So where are we going?' asked Leo Haddad.

Jason Walker gave him the building's address.

'But I don't understand why we're going there,' he added.

'We are a surveying crew. We are going to survey the situation.'

'But why?'

'It is important to know one's enemy. Chad Armstrong knows much more about us than we know about him. I would like to close the information gap, you might say.'

'But why do you need me?'

'We are not so many, Jason. I do not need just your mind and your information, I need your body.'

'But what are we going to do?'

'First we will look around. Second, we will eat breakfast.'

Marid said something to Abdul in Arabic and both men laughed.

'Don't they speak English?' asked Jason Walker.

'Of course,' said Marid.

Then both men laughed again.

Leo Haddad gave him a white coverall, a yellow hard hat, a clipboard, and a small digital camera. There were other props, which looked to him like genuine surveying equipment, already stowed in the van. He hoped the other men knew how to use the gear or at least how to make it look convincing.

Bracing himself against the bumps and lurches of the van, he pulled on the coverall and adjusted the plastic headband inside the helmet. Leo Haddad pulled on a coverall, too, and buckled a tool belt around his waist. Marid and Abdul were already wearing coveralls and had put their helmets on the dashboard.

'I must confess that I do not know whether surveying crews wear boiler suits,' said Leo Haddad. 'But I find that any kind of uniform makes people more likely to believe that you are what you say you are.'

Then he explained the plan. It seemed simple enough. They would park the van and set up their equipment one block east of the building. Then three of the men would take surveying markers and work their way down to Communication Consultants, Incorporated. The idea was to look as if they were surveying property lines for whichever business happened to be closest. But Leo Haddad wanted photos of the building site. And if any cars happened to be in the lot, or if anyone came or went, all the better. He wanted photos of them, too.

'They will be looking at the big tripod and the markers and our yellow helmets,' said Leo Haddad. 'They will not notice a small camera. But its zoom is quite powerful, as you will see.'

The plan seemed too simple. It was crude and clumsy. But then again, what did Jason Walker know about how such things were done?

They arrived at the site. Marid drove past the building, then circled around and parked one block to the east. They opened the rear doors of the van and set up a tripod-mounted scope on the sidewalk. They ringed the area in orange traffic cones. Abdul squinted through the scope and fiddled with some dials. He nodded at Leo Haddad.

'Jason, Marid, come with me.'

They walked down the empty sidewalk toward the building. Jason Walker thought nervously of Chad Armstrong's abrupt exit the day before. But when they got there the parking lot was empty. If the lot hadn't been well-swept and weed-free, the building might have looked abandoned.

'This is it? You are certain?' said Leo Haddad.

He nodded.

'Take pictures, then. Marid, hold up the reflector for Abdul.'

While the other three men went through the motions of

surveying, Jason Walker began taking photos with the small camera. He didn't see any surveillance cameras, but just in case anyone was watching, he first took photos of the block and street adjoining his real target. Then, casually, he took several photos of the building. He walked fifty feet away from Leo Haddad and Marid and photographed the building straight on. He couldn't see what use the photos would be. He walked back.

'Photograph the side street and the alley, too,' said Leo Haddad.

'Isn't that risky?'

'I do not think so. It does not look as if anyone has arrived for work.'

He moved off down the side street. The building wall was blank on that side, but he dutifully photographed it anyway. It was an odd feeling to use a digital camera. There was a small screen on the back where he could see the image immediately after he captured it.

In the back alley, a gate in the chain-link fence led to a pair of large doors set in the building's back wall. The gate was shut but not locked.

He looked up, scanning for cameras mounted on the building wall, on the fence, on telephone poles. He didn't see any. He opened the gate and walked through. The back doors were made out of steel but had a standard locking doorknob. Curious, he tried the doorknob.

It turned. The door was unlocked.

He let go as if the doorknob was hot. Backing up, he turned to go.

Marid came around the corner of the building, walking inside the fence. He had walked through the front gate and the parking lot.

'Ah, there you are,' he said. 'Does it open? I tried the front door, but, locked.'

Without hesitation Marid walked up and turned the doorknob. He raised his eyebrows in an expression of surprised pleasure.

'Always try the doors,' he whispered.

Marid cracked the door open and peered inside, then

opened it the rest of the way. They looked into a concrete
utility area with garbage cans, broken-down cardboard
boxes, and janitorial equipment. There was a door to their
right and another set of double doors directly ahead. Marid
walked to the double doors.

'Wait, stop,' said Jason Walker.

Marid ignored him.

Leo Haddad walked in.

'This is dangerous,' said Jason Walker.

'Yes, it is.'

'Shouldn't someone at least wait outside?'

'Abdul is waiting outside.'

Marid rattled the handle on the double doors. They were
locked. Jason Walker felt like clicking his heels. Then Marid
started looking through the janitor's tools. He found a long
pry-bar. Slipping the flat end between the doors, he pulled
back hard with both hands. The doors bowed outward.
Working the pry-bar back and forth, he pushed it in more
deeply. Then he pulled again and the doors broke open with
a booming crack.

Jason Walker was ready to run.

'No one is here,' said Leo Haddad. 'We will look for five
minutes and then we will go.'

The doors opened on to a bland, corporate-looking
hallway. The floor was covered in blue-and-gray carpet tiles.
The drop ceiling was filled with acoustical tiles. The walls
were white. Most of the lights were turned off, but he could
see that the hallway went straight through the building to
the front doors. A semicircular receptionist's desk with flickering video screens sat in a darkened lobby at the opposite
end of the building.

Leo Haddad and Marid had walked swiftly ahead. They
were trying doors, peering inside rooms, and muttering
when the doors they tried were locked. Jason Walker
followed as if half-asleep. He saw a meeting room with a
table and eight chairs. He saw a lunch room with vending
machines, a food-stained couch, and a smaller table with
only four chairs. He saw a room with a bank of computer
terminals and phones with headsets. There was nothing to

indicate that the building housed anything but a legitimate business.

Until he saw the bulletin board. The sheets posted on it all had Department of Homeland Security letterhead. They listed duty rosters, security procedures, urgent tasks.

He scanned the duty rosters, looking for Chad Armstrong's name. He didn't see it. Either Chad Armstrong was too important to put on the schedule, or Chad Armstrong wasn't his real name.

Was this where the Acme Messenger Service calls were answered? And if so, why was the building empty? It seemed as if there had been somebody responding to messages at all hours. He looked again at the duty rosters. He saw a note indicating that the 8 P.M. to 8 A.M. hours were covered by 'remote agent.' Did that mean they were telecommuting? The day shift would arrive by 8 A.M. The clock on the wall said 7:20. But what if someone came into work early?

He ran back into the hall. It was empty. Afraid to raise his voice, he ran down the hall looking into rooms. He didn't see anyone.

The elevator indicator showed a two. They were on the second floor. He burst into the stairwell and ran up the steps. Halfway down the hall a door was open and light was spilling out.

Inside, a lectern faced several rows of chairs. A door led to an adjoining office. At the back of the room was another door that had been taken off its hinges and now leaned against the wall. He could hear voices inside. He ran to the doorway.

'People could start arriving at work any minute,' he said breathlessly. 'We need to go.'

Leo Haddad and Marid looked up.

'He is right,' said Leo Haddad. 'We should go.'

They were in an armory. One wall was lined with assault rifles and shotguns. Sturdy metal cabinets had their contents labeled with chilling simplicity: *Grenades*, *Tear Gas*, *Rubber Bullets*. There were ammunition sizes that didn't mean as much to him. The guns were locked to their brackets with loops of hardened cable, and the cabinets and lockers seemed locked down tight. But Leo Haddad and Marid were more interested in eight shoebox-sized containers stamped *C4*. The sides of the boxes said *Danger High Explosive* and *Keep Away from Electric Current*.

Marid picked up half of the boxes. Leo Haddad picked up the other half.

'What are you doing?' said Jason Walker.

'We are taking these,' said Marid. 'Excuse me.'

They began walking out of the room.

'It is better that we have this than the government,' said Leo Haddad.

'But how can you protect yourself with a bomb?'

'Jason, we need to go.'

They were at the elevator. Marid pushed the call button with his elbow and the doors opened.

The van was waiting for them in the alley, Abdul at the wheel. They climbed in and drove away.

Jason Walker continued to ask Leo Haddad why he wanted the explosives. Leo Haddad refused to elaborate. He seemed weary. When Jason Walker demanded that they take the explosives back, Marid tapped the clock on the van's dashboard.

'If you take them back now, I think you would just meet them arriving at work.'

He slumped in defeat. He gave them the camera. They let him out on a street corner and he rode the bus home.

He stood in the shower for nearly an hour, leaning against the tiles, letting the steaming-hot water soothe his muscles. He felt sleepy and jittery at the same time. Everything was moving too fast. And he couldn't stop thinking that he had made the wrong decision.

The phone rang a half-dozen times but he ignored it. When he turned off the water he spent an unusually long time shaving and grooming. He sat in his underwear in the dark living room and ate a sandwich. Then he put on his suit and tie and got ready to go downtown.

He was at the door before he remembered the ringing phone. He retrieved the message from his voicemail. It was the woman from the Acme Messenger Service.

'Lincoln Park, between Montrose and Wilson, east of Lake Shore Drive,' she said. 'On top of the hill. Three o'clock this afternoon. Call back and confirm that you understand.'

He froze. Why was Chad Armstrong suddenly summoning him to a meeting? Had someone witnessed the theft of the explosives? Would he be arrested when he arrived? Or worse, abducted again?

Still, he had no choice but to go. He dialed the number with shaking hands. He left a message saying that he understood.

The plan was to meet at a nearby coffee shop and then proceed to the television studio. When Jason Walker arrived twenty minutes early, Gina Saraceno was already there. So were Scott Fink and Demeter.

Gina Saraceno gave him a hug and a kiss.

'You're so early,' she said happily. 'And so clean-shaven.'

'I want to look good on camera when they break my nose,' he said.

'Not going to happen,' said Scott Fink. 'George Libby had what he called "constructive dialog" with the cops. He's good at candidate-speak when he needs to be.'

'Where is he now?'

'He went to his hotel room to freshen up. He'll be here in a minute.'

The rest of the Libby Lobby, including the new recruits, trickled in. Jason Walker had to admit that he felt a grudging affection for them. His first impression had been incredulity, thinking that they were not people who were going to change the world. And while he'd seen nothing to revise his opinion—the people who changed the world were those who met in secret and who viewed human beings as game pieces—he had to admire them. They at least tried to make things better. Maybe it didn't matter that they were too naive to know they couldn't. Or maybe they did know, and they tried anyway. He felt suddenly proud to be part of the group, as unwilling and as complicated as his role was.

He pushed his chair closer to Gina Saraceno's and gave her hand an affectionate squeeze. She smiled and squeezed back. She could have no idea what he was thinking, but she was happy, trying to do good.

Scott Fink was watching the door and Jason Walker saw him suddenly brighten and start to stand. They all turned. George Libby walked in.

At first he was disappointed. Despite all the photos he'd seen documenting the candidate's ordinary looks, he had expected something different in person. Charisma, gravitas, an aura that electrified the room. Or at least an entourage, a support team that showed that the man they followed was an important person. But the candidate had one companion, a young man with thick black glasses and a digital organizer. When George Libby walked in, he looked like a salesman in a hurry to get a cup of coffee.

While his assistant ordered the coffee, Scott Fink eagerly introduced him. He made a better impression when he opened his mouth.

'Hi, I'm George Libby,' he told them, as if they didn't know.

He repeated each of their names, making eye contact as he did so. But there was something else. He had a smile that crinkled the corners of his eyes, and Jason Walker could tell that he was paying attention. He seemed not like a politician but like a real human being. That was what they needed. But could a real human being beat the president?

'It's nice to meet you all,' said George Libby. 'And I look forward to getting to know you better at our meeting this afternoon. I'm humbled by the work you've done on my behalf and on behalf of your country. And it hurt me deeply to learn that some of you were injured in the violence. I can't blame you if you're a bit nervous to go out there again, but I think it's crucial to show people that we don't go for violence, and also that we won't go away. Are you with me?'

The small group cheered, drawing quizzical looks from the other patrons in the coffee shop.

'Now let's go out and bring democracy to America!' said George Libby.

When they reached State Street things were very different

from the first time they had campaigned there. Television cameras were waiting for them, not only from ABC-7 but from a half-dozen other networks as well. There were photographers from newspapers and magazines, too, and reporters ready with notepads and small audio recorders. A dozen police cars lined the curb and two paddy wagons were parked across the street. Jersey barriers sealed off the block from automobile traffic, and wooden barricades formed a rectangle in front of the studio windows.

'That's the designated "free speech zone,"' said Scott Fink sarcastically. 'We had to agree to it.'

Despite the elaborate preparations, the waiting crowd was small. Two dozen strangers had turned out to support George Libby, some of them holding homemade signs or wearing homemade T-shirts. An equal number of passersby lingered, waiting curiously to see what would happen.

When they entered the barricaded area, the media people surged forward. Standing one-deep, they completely surrounded the area. It was difficult for passersby to see in, and nearly impossible to hand the campaign brochures out.

George Libby took it in stride, gamely thrusting brochures past the reporters even as he answered their questions.

'What brings you to Chicago?'

'As you're aware, my campaign volunteers were attacked and then arrested and charged with inciting their own attack. I'm here to draw attention to the situation and to reiterate that we stand for peace. Both in the big picture and in the little picture. We oppose violence.'

'What about the construction worker who received a head injury?'

'Whoever hit that man was not a part of my organization. We're concerned about his injury and hoping for his speedy recovery.'

'You've been accused of being a threat to national security. How do you respond?'

'I'm not sure when it was that democratic debate became a threat to national security. I'm simply asking the president to restore the people's constitutional right to decide.

They can reconfirm his mandate or they can choose a new course.'

'Do you seriously believe that, if elections were held, you could be elected president?'

'I do. I think that Americans are ready to stop living in fear. I know I am.'

The decision to campaign on State Street, despite the bloodshed, seemed to be paying off. Or maybe it was because of the bloodshed. If the fighting had, as Scott Fink suggested, been incited by undercover agents, then whoever had ordered it may have made a miscalculation. Bloodshed was one thing the media wouldn't ignore. And now here was a well-spoken, thoughtful response. It was easy to cast a chaotic fight in any light, but it would be hard to distort George Libby's remarks.

Jason Walker thought that the candidate struck an interesting balance. On the one hand, he followed the time-honored political tradition of avoiding inflammatory comment and refusing to be drawn into defensive-sounding remarks. He didn't even address the legitimacy of the president's third term or demand that the president not run for a fourth. On the other hand, he plainly said what was on his mind, without couching it in a lot of jargon.

George Libby wouldn't win, but Jason Walker would Vote Libby if he was given the chance.

At the end of the hour, they hadn't handed out many brochures, but everyone felt the effort was a success. They had gained publicity for the candidate and no one had been hurt. Still, Jason Walker thought that some of the policemen may have been disappointed. They had prepared for everything and nothing had happened.

The Libby Lobby went to a nearby restaurant for lunch. Their namesake sat at one table with his assistant, Scott Fink, and Eric. They had been followed in by several reporters, and George Libby seemed hard-pressed to eat his lunch given their steady stream of interruptions.

The rest of them sat at two nearby tables. With their attention focused on the candidate's table and their ears straining to pick up what he was saying, they didn't talk much.

Afterward, on the sidewalk outside the restaurant, Gina Saraceno looked at her watch.

'Well, we'd better get my car before the meter runs out. Dorothy and Cornelius rode the bus up, so I told them we'd give them a ride.'

Once again, he wasn't going with her. She read his expression.

'Oh, don't tell me,' she said.

'There's something I have to do,' he said. 'But I'm going to tell you all about it tonight, OK?'

He meant it, too. It was time. Provided that he was still a free man that night.

She elbowed him in the ribs.

'What are you, the man of mystery? Tell me now.'

'I can't. Later. I promise.'

She sighed theatrically.

'All right. But this had better be better than good. This better be great.'

'It's . . . complicated.'

'Big surprise. OK, call me later.'

She drew him in and kissed him on the mouth. He kissed her back. She turned and went to collect Dorothy and Cornelius.

He rode the 146 bus north on Lake Shore Drive, feeling as if he were riding to prison. Perhaps he should have splurged on a limousine. Or at least a taxi. Outside the bus the day was bright and cool. The lakefront path was busy with scantily-clad men and women jogging, bicycling, and rollerblading. Two girls flew a kite shaped like a dragon. A man used a plastic scoop to hurl a tennis ball for his dog. The dog bounded after it, an undulating, golden flash of fur.

He got off the bus at Montrose and crossed under Lake Shore Drive to the park. On a workday afternoon, the park was in only scattered use. Two boys and a girl practiced shooting goals on the soccer field. The girl, the smallest of the three, had been given the job of chasing down missed shots. After her third dutiful run for the ball, she sat down in the grass and started picking dandelions.

There was no one on the hill. He climbed slowly, trying to think of the reasons Chad Armstrong might have called. Only one came to mind. The theft of the explosives had been uncovered. Someone had been watching.

What kind of defense did he have? He had broken into a government building with suspected terrorists and watched them steal explosives. He hadn't aided them, but he hadn't turned them in. Perhaps he should. His idea of helping Leo Haddad, after all, had not included weapons theft. He could tell Chad Armstrong that, as part of his undercover work, he now had definitive evidence that Leo Haddad and his group were terrorists with a bomb. But were they? Leo Haddad had simply said that it was better for them to have the explosives than the government. He'd never discussed a desire to hurt anyone. Which was probably because he didn't trust Jason Walker.

He reached the top of the hill. He was tired. Tired of not understanding what was happening. Ever since he had stepped out of the movie theater, it was as if he had been caught in a wave, tumbled over and over, never breaking the surface of the water. Was this what life really was, he wondered, finally understanding that you have no power over anything? Or had he simply been too weak to control his own destiny?

It was difficult to make good decisions without knowing all the facts.

He waited and waited but Chad Armstrong did not appear. After a while he sat down. Then he lay down in the grass, watching the planes coming in from over Lake Michigan, their engines growing louder as they made their descents toward O'Hare.

Finally, over an hour later, he walked home. Chad Armstrong's failure to show was even harder to understand than his request to meet. He felt surprisingly disappointed at having missed the meeting with George Libby. He would have been interested to hear what the man had to say in a small, private gathering.

But he was free, for one more night at least. He would call Gina Saraceno and find out how things went. He would spend the night with her.

Schatzi woofed furiously, her claws scratching the wall as if she was trying to dig her way through. He dropped his keys in the dish, then sat down to take off his shoes. He moved to a chair by the window and sat looking out. As soon as the dog stopped barking, he would call her.

The dog quieted down. But before he could call Gina Saraceno, the phone rang. The cell phone. He fumbled it out of his bag and pressed the receive button.

Someone was shouting.

'Get out!'

'Leo?'

'Get out!'

Twenty

The line went dead. He stared at the phone. Of course it had been Leo Haddad. No one else had the number.

He looked out of the window. A half-dozen white vans pulled into his building's driveway and stopped. Men got out and moved swiftly toward the guardhouse. They were wearing body armor and carrying assault rifles. There were several men wearing plain clothes, too. He glimpsed tousled blond hair.

Something was horribly wrong. They were coming for him. He saw flashes of the cells where he'd been tortured. This was no time to give himself up. Leo Haddad was right. He had to run. But how?

He stumbled toward the door, then stopped. He was on the thirteenth floor. They would guard the exits. There was only one way out of his apartment: the front door. There were two stairwells in his tower, but they wouldn't overlook those. If they were smart, they would lock down the elevators and climb the stairs.

He ran to the window and looked out again. Two men stood guard in front of the building, scanning the yard alertly, their rifles at the ready. The others were already inside the building. They were probably already on their way up.

If his building had been built in 1920, not in 1950, it might have had a window ledge that he could have crawled out on. As in the movies, he could have crawled into another apartment. But the sheer brick walls fell straight to the ground.

He imagined the agents climbing the stairs. Where would they be? The third floor? The fourth?

He suddenly understood where he needed to hide. He

crept to his door and quietly turned the handle. He stepped out into the hall, letting the door lock behind him.

He tried the handle on Richard Zim's door. It was unlocked. It was always unlocked. And Richard Zim wasn't home, because Schatzi had been barking.

He opened the door and stepped inside.

As he stood in the foyer, his eyes adjusting to the dim light, he heard the scrabble of Schatzi's toenails on the hardwood floor. He looked up and saw the eighty-pound Rottweiler at the far end of the apartment. It was charging down the hall, a rope of slobber swinging from its bared teeth.

Richard Zim's apartment was the mirror opposite of his. There was a coat closet on his right. He opened it, squeezed in, and pulled the door shut behind him.

The sound of the dog attacking the door was like an explosion. He tripped on something and fell into hanging coats and sweaters, keeping a death grip on the doorknob. It was dark. The dog's noise was deafening. He felt what seemed to be a vacuum cleaner stabbing the small of his back. Struggling, he regained his feet and then crouched, listening quietly. He wished Richard Zim kept a cleaner closet.

Someone pounded on the door. His door, next door.

'Homeland Security! Open the door!'

Now Schatzi went truly berserk. She seemed to be rebounding between the front door, the closet door, and the adjoining wall. Between volleys of barks she caught her breath with a wet, rattling sound.

More pounding.

'Homeland Security! Jason Walker, open your door.'

They waited perhaps ten more seconds. Then there was a sound of splintering wood. Then shouts and thumping boots. Loud as they must have been, it was still hard to hear over Schatzi.

Then, for a while, he couldn't hear anything but the dog. He assumed that the Homeland Security men were used to hearing dogs bark when they broke down doors. Perhaps sometimes they brought their own dogs.

After five or ten minutes someone pounded on Richard Zim's door. They tried a second time, but Schatzi's barking must have convinced them that the neighbor wasn't home. And at any rate, the neighbor's apartment was protected from intruders by a terrifying dog.

Over the next half hour he occasionally heard voices, or the crackle of a radio, but he couldn't understand what was being said. Then he couldn't hear anything. He didn't know if anyone was still in his apartment or not. There was no door for them to close.

Schatzi finally quieted down. She lay down in front of the closet door, whining in frustration, once in a while giving a random yelp. He could hear her breathing. He could feel her weight against the closet door.

He wondered when Richard Zim would get home from work.

The dog was snoring. Jason Walker was wondering whether he would have to finally give up and urinate in his neighbor's golf bag. He had escaped one problem and now had to escape another. He contemplated throwing the door open, hoping to stun the dog, then wrenching open the front door. But he wasn't sure he could even move the door against Schatzi's dead weight, at least fast enough to get away from her. If he couldn't close the front door before she got through, she would bring him down in a second.

Maybe it was better to wait for her owner to come home. Jason Walker could explain things. Explain things and wait for Richard Zim to call the police.

Where was Richard Zim? Didn't his dog need to be walked?

Finally, Schatzi stirred and whimpered. Jason Walker heard someone in the hall.

'Holy crap!'

Richard Zim was home. He'd seen Jason Walker's door. Schatzi stood and yelped, agitated, but Richard Zim's door didn't open.

'Jason? Are you all right?'

Hearing her master's voice, Schatzi yelped again. She began whining steadily. It became hard to hear Richard Zim. But he heard an exclamation of fright, then an apology, then two voices. There was someone waiting in his apartment. Waiting to see if he would come home.

Richard Zim opened his own door. His dog leapt on him, relieved.

'Hey there, girl. Who's my good girl? Some excitement around here, huh?'

Schatzi scratched the closet door and barked.

'Schatzi,' he admonished her. 'Don't scratch the door. Do you want to go out?'

The dog scratched the closet door again. Jason Walker's feet had fallen asleep, but he got ready to run anyway.

Schatzi barked.

'What, is your ball in the closet? You want to take it outside?'

Schatzi barked. Richard Zim turned the door handle. Jason Walker would have to shoulder the door open, stunning both man and dog, if he had any chance of escape. He took a deep breath.

'Wait a minute. There's your ball. Over there, by the TV. Go get it.'

Schatzi didn't move. It sounded as if she was trying to burrow under the door with her nose. Richard Zim sighed in exasperation.

'Fine, I'll get the goddamn ball.'

His footsteps went away and came back. There was a jingle as a leash was lifted off a hook.

'OK, let's go.'

Richard Zim clipped the leash on to his dog's collar and dragged her, resisting, out the door into the hall.

'What's got into you?' he said.

And then the heavy door to the freight elevator banged shut.

Jason Walker breathed a huge sigh of relief. He opened the closet door and hobbled out, his muscles stiff from crouching so long. He gave himself five minutes before his neighbor came back.

He needed shoes and a jacket. He needed money. He needed his passports.

He found a navy-blue light canvas jacket in the closet. It was too big on him, but that was fine. In the bedroom closet he found a messy pile of shoes. They were two sizes too big, but the athletic shoes could be laced tight enough that his feet didn't slide around in them too much. In a junk drawer in the kitchen he found an envelope holding several hundred dollars in cash. After a moment's hesitation, he put the money in his pocket.

Fortunately, his own wallet was in his pants pocket. It contained only fifty dollars, but it held his identification, his bank card, his credit cards, and his transit pass. All of which, it occurred to him, were now essentially useless. If he used them it would be as good as leaving a written itinerary behind.

He put that out of his mind. He needed his passports. Fortunately, he didn't keep them in his apartment. If they had been there, they would have already been confiscated. They were in a safety-deposit box at Bridgeview Bank, a short walk away. But the key to the safety-deposit box was in his key dish.

It was time to leave Richard Zim's apartment. Carrying the shoes, he opened the door as quietly as possible and stepped out into the hall. He closed the door and turned the handle until the spring set into the latch.

The door to his apartment was open, hanging precariously from one twisted hinge. The doorjamb was splintered and the wall behind it was deeply gouged.

He held his breath and listened.

'. . . sources say that at this time the nature of the alleged plot is unclear, but defense attorneys have been unable to challenge key incriminating facts, namely . . .'

The agent in his apartment was watching television.

He crept into the foyer. He knew which floorboards creaked and how to avoid them. Peering around the corner, he saw a man sitting on the couch, watching television. An assault rifle was lying within easy reach on the ottoman.

The key dish was three feet, maybe four, inside the living

room. He would have to expose himself. His heart thudding in his chest, he crouched and slid one sock-clad foot forward. He lifted his arm and extended his fingers. The key ring he needed was under a letter opener and a metal box of mints. There was no way to lift it without making noise.

The dish was broad, green with a brown rim, an old piece of pottery he'd picked up at a yard sale. It was about a foot in diameter. He picked the whole thing up and then slipped back into the foyer. The agent didn't take his eyes off the television screen.

In the hall, he finally exhaled. He was heading for the stairwell with the dish in one hand, the shoes in another, when the freight-elevator door opened and Richard Zim and Schatzi came out.

'Hi,' said Richard Zim cheerfully.

Then he realized who he was talking to.

'Jason—'

Jason Walker was already running for the stairwell. The dog broke from her owner's startled grasp and bounded along the carpet. He pushed through the stairwell door and forced it closed, using the whole weight of his body against the stately pace of the tension arm.

The dog thudded against the door, woofing, berserk.

He sat down with his back against the door. He put the shoes on, pulled the laces tight, and tied them.

Richard Zim pounded on the door.

'Jason! There's a man who wants to talk to you.'

Shut up, shut up, shut up! he thought.

He dug through the contents of the dish until he found the key he needed.

Richard Zim dragged his protesting dog away. If the agent was not already coming down the hall, he would be soon.

Jason Walker looked down the stairwell. He took the key dish and tossed it downward. It shattered when it hit, scattering coins, mints, keys, and paperclips down the steps.

He turned and started climbing. He went up one floor and exited. The building was massive, designed around four towers. They either had all the exits guarded or they were spread thin. On the fourteenth floor, marked as the fifteenth, he ran from the southeast tower to the northwest one. Then he ran down the stairs as fast as he could.

On the second floor he slowed down. He crept the rest of the way, watching for shadows around corners, listening for the crackle of radios. He didn't see or hear anything.

He stopped at a service door and looked out. White vans were waiting at either end of the alley.

He heard loud voices and laughter. Four young men in polo shirts rounded the corner behind him, headed for the alley.

'What's so funny?' he asked.

'The security guard told us that Homeland Security is sweeping the building for terrorists,' said one of the men.

'That is funny,' said Jason Walker.

He walked out with them, all of them laughing. They turned north in the alley and squeezed past the white van. An agent scanned all five of their faces and then turned again toward the building. On Argyle Street, the four men turned left toward the train station. Jason Walker went straight, crossing the street north and plunging into another alley.

A block later, he turned east toward the park. He went under Lake Shore Drive and walked south through grassy fields, keeping between the bike path on one side and the parking lots on the other.

He looked at his watch. It was a quarter to five. If he wanted to get his passport out of the bank, he had to do it now or wait until the morning.

It was possible they would be waiting for him at the bank, he thought, but unlikely. If they knew about the safe-deposit box, they would have simply taken the key. Unless it was a trap. But they had had no way of knowing he was still in the building while they searched his apartment.

Everything could be a trap. But he had to move. He started running. It was a short way to Lawrence Avenue. He went west again, away from the lake, under Lake Shore Drive. He jogged past Marine Drive, past Clarendon, to Sheridan Road. Winded, he slowed to a fast walk. His watch showed seven minutes left. He started to run again. His breathing was ragged.

A police cruiser rolled toward him, part of the creeping line of cars. He slowed to a walk, cursing the rush-hour traffic. Finally, the cruiser went on. He started running again. Four minutes left.

He reached the bank with one minute to spare. He ran through the doors, down the hall, past a security guard, and down the curving stairs to the basement. His watch showed five o'clock exactly. The safety-deposit department was still open.

The woman at the counter, who usually seemed to be half-asleep, stared at him as he caught his breath. She waited until he panted out his request.

'We close at five,' she said pointedly.

'I'm sorry. Your door was still open.'

'We have strict rules about closing the vault door.'

'I wouldn't bother you but it's urgent. All I need is thirty seconds. Just to take something out.'

She let him sweat, then snapped a file card on to the counter.

'Fill this out.'

He filled out his name, box number, and the date. He signed it and gave her his driver's license. She scrutinized both signatures. Sighing, she conceded that they matched.

'Raul!' she called.

The door to the vault buzzed open and he went inside. The door clanged shut behind him. A middle-aged Latino man with gray hair took his key and then searched for the correct box as if his feet were hurting him.

Jason Walker felt claustrophobic. If they were anxious to go home, why didn't the guard hurry?

Finally the guard turned the key and pulled out the long, thin metal box. He handed it to Jason Walker and pointed through a doorway toward the cubicles where box-holders could add or remove items in private.

'It's all right,' said Jason Walker. 'I just need to grab something.'

He started to open the box's hinged lid.

The guard stopped him.

'Please, sir. Our rules. You have to open your box in there.'

Jason Walker walked to the nearest cubicle and opened the door. The desk light was already on. He closed the door and, without sitting down, opened the box lid, half expecting to find it empty.

Relief surged through his tense body. Everything was there. Five thousand dollars in savings bonds, a few pieces of his mother's jewelry, and his two passports. He put everything in his pockets, closed the box, and turned to go. He opened the door.

Chad Armstrong was standing in the doorway. He was smiling. He held a sleek black pistol in his hand.

'You know, we've been missing each other so much lately, I'm glad we finally connected.'

Jason Walker looked left and right. There was nowhere to run.

'Yup, only one way in and out of a bank vault,' said Chad Armstrong. 'I gotta say, Jason, I have no idea how you got out of your apartment, but I'm really glad you decided to drop by the bank. My boss was *pissed*.'

'Why did you come after me?'

'Why did you run? If you didn't do anything, you could have just let us bring you in.'

'It was the explosives, wasn't it? I swear I never—'

'Everybody swears they never, and then they do. You could say it was the explosives. They have a habit of going off. But listen, the nice people who work at the bank want to get home in time for the news. Here's what's going to happen: I'm going to step out of the way and you're going to walk past me. Then, with you in front and me behind, we're going to go out of the vault, up the stairs, and out the east door. I have a ride waiting for us.'

Chad Armstrong stepped into the room and turned sideways, then motioned with the gun for Jason Walker to go past.

He hefted the box. He wondered if he could swing it fast enough.

'Hup, two, three, four,' said Chad Armstrong.

Jason Walker walked toward the doorway. As he neared it, Chad Armstrong stepped back out of reach. They went into the main room of the vault. What did he mean about the explosives?

'Did you get everything out of the box?'

'Yes.'

'Got it all in your pockets?'

'Yes.'

'Good, good. Go ahead and put the box on the guard's desk.'

The guard was gone. Through the bars he saw that the clerk was gone, too. He put the box on the guard's desk.

'By the way,' said Chad Armstrong, 'that was a nice move yesterday, pretending to be a passed-out bum. It almost makes me think you could have had a future with us.'

It was information he didn't have time to process. Chad Armstrong gestured with the gun.

'Right up to the door. Nice and slow.'

He walked to the vault door.

'Now turn the handle.'

He turned the handle. It didn't give.

Chad Armstrong swore.

'Forgot about that part. OK, take two steps back.'

Jason Walker took two steps back. Chad Armstrong went back to the guard's desk and opened a drawer.

'Now, when I hit the buzzer,' he said, 'grab the door and hold it open.'

Was Chad Armstrong going to shoot him? If so, he could have done it in the vault. But then there would have been a mess. It would be easier to drive him somewhere private and shoot him there.

The buzzer sounded. The lock released with a click and the door opened a quarter of an inch.

Jason Walker grabbed the handle, pulled, and ran through. If Chad Armstrong was going to shoot him, he would find out now.

'Hey! Jason!'

Chad Armstrong was halfway to the vault door when it

slammed shut. He ran sideways along the steel cage, the narrowing angle closing the space between the bars.

Chad Armstrong shot at him anyway, two times. The sound was deafening. There were sparks and then high whines as the slugs ricocheted crazily around the armor-clad room.

He was out the door. Behind him, Chad Armstrong cursed and ran back to the desk. The front doors to the vault area were made of shatterproof glass. A mop in a yellow bucket stood nearby. Jason Walker grabbed the mop and slid the wooden handle through the door pulls. He ran up the stairs.

At the top he stopped and walked nonchalantly toward the west entrance, where a bank guard was letting bank employees and late customers out. He stood in the line, waited his turn, and pushed out through a revolving brass door on to the street.

Hands in his pockets, he turned south on Broadway Avenue and started walking away.

Twenty-One

During his short walk through Uptown it was as if the city had come under siege. Police cruisers crept slowly down the center of the streets, their flashers blazing. An olive-green truck dropped National Guardsmen off at the Wilson El station, where loudspeakers on the platform above crackled with urgent but unintelligible messages. Every few minutes, a white Homeland Security van sped by, cleaving the traffic with siren bursts. As he turned east on Montrose, he saw police setting up a roadblock in the intersection.

He stayed on the main streets, walking always on the busiest part of the sidewalk, working his way back toward the lake. It wasn't safe to ride the bus or train. Hailing a cab was out of the question. And he didn't have the tools to steal a bicycle.

While he walked, he tried to sort out what Chad Armstrong had said. Chad Armstrong knew that he'd been followed. Had he known yesterday or only figured it out later? If Chad Armstrong had seen him sprawled on the sidewalk, why hadn't he stopped? Had he wanted to see what would happen?

Had he allowed himself to be followed on purpose?

Even if he had, it wouldn't have made any sense. Unless he wanted Leo Haddad to know the address, too. But allowing someone to steal explosives seemed like a terrible risk. Unless they weren't real explosives.

Had it all been an elaborate plan to frame Leo Haddad? If so, it had worked perfectly. But then what had Chad Armstrong meant about explosives going off?

A loud whoop made him jump. Behind him, a police

cruiser was nosing toward the curb. He quickened his pace, ready to run. This was it.

'Move along,' crackled a voice through the loudspeaker. 'Come on, get going.'

There were three black teenagers behind him, too. They were leaning against a fence. He hadn't noticed them. Grumbling, glaring, they started to walk away with exaggerated gaits, as if they were running in slow motion.

He kept walking. He crossed Clarendon Avenue. He passed the Maryville Academy, then walked alongside a park with soccer fields and softball diamonds. He crossed Marine Drive, went under Lake Shore Drive, and then was in the park once again. His shadow stretched out in front of him, leading him toward the lake.

He left the road for a footpath and followed it to Montrose Harbor. The slips were still full of sailboats and powerboats. There were a few more weekends of good sailing left. But apparently, the National Guard didn't see boats as a transportation risk. There was no armed presence here, just a light in a guard shack and a small Coast Guard tender that was already motoring out of the harbor.

Trying to look as if he were admiring the boats, he circled the harbor, looking for a way to steal one. The big slips were well-protected, their gates ringed with long spikes. He could drop into the water, though, then swim to a boat and crawl up its ladder. But how would he start a boat without keys? And now was no time to learn how to sail.

He started circling back. He had wasted precious time on a stupid idea. He would just have to walk.

In front of the guard shack there was a small motorboat, just a fiberglass hull with an outboard motor stuck on the back. Tied to the cleats with a dirty white rope, it bumped lazily against dirty white fenders.

He looked at the guard shack. He couldn't see anyone looking out. He climbed down the ladder.

It was five feet down. Once in the boat, he couldn't be seen from the guard shack.

The motor looked simple enough. It started with a pull cord, like a lawnmower. He grabbed the T-shaped handle and pulled. The motor turned listlessly. He pulled harder. It chugged several times. He pulled as hard and fast as he could. The motor chugged several times more. It didn't sound as if it was going to catch.

He had forgotten to prime it. There was a bulb in the black rubber feed line. He pumped it a dozen times, then pulled the cord again. The engine stuttered but didn't catch.

At any moment he expected to see a face peer over the edge of the dock at him.

He kept trying, pumping the bulb, pulling the cord. The engine wouldn't catch.

A new sound came from above, the steady chop of a helicopter. It grew louder and louder. He couldn't see the helicopter.

The boat wouldn't start. He climbed up the ladder. A park district employee was standing in the doorway of the guard shack, shading his eyes at the sky. He saw Jason Walker climb out of the harbor. His lips formed inaudible words.

Jason Walker smiled and waved, then turned and walked off. He started to run. There was a golf course ahead. He climbed a low fence, skirted a putting green, stumbled through a sand trap, and reached the treeline between fairways.

The helicopter finally came into view over the lake. Moving slowly, it was a big, orange Coast Guard craft that looked as if it could winch a small boat right out of the water. There was a higher-pitched whine and he whirled the other way. Pushing aside weeds and branches he saw a small police helicopter speeding south along the wall of high-rises lining Marine Drive.

He had to go south, too.

He worked his way through the golf course, surprising a few after-work foursomes, then past tennis courts, another harbor, a driving range, more tennis courts, another harbor. South of Fullerton he walked through the public zoo, doing his best to blend in with the strolling, chattering families. He bought a hot dog and ate it standing, then bought another before walking away. He used the toilets in the big-cat house, then combed his hair with his fingers and tried to wash the hunted look off his face.

Helicopters buzzed angrily overhead. Sirens echoed off city buildings.

The tree cover grew thicker and then the park petered out. He was forced to backtrack, then cross a pedestrian bridge over Lake Shore Drive, then walk along the bicycle path as it followed the sandy beach. But this was better. The beach was dotted with people. There were office workers carrying their jackets and homeless people lying on sleeping bags. There were swimmers and joggers, jugglers and dog walkers. There were police cruisers parked every few hundred yards along the path but the officers inside didn't seem to be stopping anyone.

He followed the pleasure seekers, all of them seeming determined to wring out the last of the fading daylight, until he reached Navy Pier. From there he followed the odd patchwork of trail, sidewalk, and bridge over the Chicago River. In Grant Park, the city's formal front room, he faded into the darkness under the trees.

At the far south edge of the park he stopped and looked back at the sweeping wall of buildings facing the park. Called the 'Michigan Avenue Cliff,' it had never failed to thrill him. Especially now, twinkling with light against the purple sky, the last time he would ever see it. He sat down to rest, hoping to print the scene firmly in his mind.

He considered going to Gina Saraceno's house. It wasn't far away. But they would expect him there. If he came, he would involve her even more than he already had. He wished he had known he was saying goodbye. He would have told her that he loved her.

Stiff and sore, he climbed up and set out once more on his aching feet.

It was a long way to go on foot. He worked his way past the museum campus, Soldier Field, and the mammoth convention center. Then the park spread out emptily. He went slowly, stopping at water fountains to slurp tepid water. He had never been to the lakefront on the South Side, to

Burnham Park. The facilities were few and far between, but it felt more peaceful than Lincoln Park. He wished he could have visited under different circumstances.

Finally, below Seventy-First Street, after he had passed the University of Chicago, the Museum of Science and Industry, and the South Shore Country Club, the park ran out for good. He threaded his way through unfamiliar streets lined with brick three-flats and apartment buildings into a quiet neighborhood of wooden frame houses and overgrown shrubbery. He peered through the fence at an abandoned steelyard, but he saw acre after acre of flat, razed land, and no place to hide.

He walked and walked. His feet were swollen and sore. He thought that they might be bleeding. He was afraid to take off his shoes and look. He found himself on a bridge over an industrial canal, frighteningly exposed, and then he passed under an expressway and into yet another working-class neighborhood. Then he wandered through a seemingly endless landscape of spent industry. The numbered streets had passed one hundred and kept climbing. He watched for a sign saying that he was entering Indiana.

After midnight, on a street called Avenue M, he saw a tavern, its door spilling light out into the night. He was desperate for food and a comfortable seat. Collecting himself, pasting a smile on his face, he hobbled inside.

No one noticed. Everyone in the half-full room was watching the televisions over the bar. They were talking in low murmurs. Even the bartender had his back to the door.

Jason Walker slipped into an empty booth. He scooped a handful of peanuts from the bowl on the table and began to crack the shells with his teeth. Then he heard what anchorman Joel Devonshire was saying.

'Welcome back to this special ABC-7 news bulletin. Our top story tonight, the only story, is the apparent assassination of self-declared presidential candidate George Libby. Libby was in town following a protest in his name—outside the window of this very studio—that turned violent. He was meeting with his supporters in a Hyde Park three-flat when an explosion occurred, killing everyone in the room.'

He gasped. Several people looked at him but then quickly looked back at the television.

'The death toll is believed to have been at least fourteen. The names of the dead have not been released pending identification of the bodies and notification of the victims' families. Earlier this evening, a Homeland Security spokesman stated that the attack was, and I quote, "definitively an act of terrorism." More now from that press conference.'

The scene changed to a podium with the Homeland Security logo on the front. Behind the podium was a spokesman he'd seen before.

'Today's assassination of George Libby was especially regrettable in that it could have been avoided. The bombing was carried out by a terrorist operative known to our offices and whom we had been tracking for a number of weeks. However, the speed with which he carried out this heinous crime gave us no chance to stop him. Our hearts go out to the family of George Libby and also to those who were killed with him. Once again, this reprehensible deed highlights the fact that America will not be safe until we vanquish terror from our midst.'

Joel Devonshire returned.

'At that press conference, videotaped a few hours ago, Homeland Security officials stated that they believed the attack was carried out by a suicide bomber who died in the blast. We have recently received word that they now believe that this was not the case; that the bomber escaped and is still at large.'

The screen filled with pixellated footage from a security camera. Jason Walker, Leo Haddad, and Marid, and eight boxes of explosives. Then a still photograph of himself walking with Leo Haddad, the two of them in intent conversation. Then video of himself, handing out a George Libby brochure on State Street.

A dull roar filled his ears.

'Homeland Security officials identified this man, Jason Andrew Walker, as the bomber. Lebanese by birth, he was a disciple of this man, Leo Haddad, and had infiltrated the George Libby campaign in order to get close to the candidate. Other evidence against him includes secret, detailed notes of campaign meetings and audiotape of phone conversations. Homeland Security officials now further believe that the bomb was carried by Walker's girlfriend, Gina Saraceno, although it isn't entirely clear whether she was a willing participant or not.'

There was an audio clip. From the background noise, it had been made in a restaurant. Gina Saraceno's voice sounded as if it was coming from inside a tin can.

'I'm just so pissed off,' she said. 'I can't believe what they did to us. I understand now how people are radicalized.'

Jason Walker's driver's license photograph filled the screen.

'Officials are asking for the public's help in locating Jason Walker,' said Joel Devonshire. 'Anyone seeing him should call 911 immediately. Because he is believed to be armed and dangerous, officials caution that under no circumstances should any member of the public attempt to speak to or approach Walker on their own.'

He stumbled out of the tavern. He didn't see whether anyone noticed him. His eyes were too full of tears.

Oh Gina, he thought.

He fell to his knees in an alley. He imagined Chad Armstrong handing a gift-wrapped shoebox to Gina Saraceno and asking her to take it to the meeting. Jason Walker had called Chad Armstrong his friend, after all.

He crawled behind some trash cans and lay down on his side, sobbing convulsively.

Oh Gina, he thought, I'm so sorry.

When he screamed, the sound was covered by the wail of an approaching siren.

He reached the Gary, Indiana bus station at dawn. Two empty buses idled near the departure doors. A janitor swept the pavement with a push broom. A newspaper deliveryman lifted a stack of papers out of the back of his van and dropped them on the curb. Dropping fifty cents in a red vending machine, he opened the door and pulled out yesterday's papers, then cut open the new stack of papers and pushed them inside, making sure to slide one into the display window. Whistling, he got in his van and drove away.

THE MAN WHO WOULD BE PRESIDENT—ASSASSI-NATED, read the headline. There was a photo of George Libby next to a photo of Jason Walker.

He waited until the janitor rounded the corner, then put his own coins in the newspaper box. He took out all the newspapers and dropped them into a nearby trash can. He took a copy of the *Auto Trader* out of another box. He went into the station. He could barely lift his legs.

There were only a dozen people waiting for buses, half of them from the same large family. The ticket window was still closed.

He sat down and opened the *Auto Trader* in front of him. It was a feeble disguise but he had to be there. He wasn't so sure he wanted to get away. But he couldn't bear to see Chad Armstrong again.

There was a television on. Of course. Cable news. The blonde anchorwoman said something grave, and then there was the president, sitting at his desk in the Oval Office. With his salt-and-pepper hair, his red tie and his navy suit, he looked the same as always. The expression on his face was familiar, too. He looked slightly bored, like a man struggling to reconcile himself with the seriousness of the situation. The president started to smile but stopped. It looked like a smirk.

'My fellow Americans,' he said. 'Our country has endured many tragedies in the last few years. We have seen many lives put at risk and some of them lost. Many of you are afraid. And yesterday we saw a terroristic political assassination in the city of Chicago. Our hearts grieve for the slain, and our prayers are with their families.'

Jason Walker was afraid that at any moment his photo would flash across the screen. But it may not have mattered. The people in the bus station were not paying very close attention to the president. A runny-nosed little girl in a red dress was playing with a dirty newspaper on the floor while her mother, holding an infant, tried to swat the newspaper out of her hands.

'We do not yet know everything about the group behind the attack. But we do know one thing: these terrorists carry out their attacks because they hate freedom. They live among us. They look like law-abiding citizens. But their hearts are black, and their minds are filled with poisonous ideologies.'

The newspaper on the floor was yesterday's evening edition. It also had a photo of Jason Walker splashed across the front page.

'My message to you tonight is brief: be strong. Be resolute. We will not give up the fight against the enemies of freedom. Though we make sacrifices now, we will emerge victorious at the end of the day. And if you live in one of the cities where I've declared a curfew, I urge you to respect your local law enforcement authorities as they enforce it.'

The little girl was looking from the photograph to Jason Walker and back.

'May god bless us all.'

Jason Walker got up and walked to the toilet. If he was forced to leave the bus station he would have no way of contacting Leo Haddad. He had dropped the cell phone on the floor when he fled his apartment.

The toilet door started to open. He stepped into a stall and closed the door. He sat down on the lid.

The man who walked in used a urinal and flushed. He washed and dried his hands. But he didn't leave.

Instead, his footsteps tapped closer.

'It is all right. You can come out, please.'

'Who is it?' Jason Walker asked.

'A friend. It is all right.'

There was no point in staying hidden. He opened the door. A short, thin man with brown skin was waiting for him.

'Our friend is waiting outside for us,' said the man.

He followed the man out of the toilet and through the departure lounge. The small girl pointed at him excitedly and tugged on her tired mother's sleeve. They went outside.

They walked away from the bus station. A block away, there was a white car waiting in an alley. The car had once been a taxicab. There were holes in the roof where the top-light had been bolted on, and house paint had been used in an unsuccessful attempt to paint over the cab's medallion number and the cab company's logo.

The thin man opened the back door and Jason Walker got in. Leo Haddad gave him a wan smile.

'I am glad to see that you escaped,' he said.

The thin man climbed into the front seat. Ghassan was at the wheel. He started driving.

'I am sorry for your loss,' said Leo Haddad. 'I hope you are not angry with me for taking the explosives. I see now that it was a mistake. I am glad that I trusted you, though I underestimated our opponent. But you must realize that they would have accomplished their plan one way or the other. They are skilled at creating the appearance of truth.'

Jason Walker looked out the window. In parts of downtown Gary it looked as if a bomb had gone off. Once a thriving steel town, now the city tried to lure Chicagoans to spend their money at its casinos. Other countries, in the Far East, made cheaper steel now. It was cheaper even after it had been shipped across the Pacific Ocean. Many of the people who made the steel hated America.

'We do not have much time,' said Leo Haddad. 'It will be very embarrassing to them if we live. I must go one way, and you must go another. I believe I can help you, but you must do precisely what I tell you to do. Do you trust me?'

Jason Walker looked across the back seat at Leo Haddad.

'Did they take back the plastic explosives?'

'No,' said Leo Haddad. 'The bomb they set off was their own.'

'Where is it now?'

'Safe. You are sitting on it.'

Involuntarily he looked down at the seat. The worn vinyl upholstery told him nothing.

Leo Haddad looked at him earnestly.

'You are one of us now. You have my full confidence, but I must also have yours. Do you trust me?'

The car glided past the hulking wall of a ruined factory.

He didn't know, but what could he say?

Twenty-Two

The sun was already high when he woke up. It made the red-curtained window glow orange and turned the unmortared rock walls into a jigsaw puzzle. He laid on the rug for a while without moving, watching dust float lazily through shafts of light, listening to the buzz and scratch of insects in the bushes outside. There was a cough in the other room and a clank of pans as the midday meal got underway.

Eventually he sat up and threw the blanket off. He rolled up his rug and blanket and put them against the wall. The stone floor was cold under his feet and there was a lingering chill in the air. Coughing the night's dust out of his throat, he poured water from a pitcher into a basin and splashed his face until he felt reasonably alert. There were a few dead bugs in the water but he didn't care. He felt too tired to go outside for fresh water.

In the next room, Udail Abaid stared at him, then jerked his head toward a cold cup of coffee. Udail Abaid had been unfriendly from the start. Jason Walker suspected that he resented his job, caretaker of the American. And the later Jason Walker slept, the more casual his hygiene became, the more disgusted Udail Abaid appeared to be. But perhaps it was also because Jason Walker did not pray toward Mecca five times a day.

'Thank you, Udail,' he said.

He took the cold coffee and stepped outside.

He hadn't known what to expect of Lebanon. Probably he had imagined sand dunes and camels. And maybe those could be found in some other part of the country. Here, wherever he was, it was dry but also surprisingly green.

Trees shaded the old house, bushes clumped along the path, and in a neglected garden vegetables fought weeds as they climbed toward the sun.

It was warm in the sun. He sat down on a flat rock and let the sun's rays beat down on his head. He sipped the coffee. It wasn't so bad.

There was a village just a few hundred yards away. The first couple of weeks, he had gone to the village every day and made earnest attempts to communicate with the people there. Udail Abaid's English wasn't too bad, but he didn't seem inclined to help. So Jason Walker had tried to find others who spoke his language. He didn't have much success. He tried pantomime, stick drawings, and more desperate means, but he didn't find anyone who admitted to understanding him.

At first the people had been amused by him, and brought him food and drink in the cafe and sat to watch his child-like attempts to communicate. But after a few days they grew bored. And then they began to ignore him. Again, he wondered if it was the lack of prayer. Or maybe Udail Abaid had told them he was a Maronite. Which wasn't true, of course. As he had told Leo Haddad in Chicago, he wasn't anything.

It had been a strange trip to get there. After saying goodbye to Leo Haddad, he had gotten into another car, a tiny blue compact, with the thin man. The thin man didn't introduce himself. The thin man hadn't spoken much at all. He drove north into Wisconsin, then west into Minnesota. They stopped only for gas and food. They ate in the car. Late that night, they passed through International Falls, a town on the Canadian border. They drove through town, then drove some more. They drove into a state park and parked in an empty campsite. The thin man told him to sleep. He slept.

They were awakened at dawn by a gentle tapping on the window. A bearded man with a backpack and a walking stick was smiling at them. They got out of the car, Jason Walker shivering in the frosty air. The man with the backpack gave him a sweater and the two of them hiked into the woods.

After a few hours the man said, 'Here we are.'

The narrow game trail looked exactly the same. He presumed the man meant that they were in Canada.

A few hours later, they hiked out of the woods on to a graveled road. There was a battered white sport-utility vehicle waiting. They got in and the man started the car. Jason Walker fell asleep again.

They drove back east that day, finally reaching Toronto after dark. They stayed in a small motel on the outskirts of the city. The next morning they drove to a mall. Jason Walker bought a suitcase and a week's worth of clothes. He bought several books and magazines, too. Then they drove to the airport. The bearded man told him which airlines and flights he was to take, said goodbye, and drove off.

Jason Walker's Lebanese passport concerned the Canadian customs official. She wondered why there weren't any stamps in it. How had he arrived in Canada?

He explained to her that he had dual citizenship, that he had homes in both America and Lebanon. His American passport had been stolen from his hotel room last night, so he was forced to travel to Lebanon under his Lebanese passport.

He wouldn't have believed it himself, but she stamped him through.

'I guess it's not like they won't take you back,' she said, smiling.

'Exactly,' he agreed.

He had half a day until his flight departed. In an airport restaurant, he ordered a steak and a bottle of wine. He drank most of the wine, then fell asleep in the departure area. A gate agent woke him just before the flight finished boarding.

'Sir? Sir? Are you on this flight, sir?'

He flew direct to Frankfurt, then to Istanbul, then to Damascus.

In Damascus he stood there looking lost until a man took his arm and called him by name. The man drove him over the border into Lebanon.

*　　*　　*

After a while the sun felt hot. He had finished his coffee. Udail Abaid brought a plate of food to the door and stood there without saying anything.

Jason Walker took the food and sat in the dirt under a tree. Flies, still slow-moving from the cold night, tried to land on the plate. He swatted them away.

He dreamed about Gina Saraceno every night. In some of the dreams they were in her kitchen together, talking while they cooked and drank wine. In some of the dreams she was lying in the rubble of Scott Fink's ruined living room, her body torn to pieces and covered with blood. He had learned how to will himself awake from those dreams. But then he was always afraid to fall asleep again.

He felt desperate for news from Chicago. The only newspapers in the village were in Arabic. Several of the houses had satellite dishes on their roofs, but the house where he was staying did not. Udail Abaid ran a generator for a couple of hours each night, using it to light the house and to listen to the radio. When he was done, he let Jason Walker fiddle the dial until he found the BBC. He learned that the Chicago curfew had been extended to other large American cities and heard a brief mention of George Libby's assassination. But then the news had moved on to the usual, sporadic attacks against Americans. He wondered if some evening he would hear that a tall building in downtown Chicago had come crashing to the ground.

A few nights later, a man he hadn't seen before visited Udail Abaid. They spoke for an hour and then the man went away. Udail Abaid came into Jason Walker's room. He explained that it was getting too difficult to keep Jason Walker hidden there. In such a small village, an American stood out. People were talking. They had no desire to bring foreign commandos here. It was time to move again. It would be easier to hide in a city.

Tomorrow they would go to Beirut.